CRITICAL ACCLAIM FOR
DECEPTION SPECIALIST

"I've always been a sucker for a conman, and it's a joy to be taken in by reformed grifter Jack O'Shea as he turns the tables on a murderous conspiracy."

—Dennis Tafoya, author of *Dope Thief*

"Won't get fooled again, not with Jack O'Shea on the case. Master con man turned PI, O'Shea isn't exactly on the side of the angels, but he's our kind of rogue."

—Reed Farrel Coleman, *New York Times* bestselling author of *Sleepless City*

"A good, old-fashioned mystery thriller powered by a completely original and compelling protagonist, John Shepphird's *Deception Specialist* speeds along at a breakneck pace while also tugging at your emotions. I read it in one sitting."

—David Housewright, Edgar Award-winning author of *In A Hard Wind*

"Scammers, schemers, and scoundrels are no match for former con man-turned-private eye Jack O'Shea. This Deception Specialist navigates a murderous conspiracy while confronting the ghosts of his swindling past in this edge-of-your-seat page turner."

—Steve Jankowski, author of *Below the Line*

"Tragedy turns a former conman into Shepphird's *Deception Specialist*: A force for good in a world gone murderously bad."

—Lawrence Maddox, author of *Fast Bang Booze*

DECEPTION SPECIALIST

BOOKS BY
JOHN SHEPPHIRD

The Shill
Kill the Shill
Beware the Shill
Bottom Feeders

The Jack O'Shea Novels
Deception Specialist

JOHN SHEPPHIRD

DECEPTION SPECIALIST

A Jack O'Shea Novel

Crimson Gate Books

For Maggie and Evelyn

CHAPTER 1

Three Years Ago
Napa Valley, California

I made a killing that day.

The convertible top of our fast getaway was down. Mona's blonde hair whipped in the wind, backlit by golden sunlight. There was that look of mischief in her eyes.

She was so incredibly smart, and so beautiful. Mona was the most gifted shakedown-artist I've ever seen, and the love of my life. It wasn't about the money with her. My partner-in-crime lived for *the game.*

Her wide-brim hat blew off. In the rear-view mirror, I saw it rolling across the pavement. I didn't see the semi pull out ahead.

An hour earlier, Kenneth Coleman thought he'd bought the most expensive champagne in the world. Mona found the Greenwich, Connecticut hedge fund wizard, and she masterminded the caper. She played into his fantasy to show off the prized bottles to his wine-snob friends. The master negotiator forked over a half a million dollars for two bottles of counterfeit champagne.

One second, I was on top of the world. The other...

I stomped the brakes. The convertible veered sideways before it slammed under the tractor trailer.

I killed Mona that day.

CHAPTER 2

Present Day

None of the "before" pictures looked as severe as my face.

On his iPad, the plastic surgeon showed me his former patient's progressions. "The treatment involves various stages," he said. "It'll take a combination of techniques—from injections, derm-abrasion, and laser-resurfacing. I'm confident our team can bring you back to your true self."

My true self.

It's not like I'm a circus freak, but hitting that windshield face first changed my life forever. The deep, hideous scar which cuts across my face is the ever-present reminder of Mona, and my mortal sin. I can't help but think of her every time I look into the mirror.

The facial reconstruction was not covered by health insurance—they deemed it elective surgery—so I asked to the doctor, "What do you estimate this will set me back?"

"Depends on how many sessions are required."

"Ballpark."

"I'd say roughly eighty-five to one-hundred thousand dollars, give or take, not including the cost of medications." He handed me a pamphlet. "Most of my patients opt for our no-interest payment plan. We're very flexible."

I wanted to say, *You obviously haven't run my credit score,* but I held my tongue.

I considered his sleek Manhattan Beach office with its Pacific Ocean view. Doctors don't get rich removing your appendix. Elective surgery has got to be the most lucrative path. But I didn't have a spare one-hundred thousand dollars, with or without his payment plan. There was a time I could have easily afforded it—a drop in the bucket. I was foolish to gamble away the money I'd gained over the years. Instead, I'd hemorrhaged cash like a drunken sailor. Didn't have the willpower to walk away from the seductive felt of casino tables.

I let the doctor know I'd think about it and got the hell out of there.

Con men can't be disfigured. We're supposed to be appealing. Charismatic. Aspirational. I used to get plenty of smiles from the young ladies. Now once they see the scar on my face, they avoid me. I can't blame them. A con man can't work without confidence, and I've lost mine.

I had no choice but to change my profession. Now I work for the other side. They pay me to root out deception because *it takes one to know one.*

But more so, I was tired of lying.

I'd lied to everyone. My life was one lie piled upon another. Juggling all those balls and dodging the long arm of the law was exhausting. I'd come to a newfound freedom by being honest with others and myself.

To earn one-hundred thousand dollars, I needed to step up my game as a private eye.

CHAPTER 3

You can't escape your past. Not entirely.

On the drive back to my office, I noticed the white van in my rear-view mirror. Was it the same one I'd seen the other day? Almost every plumber, florist, and dog groomer travels in some sort of white panel van. I wondered if I was being paranoid. Those I had swindled are out there, licking their wounds. The embers of deep hatred and bruised ego still smolder. I always suspected one day there'd be a knock on the door.

After the car accident, while I was in recovery, I started writing a book about my life as a con man. Getting it all down on paper was therapy—my tell-all confession. When the memoir was finished, I gave it to my friend Hector to read. He teaches screenwriting at USC and hangs out with literary types. Hector cleaned up my bad grammar, connected me with a literary agent, and before I knew it, the manuscript was on the fast track with a publisher.

When my book came out, I was surprised by the reception. People love to learn the secret behind tricks. But *the grift* is rarely sleight-of-hand. It comes down to storytelling, much like the narrative Mona and I spun about those fake bottles of champagne. You create fiction, fine-tune the story, and tell it so many times after a while even you believe it.

Because of the book Oscar Lang approached me to serve as an

expert witness. Oscar is an old-school attorney with an office in a downtown Los Angeles high-rise. He represents insurance companies and pays me to come to the courtroom and explain the mechanics of various schemes, in layman's terms, to judges and juries. Oscar pays me surprisingly well. He introduces me in the courtroom as a "Deception Specialist."

Six thousand hours are required to be licensed as a private investigator in California, but Oscar had connections in Sacramento and somehow was able to circumvent all that. I asked him, "How did someone like me, with no experience in security or law enforcement, get licensed as a private investigator?"

With a wave of his chubby fingers, Oscar said, "If a crooked, retired cop collecting a fat ass pension can be licensed as a private eye, why not you?"

I passed the written test. The state ran a background check. Thanks to my father not squealing on me, I'd avoided felony convictions throughout my life of crime. God knows there were close calls.

My dad? He literally sold swampland in Florida. No kidding. He taught me how to lie, cheat and steal. My mother left when I was young, so I was raised by a ne'er-do-well gambler with a revolving-door of live-in girlfriends. He was gone often, so I watched a lot of TV, and learned how to get by on my own. After rebellious teenage years, I followed in my dad's footsteps, like father, like son, as an apprentice grifter. More on him later.

It became clear the white van was following me. I kept an eye on it while I planned my next move.

I drive a Chevrolet Super Sport, what's known as a *sleeper*—a wolf in sheep's clothing. The unassuming, four-door sedan was my dad's car. I inherited it when my father was sent to prison. In Australia, they sold the car as the Holden Commodore. It can outrun most anything, but you'd never know at first glance. I disguised it even more by having the flared wheel-wells trimmed. It looks like something you rented at Avis.

The jokers at General Motors must have had a sense of humor

when they put a 650 horsepower super-charged Corvette V-8 with a six-speed sport manual transmission onto the frame of a four-door family sedan. What's odd is the model has no name—simply the Chevy SS—which is the acronym for Super Sport. It's a shame GM stopped making the model.

Mona once asked me what the chrome double S insignia inside the door panel meant. "Let me show you," I said, and took her on a high-speed demonstration. "Super Sport," I explained.

White-knuckled, Mona said, "I think it means Secret Sauce." We laughed for hours, grinning in the wind. Most days were like that with Mona.

With the white van on my tail, I cut into a residential neighborhood in Westchester, a suburb adjacent to LAX. The van did too. I gave the Chevy a little "ask" and the van could not keep up.

My office is another sleeper—on the second floor of a drab, two-story stucco building in Culver City. The business directory in the lobby downstairs reads, *Jack O'Shea, Deception Specialist.*

I slid into my desk and got back to what I was doing before my visit with the plastic surgeon—editing surveillance video for one of Oscar's workers' compensation cases. That had become my bread and butter.

When a business has a loss history, the premium of the California's Workers' Compensation Insurance shoots through the roof. In this case, the subject was a high-end chef who supposedly suffered a debilitating back injury slipping on the job. Earlier that day, I'd captured video of the guy at the gym, and then swinging a Big Bertha at the Wilson & Harding Golf Course in Griffith Park. The golf bag I'd rented in the pro shop turned out to be a pretty good tripod. I was able to get steady shots from a distance.

From there, the chef drove to the Griffith Observatory. With his golf partner, a slender lady friend, they took in the view of downtown Los Angeles, then spread out a blanket for what looked like a picnic on the sprawling lawn. He moved with ease and grace. And it looked like he had *game.* It was clear his mobility was not impaired, but who am I to judge? As a detective, I simply collect the evidence.

I uploaded the video and added the hours to my invoice for the day. I never pad my bills. I suspect Oscar marks up my services on the statements he submits to the insurance companies, but I play it by-the-book. In my previous life, I would have cheated for sure, but since I've turned over a new leaf.

Late that afternoon, in the reflection of my office window, I caught the reflection of the hideous scar—the ever-present reminder of Mona.

I may look like a monster, but...

CHAPTER 4

My friend Hector Garcia texted me. *"I need advice. Let's grab a beer."*

I replied, *"???"*

"I'm buying. Meet me at Backstage at 4."

I read into Hector's angle—wait until four o'clock, the beginning of happy hour.

The Backstage Bar & Grill sits directly across from the Sony Pictures Studios lot which used to be MGM. The bar claims to be the oldest watering hole in Culver City. Spencer Tracy, Hedy Lamarr and the Wizard of Oz munchkins drank there. Now it's a cozy neighborhood bar across the street from one the studio's parking structures. Countless liquid lunches had been served there.

I entered the establishment. Only after my eyes adjusted to the darkness did I notice Hector seated at the bar. He wore his usual button-down Oxford and khakis, attire he refers to as, "the uniform of academics and middle management."

Hector teaches screenwriting and is a part time development executive for one of the mid-list streaming services. His professional credits include a few low budget action movies starring aging, has-been stars. After I took a seat on the barstool and settled in, Hector asked, "When you're working as a P.I., do you carry a gun?"

"It's not like in the movies," I said.

"Jim Rockford had a gun."

I said, "I think he kept a Smith & Wesson in the cookie jar of his trailer."

"Yeah," Hector said nostalgic, "love that show. But you have one, right?"

I tried to remember where I'd stashed the Colt Model 1903 Pocket Hammerless .32 pistol—the vintage automatic I'd inherited from my grandfather, another item passed down by my dad before his incarceration. He said it was the same model John Dillinger carried the day he met his demise outside Chicago's Biograph Theater. The .32 doesn't offer a lot of punch, but the pistol is slim and easy to conceal. I asked Hector, "You need a gun?"

"Nah. Just curious."

"Writing something with a private eye?"

"Hoping you can look into something. I've told you about my crazy sister, right?"

He'd mentioned her a few times. I nodded and sipped my beer.

"Well...her husband died in an accident, but Madeline's convinced he was murdered."

"Why does she think that?"

"Because she's batshit crazy. Madeline lives in a fantasy world. Makes sense since she's a performance artist. Lives up in Argonaut, this funky college town in the mountains above Sactown. Teaches drama. Her husband Mike fell down a mineshaft. My sister is convinced he was pushed."

"By who?"

"She's got theories. You'd have to talk to her. The coroner claimed it was an accident, but my sister says that's total bullshit. She hired this private eye, but the guy's giving her the runaround. He took her retainer and split, doesn't return phone calls. Ghosted her."

"Who'd she hire?"

"Some douche."

"She needs to call the Better Business Bureau."

He shrugged.

"Tell me about your brother-in-law?"

"I'd see him at Christmas when they came down to stay with the folks."

"What kind of guy was he?"

"Mellow. Wouldn't hurt a fly. Maybe you can look into this private eye she hired, and then while you're up there ask around to see if there was anything weird about the accident?"

"Up there?"

"In Argonaut. The college town."

"Fraud detection is my racket," I said. "A retired homicide detective would be best for something like this. Someone with experience."

He considered that. "Yeah, you're probably right. Can you at least look into this asshole who took her money? I mean, what kind of asshole collects on a job then skips out? We can pay you."

"Hector," I said. "I can't take your money."

"Why not?"

"You're a broke college professor and the walking encyclopedia of bargain happy hours."

"My sister and I inherited a little money after my dad died. I wouldn't be paying you. It'd be my sister's."

"I can't take it."

"Then give us the friends-and-family rate. I'd do it myself, but teaching keeps me in town, and I've got a rewrite with ridiculous producer notes to deal with." Hector looked me in the eye and said, "I don't want you to do this for free."

I'd known Hector for years. He'd always been broke. We met when he moonlighted as a limo driver. He became my regular driver, street smart, and a jack-of-all-trades. He helped me in various schemes I was pulling at the time and didn't ask questions. We became friends.

When I was in the hospital, he visited every day to keep my

spirits up. He brought vintage paperbacks. Charmed the nurses. If Mona and I had gotten married, Hector may have been my best man. I said, "I'll do it as a friend, but I won't take a fee."

"Expenses then. Gas up there and back, plus per diem and hotel. You'll want to stay overnight because it's a seven-hour drive."

"We'll see."

"Are you going to help me or not?"

I reluctantly said, "Alright. I'll find a cheap flea bag."

"Splurge, my friend. Go for a Holiday Inn Express with that complimentary continental breakfast thing. You know what I'm talking about...watered-down coffee and a waffle machine."

"Will I need my gun?"

"Nah. These are pseudo-intellectuals. Wood-cookies."

"Wood-cookies?"

"Tree huggers. Birkenstock-wearing professors."

"You're a professor."

"Adjunct, not full-time," he reminded. "There's a difference."

"I guess teaching runs in your family, huh?"

"What can I say? Our parents over-educated us."

What I knew about Hector's folks is they came from Mexico to work as migrant pickers in the Central Valley before settling in El Monte, a Hispanic suburb of East Los Angeles. His parents worked multiple jobs to afford private Catholic school, and then college for their kids.

Hector flagged the bartender to order another pair of rounds, and said, "Just look into this joker she hired. Maybe you can get that money back."

"Have your sister call me."

CHAPTER 5

Three Years Ago

Months before the fatal car accident I was in downtown Vegas, crossing Fremont Street between Binion's Horseshoe and the Golden Nugget, when Mona tried to lift my wallet.

I grabbed her arm and said, "Not cool, little lady."

"Excuse me, mister...I'm *so* sorry," she said, faking a drunken slur, "I didn't see ya, and—"

"You were going for my wallet."

"What? No. I'm sorry, but—"

"—Working alone?"

She eyed me with daggers. "Working?" With prostitution legal in the state of Nevada, she'd misinterpreted what I'd meant. I estimated her to be in her late-twenties—hardened beyond her age.

At that moment, a pair of Clark County Sheriffs walked past, and Mona stiffened. The female officer gave her a double-take, and Mona turned away.

Hushed, I said, "Know them?"

She glanced over her shoulder to make sure they'd moved on before, "I'm just...not super friendly with cops."

"Let me offer some advice," I said. "Whatever you do, don't pick pockets inside the casinos." I motioned to the entrance of

Binion's Horseshoe. "Cameras everywhere. Get caught lifting in there and security will make your life a living hell." I looked at her meaningfully before another thought occurred to me. "And another thing...do your homework. Go for whales."

"Whales?"

"After the beating I took at that craps table...you're harpooning a minnow with me."

She tilted her head to one side and a strand of blonde hair fell to cover one eye. "I wasn't trying to take anything from you."

In a lowered voice I said, "What I meant by working alone...the real pros, like Gypsies in Europe, work in teams. First there's the *bump*, a kid or attractive girl like you, a distraction. Then someone else, the *hook,* snags the wallet. Often, a *pass* will take the prize, so it's long gone. That way, the victim doesn't sense the actual pickpocket quickly scurry away, especially if they feel something. It's not a bad idea to have a *lookout*, too."

"What makes you think I was trying to take your wallet?"

"Because you were."

She knew it. I knew it.

Mona brushed hair from her face and gave me a playful salute. "Whatever. Peace." She spun on her heels and moved on.

I crossed to the Golden Nugget to see if I could change my luck. I found a single-deck blackjack table with a seat at the far end, what's known as third base. By counting cards, combined with a bit of old-fashioned luck, I won back some of the money I'd lost across the street.

I was starving and figured I'd head back to my hotel on the strip. I cashed the chips at the cage and was waiting at the cabstand when I saw two sheriffs questioning Mona across the street. One of them had cuffs out. There was a portly, middle-aged couple standing aside, arms crossed and defiant. I assumed she tried to pick one of their pockets.

I dug out one of the fictitious business cards I carried at the time, the doctor one, and crossed the street. "Cindy, there you are. I told you to stay in the car." I turned to the sheriffs, "Is there a problem?"

"Know this woman?" asked the female deputy.

"I'm Doctor Monroe and this is one of my patients."

Mona eyed me.

The deputy said, "She has no identification."

I nodded and said, "She wouldn't because it's all at the treatment center."

"What treatment center?"

Without answering, I turned to Mona. "Cindy, have you been bothering people again?"

At that moment, the Sherriff's radios squawked. The male deputy responded. It was clear they were being summoned to a more pressing matter. The female deputy had a few words with the waiting couple, and I overheard something about pressing charges. They shook their heads no, and that was that.

The female deputy returned to Mona and said, "If we see you out here again, we'll run you in." With that, the sheriffs moved on and the couple waddled on back to Fremont Street.

Mona muttered, "Thanks."

"What did I just say about only going after whales?" I motioned to the pathetic couple blending into the crowd. "What little you'd get from those two is not worth the risk."

She shrugged, brushed the hair out of her eyes, and with a half-smile, said, "A girl's gotta eat."

CHAPTER 6

We sat at a booth in a diner around the corner from Fremont Street. When the waitress arrived, Mona ordered apple pie and a Diet Coke. Considering her emaciated look, I suggested she go for something with a bit more sustenance. Mona waved me away, shook her head no, and pecked at her phone, texting someone. I ordered a club sandwich, figuring I'd offer her the other half.

I could see she felt uncomfortable sitting with a stranger, somebody who only moments ago she was trying to rip off, so I started talking about myself to break the ice. I told her I'd grown up in Florida.

"Never been there," she said.

"A lot of things can kill you in the Sunshine State. Poisonous snakes. Spiders. Gators. Cretins."

She raised an eyebrow. "Cretins?"

"Stupidshits who will gut and dump you in The Everglades for the loose change in your pocket. Lots of desperation there."

"Sort of like here," she said with a glance out the window.

Something about her made me want to tell the truth, so I confessed, "My dad hustled cheap condos built on swampland. Hurricanes and floods took out most of them. Florida is all that."

She asked, "Your mom?"

"When I was five, she packed a suitcase and never came back."

Mona couldn't believe it. "She left her little boy?"

"She had a guy on the side. And he didn't want a kid."

She considered that before asking, "What kind of mother runs out on her child?"

"It happens."

In a lowered voice, she asked, "How do you know so much about picking pockets?"

"My dad taught me. The teamwork I told you about...we used to crew that way when I was a teenager. We preyed on tourists and worked conventions when they were in town."

"Your dad taught you how to pick pockets?"

"Among other things. You can't really do that now. Nobody carries cash anymore, and with all the surveillance cameras..."

"Gamblers carry cash," she said. She'd pegged me as a gambler.

"True," I replied. She was right. At the time, I gambled all the time, and chased my losses. Another vice I learned from my dad. The sole reason I was gambling downtown, as opposed to on the strip, was because those craps tables offer higher odds on the pass line.

The food arrived. She gobbled down her slice of pie. I asked the waitress for another plate. When it arrived, I offered her the other half of my sandwich. At first, Mona refused, but then she picked out the bacon and chewed on that.

"Where do you live?" she asked.

"L.A."

"Near the beach?"

"I have a view of the water."

"What brings you here?"

"The green felt," I confessed, "what else?" and asked her, "How long have you been in Vegas?"

"Couple months. I'm here with friends. When it gets too hot, we'll get out of here."

"You talkin' about heat from weather...or heat from cops?"

"Both."

We shared a smile.

Seemingly more at ease, she told me how she grew up in Mill Valley. I was familiar with the upscale suburb north of San Francisco's Golden Gate Bridge. I wondered what path had led her from moneyed Marin County to picking pockets in Vegas. Pulling out a couple of one-hundred-dollar bills, some of what I'd cashed at the Golden Nugget, I said, "Look, it's obvious you're living on the street, so—"

"—What makes you say that?" she said, defensive.

"Am I wrong?"

Her eyes said it all.

"Check into a hotel for a night," I said, suggesting, "Take a shower and get a good night's sleep. Don't use this to party. Take care of yourself. Will you do that?"

"What makes you think—?"

I pointed to the track marks on her arm and said, "Because you're using."

Ashamed, she ducked her arms under the table.

I set the money between us and said, "If you make it out to Los Angeles, I can probably find you work."

"What...you some kind of pimp or something?"

"That's *not* what I'm talking about."

Mona eyed me, unsure. I couldn't blame her. I was a complete stranger. It made me think about the age-old proverb, *you can lead a horse to water, but you can't make it drink.*

Her phone chirped. She checked a text, then something outside the window caught her eye. There was a man and woman standing across the street. The guy wore a sleek, dark suit—dance club attire. The woman was somewhat obese, dressed in all black, and pecking at her phone.

Mona's phone chirped again. Reading the text, she said, "I've got to go."

I pulled a Keno card from the plastic caddy on the table. With the crayon marker, I jotted down my cell phone number. "If you're ever in L.A," I said, "I won't give you more money, but I can probably help find you a job. Ever wait tables?"

She didn't like the sound of that. "That's nice of you, mister," Mona said, getting up, "but I won't be in SoCal anytime soon."

I folded the Keno card in half, placed the cash inside, and handed it to her.

Mona took it. "Thanks for getting me clear of those pesky cops." She gave me a salute, then swayed out of the restaurant.

When she joined her friends, the guy put his arm around her, and they kissed. She chatted with the woman for a bit, thumbing back towards me. Mona shot one look back at the diner before they moved on.

At the time, I was certain I'd never see Mona again.

CHAPTER 7

Present Day

On the phone Hector's sister Madeline said, "The cops were no help, so I hired a detective. Sent the guy three thousand bucks, but he did next to nothing. Then to add insult to injury, the coroner recorded it as *Death by Misadventure* on the death certificate. That means it was Mike's fault, which is bullshit. He was pushed down that shaft."

I searched the detective she'd hired. A website for *Nick McClintlock; Investigator* came up. From his photo, I could see he was a weight-lifter type—bulging biceps and military haircut.

It appeared he was the author of a series of how-to books. *Side Hustle: Earn Extra Cash as a Private Eye* appeared to be the most recent, prominently featured on the home page. Others included *Camouflaged Revenge: Retaliate Undetected* and *Deep-Dive Deluxe: Find Dirt on Anybody.* The cover art of these books reeked of do-it-yourself, self-publishing. I didn't see investigation services featured on his website, and asked, "Where did you find him?"

"He was holding a seminar in Sacramento. I took him to where Mike fell in. He talked to the sheriff, then split and didn't return my calls. Ghosted me."

I asked, "When you retained his services was there a written agreement?"

"No."

"Did he send a report?"

"No."

"How'd you pay him?"

"Western Union because he said his Pay Pal and Venmo accounts had been hacked." That was bad news, and I told her so. Money wired by Western Union cannot be returned. I'd used that method of untraceable payment many times.

Under the "Events" tab on the website there was a seminar that evening at a hotel in Santa Rosa, a town north of San Francisco. I directed Madeline's attention to it.

"Should I go there?" she asked.

I owed Hector. He was like a brother to me, and one of the few friends I had. I said to his sister, "I can try to get your money back, but no promises."

"So you'll help?"

I explained I'd approach McClintlock and see what happened. She was grateful. On one hand, I regretted the decision. The travel would be a hassle. A time sink. But on the other, I saw it as a step towards my redemption. I was helping the sister of my friend and stepping out of my own self-centered ego for a change. I told Madeline I'd be in touch.

Before hitting the road, I showered and took my greyhound to the dog park before the drive north. The crowd of regulars were there—both dogs and the owners I recognized. Some of them were single, attractive women. Congenial, but they tended to avoid me. Admittedly, I'm not easy to look at.

I'd barely felt the touch of a woman since I'd lost Mona. The nasty scar on my face is the male equivalent to a chastity belt. At least the dogs don't judge.

Suzie played with an energetic black Labrador before she came to my side exhausted, tongue out and panting. We got in my car, and she curled up on the passenger side floor mat. My dog fell fast asleep as we headed up the 405, over Mulholland

Pass, and transitioned onto Interstate 5.

That's when I noticed a familiar white van behind me. I pulled off at the next exit and ducked into a Chevron station.

The van followed.

At the pump, I made a show of getting gas while the van turned around on the frontage road and parked in a position to follow once I pulled out.

I searched the glove compartment for my foldable knife. I'd only used it once before, to cut nylon marine rope back when I leased a sailboat in Marina Del Rey. The knife was brand new and razor sharp.

I left the gas nozzle in my car and made my way into the station's convenience store. I avoided the clerk and slipped into the hallway near the restrooms. At the emergency exit, I pushed the security bar. The buzzer rang.

I darted outside and hid behind the dumpster. From there, I saw the cashier peek out and then slam the door shut. From my position behind the convenience store, I could see the van hadn't moved.

I crept up behind the vehicle to the passenger side. There was a teenage boy sitting in the driver's seat, peering the other way at my car through binoculars. I opened the knife and moved to the back of the van.

In the side view mirror I saw him move. At first I thought the kid was vaping. But then it became clear once he rolled down the window and poured a paper cup of spent sunflower seeds onto the pavement. After he rolled the window back up, I plunged the knife into the sidewall of the rear tire.

There was a loud pop, followed by hissing.

I went around to the driver's side.

The kid's panicked eyes caught me in the mirror as I punctured the opposite tire. He jumped out, yelling, "What the fuck!" He was small-framed, couldn't have been more than fifteen, and appeared to be of Polynesian descent.

I asked, "Why are you following me?"

He came towards me but stopped once he saw the knife in my hand. We stared at each other for a second before I said, "If I see you again..." and raised the blade.

He considered that, then dashed for something inside the van.

That was my cue to get out of there, so I ran back to my car, replaced the gas nozzle at the pump, and could see him coming at me with a pair of nunchucks. The boy ran up, swinging the martial arts weapon made famous by Bruce Lee.

I started the car and pulled out. I heard the weapon smack my rear quarter panel before I sped for the freeway.

Nunchucks? Really?

In the rear-view mirror, I could see him running back for his van. With two flat tires, he couldn't get far. But to play it safe, for a mile or so, I put the Chevy to the test. What's great is how assured the SS feels topping over one hundred miles an hour. *Why would a kid be following me?*

Oblivious, dog Suzie lifted her head, looked around, and then went back to sleep.

CHAPTER 8

On the drive north my phone rang—the bi-weekly collect call from dad at the Federal Correctional Institution in Englewood, Colorado. Patrick O'Shea is six years into a twenty-year stint. Maybe he'll get out in twelve for good behavior. Had he squealed, the sentence would have been drastically reduced. But dad hadn't given up anyone on his crew, including me. The judge who sentenced him resented he clammed up and threw the book at him.

It was pure bad luck my dad's mark was Joseph Nazarian, a New Jersey blowhard who made his fortune with a chain of payday loan stores. Need a loan? Show up with a mere paystub and sign for high-interest robbery.

Joe Nazarian was a gambler. When he first launched his chain of stores, Joe flooded New Jersey cable television with obnoxious commercials. He posted billboards up and down the Turnpike. He'd gotten so overextended by marketing costs he needed to fly to Las Vegas for much-needed cash flow to float payroll. Had his luck playing high-stakes blackjack gone other way, the business would have crashed and burned. But Lady Luck was on Joe's side.

Joe ran out of luck when he fell for my father's real estate scheme. Dad's gang of cohorts played the parts of loan executives, appraisers, and city officials. My role was as the clueless land-owner who was blind to the true property value. In the final act of our scheme, Joe suffered a fatal heart attack.

Urgency is key in financial scams, and ours involved a false crisis.

Orchestrated by my father, Joe was urgently trying to get to the bank to halt a wire transfer when he unexpectedly keeled over into a snowdrift. The ambulance team tried their best to revive him. No luck. Unfortunately, Joe's congestive heart failure was attributed to my father's malfeasance.

Because there was a death in the act of a felony, they slapped my dad with a second-degree murder charge. The fact Joseph's family had a long history of heart disease was deemed unsubstantial. The District Attorney went after him with vengeance. Things didn't turn out so well.

My father taught me to only target people who can afford the loss—those who won't necessarily go to the cops. "Play your cards right and the mark will never realize they've been taken. They'll chalk it off as a deal gone sour and not report it out of embarrassment." The *blowoff*—one of the things I learned.

From the prison payphone, my dad said, "What's going on, Jack?"

"Driving up north on Interstate 5."

"Business or pleasure?"

"Helping a friend."

"How's she running?" referring to the Chevy SS. I inherited an appreciation for fast cars. As a kid, my fondest memories were at his side at the Daytona 500. Kentucky has its Derby. Florida has Daytona.

"Just opened her up some," I said. "Feels good."

Phone calls in and out of a federal penitentiary are recorded, so I wasn't about to tell him I was being followed by a nunchuck wielding punk. I doubt the Bureau of Prisons was listening, but I'm certain algorithms pick out buzz words and key phrases from the auto-transcription. To play it safe, what we talk about is generally on the surface, and nothing incriminating.

The prison is wired with basic cable, and they allow inmates to purchase small televisions. A lot of what he talks about are current events he sees on the news, and Notre Dame football. When it comes to sports, Dad is passionate about the Fighting Irish. I've always assumed that comes with our Celtic surname, O'Shea. He claims we're related to the O'Shea Brothers of Ireland architecture fame.

Our prison phone conversations have a fifteen-minute time limit. No matter what we are talking about, he continues to the very end, to the final cut off, milking every second. Often, in the last remaining moment, he signs off with a quick, "Don't take any wooden nickels," an inside-joke. My father had a favorite watering hole which gave out wooden nickels as promotional items. Even though I was underage, and wasn't allowed inside the joint, I collected the tokens, many found discarded in the gravel parking lot. "Those things are worthless," my dad said, but I didn't care. I thought they were cool.

Poker games with his buddies were often in our home. I'd go to sleep to the sound of them. One night, when I was eight or nine, in a lively game amongst my father's ne'er-do-well friends, I took a seat with my stack of wooden nickels. His poker buddies humored me. I ended up winning with two pairs, black aces and eights, what's known as the dead man's hand, gunfighter Wild Bill Hickock's final play.

It turned out wooden nickels were worth something after all.

While most dads teach kids how to play sports, and help navigate homework, I learned all about poker, dice, horse racing, three-card monte, scams, and card manipulation. The fix was in.

Eventually, time ran out on our call and he reminded me not to take any wooden nickels.

On the drive, I passed a lot of semis. Many were hauling produce through California's Central Valley, everything from garlic to grapefruits. I can't help it, but big trucks remind me of the tractor trailer I'd smashed into. The accident. And Mona.

Up past Bakersfield, a lone crop duster caught my eye. I found it fascinating. So much so I pulled over to watch. The small plane swept low—couldn't have been more than thirty feet off the ground. After dusting a row, he pulled up over the freeway, banked a U-turn and then dropped back down to the crops in death-defying aerobatics. You'd have to be one crazy bastard to fly a crop duster—an adrenaline junkie for sure, not to mention the cancer risk of inhaling airborne chemicals. But deep down, I understood that—living on the edge, tempting fate. That's exactly how I felt when I had a mark on the line. Once I had an angle, a *live one*, that's when my life had pulse. Mona felt the same way. All else…waiting.

I got back on the road, and in the rear-view mirror I saw a black sedan coming up fast. I changed lanes. It blew past me. The Chevy SS could easily have met that challenge, but I'd given up *life in the fast lane.*

The Flamingo Conference Resort & Spa in Santa Rosa had mid-century charm. In the lobby, a sign on an easel touted Nick McClintlock's seminar. I had to admit, the vintage hotel was a good fit for a private eye. The place sparked my imagination from classic detective fiction—Mickey Spillane's Mike Hammer or John D. McDonald's Travis McGee. Those were the dog-eared paperbacks Hector brought when I laid bandaged in recovery.

I purchased a ticket to the seminar and found a seat in the back. I could see the audience was older, mostly middle-aged folks and retirees. The lights dimmed, canned music started, and Nick McClintlock made his grand entrance.

The man of the hour dressed in pleated slacks and a sports jacket. He appeared older than the author photo on his website. Nick welcomed everyone and, with a laser pointer, directed attention to his book and a QR code projected on the screen, repeatedly emphasizing how much money he had made as a private eye. "After taxes," Nick claimed, "I bank over three hundred thousand dollars a year. And the best part, I'm my own boss, and choose my own hours."

Three hundred thousand dollars? I asked myself. *What's he doing that I'm not?*

I could see he was a gifted storyteller. He began the Power-Point presentation, which detailed his military background and experience in law enforcement. It all seemed vague. Who knew if any of it was true? What I found lacking was any information about finding clients in need of investigative services. Anyone can open a storefront or put up a website. Getting paying customers to cross your threshold is another story.

When audience members asked questions, Nick often referred to his books. He said they could find the answers there—all an obvious ploy to make a sale.

After more stories about his adventures, Nick paraded the gadgets, hidden cameras, software, and tracking devices featured prominently on the big screen behind him. These gadgets were the common things you'd find in a spy shop. Add the price of admission, his book, and any one of these toys—a sucker could drop three hundred bucks, easy.

Nick said, "As essential as these tools are, you also have to consider *you* may be under surveillance. It's more common than you think."

Nick displayed a handheld electronic device about the size of a deck of cards. "Before we take a break," he said. "I'd like to demonstrate the effectiveness of this tool. The sensor detects audio and video bugs, cellular signals, and active GPS trackers. But before we continue, is anyone in attendance wearing a court-appointed ankle bracelet? It picks those up too. I'm not one to judge."

That got a light chuckle from the room.

He went on about the importance of sweeping your home for bugs, but more importantly, hotel rooms and vacation rentals. Nick said, "Let's take a brief intermission. For those who care to stretch your legs, I have a challenge." He held up a few of the devices. "I've installed a GPS tracking device in the wheel well of my car, parked outside, but I'm not going to reveal the make and model. Find my car and report back, but don't reveal it to me until I ask. For those who get it right, we'll draw straws, and the winner walks away with one of these bad boys. Who wants to try?"

More than a few hands went up.

Nick said, "Let's take a fifteen-minute break. When we're all back, we'll look at actual surveillance from one of my biggest cases, a felony where the video was used as evidence in the court." With the tease planted, Nick's book returned to the screen, and the lights came up.

My plan was to approach Nick after the presentation and question him when he was alone.

It was more than twenty minutes later by the time everyone settled in for the second half of the presentation. Nick brought forward the few who had ventured out into the parking lot with his bug detectors. "Okay," Nick began, "Before we get started, let's see if our volunteer detectives were able to determine which car is mine." He motioned to a scrawny twenty-something in a trucker hat. "You're first, partner. What do you say?"

"A Chevy SS," he said.

My car.

That was a surprise, but it explained how the kid in the white van was able to follow me.

Nick said, "Why no…I'm sorry, but that's not my vehicle."

"But this thing went off," the guy said.

"Possibly an anti-theft system. I'll still give you a straw. You're in the drawing. Anyone else?"

"It's a black Honda Pilot," an overweight middle-aged woman said.

"That's right, young lady" Nick handed out straws to each volunteer.

So my car had a tracking device. I wondered who was watching me, and why?

CHAPTER 9

The second half of the program featured multi-media clips, surveillance video and audio recordings which were supposedly used as evidence in actual court cases.

Someone in the crowd asked about carrying a gun. Nick went into detail about how to apply for a concealed-carry permit.

By the time it all wrapped up, many walked away with books and electronics. I took a seat in the hotel lobby and waited.

After Nick settled up at the front desk, I followed at a distance as he wheeled his road case out to his Honda Pilot SUV. I went to my car. With the light from my iPhone, I checked the wheel-wells for any GPS device but found nothing.

Nick pulled out of the parking lot, so I tailed him.

He pulled onto Highway 12 and headed north on Highway 101. The Honda veered off at the next exit and pulled into the parking lot of a Motel 6. I hung back and observed.

Nick backed his SUV into a spot and unloaded his road case into a ground floor room and closed the door. I was planning to knock after he'd settled in, but he drew the curtains, turned off the light, and made his way past me to the adjacent strip mall.

I got out of my car and followed.

There was a bar, the Wagon Wheel, and Nick sauntered inside. I gave it a minute before I followed.

True to its namesake, the dive had a western theme. I recognized Dwight Yoakam's "A Thousand Miles From Nowhere" playing on the jukebox.

Nick already had a beer in front of him and was nose deep checking his phone when I slid onto the adjacent barstool. The bartender, a tired-looking bottle-blonde, approached. "What'll it be, handsome?"

I wondered if she was being facetious, considering the scar on my face. It was dark, so maybe she didn't notice. I tossed a twenty on the bar with, "Jameson. Rocks." She filled a glass with ice and gave me a generous pour. A cardboard coaster spun in front of me. She placed the glass atop before toting my twenty off to the cash register.

All the while, Nick didn't look up from his phone. I held up my drink with, "Great seminar."

He turned to me. "You were there?"

"Very informative."

"I'm glad you liked it."

I sipped the whiskey before asking, "Sell a lot of those gadgets?"

"A few," he said.

The bartender returned with my change before moving to another customer. I asked, "And those books of yours...sell a lot of those?"

"Here and there."

"But you don't actually practice," I said. "Seminars and selling that stuff is your racket, am I right?"

He clearly didn't like that and shot me a glare. "Of course I do. And I train investigators."

"You took on a case...a friend of mine, Madeline Garcia Ludwig. Up in Argonaut." I let that hang there to gauge his reaction.

"My client's confidentiality is—"

"Her husband was thrown down a mineshaft."

He countered with, "Any details of a case would be confidential between me and my client."

"Madeline says you took her retainer, then did nothing."

"And you are?"

"Jack O'Shea."

"And what is it you do?"

"Solve problems."

He glared at me.

I had my Deception Specialist business card in my breast pocket and slid it to him.

Nick considered it before he pulled at his pant leg—a gesture which made it clear he had a pistol holstered at the ankle. I know guns, and from what I could tell, it looked like a Ruger LCP .380 ACP. He asked, "What's a deception specialist?"

"Let's just say we're in the same line of work."

He leaned back, studied me for a second, then said, "Madeline retained my services. I interviewed campus security and the sheriff, but couldn't find evidence of any foul play, as she claimed. It was an accident, plain and simple."

"She never got a report."

"Have her check her spam folder."

I ignored that. "Three thousand dollars is one hell of a day rate."

"What do you want from me?"

"The return of two thousand, two hundred and fifty dollars will settle this matter. That allows seven hundred dollars for your effort, minus the fifty dollars I plopped down to sit in on your seminar tonight."

He eyed me. "If I refuse?"

"You won't."

I caught his eyes dart to the scar on my face. I'd never been one to intimidate people. My skill had always been friendly persuasion. I have to admit, there is something menacing about the scar. I could see wheels turning in Nick's head before he finally said, "I did my due diligence."

"She wants to know why you wouldn't return her phone calls."

"I'm busy."

"I'd suggest you settle now to avoid a civil case. That could be costly."

"I'll mail a check."

"Cash. Now."

"I don't have that much on me."

"You have a cash box back at the Motel 6."

That surprised him. "You're following me?"

"I found you here, didn't I?"

McClintlock pulled out his wallet, said, "I've got about three hundred on me."

"The cashbox."

He silently stewed in anger before finally nodding to himself. Nick settled his tab, and I followed him out of the bar, walking a few strides behind, prepared to run if he pulled his gun from that ankle holster. He asked, "So you're taking on Madeline's case?"

I wasn't planning on it, but said, "We'll see."

"The sheriff up there...make sure to get his perspective. He'll tell you all about what went down. People believe what they want to believe."

I said nothing. Nick entered his motel room as I stood near the doorway. He opened the road case, pulled out the cashbox, and counted what he had. Combining it with the money in his wallet, he said, "Just over two grand is what I've got."

"Throw in a bug detector and we'll call it even."

He reluctantly did, put it all in a plastic grocery bag, and set it on the bedspread. "Her husband had an accident. I told her that, but it wasn't what she wanted to hear."

"All of that is detailed in your report," I said. "The one she can find in her spam folder."

From Nick's reaction, it was clear he hadn't sent anything. I took the plastic bag. "Good luck with your medicine show."

"Medicine show?"

"Snake oil racket."

He scoffed. As I walked on, I heard the door close and the chain latch.

Down Highway 101, I found a pet friendly Best Western Plus that looked promising and got a room for the night. The first thing I did after walking my dog was fire up the bug detector. The device detected something—the strongest signal coming from the steering column. It was too dark to pull my dash apart, nor did I have the tools, so I figured I'd deal with it in the morning.

All the time I got the feeling I was being watched.

I guided Suzie into our room on the ground floor. I didn't see anyone out in the darkness, but sensed someone was out there.

There was no white van.

Had McClintlock followed me?

I texted Madeline, *Got some of the money back. Will see you tomorrow.*

A moment later, she returned a heart emoji. Another followed. This time it was an emoji cartoon caricature holding a magnifying glass and smoking a pipe—Sherlock Holmes.

CHAPTER 10

Hector was right. There was a complimentary breakfast at Best Western Plus, a sad, gluten-ridden affair of assorted packaged mini-muffins. I avoided that and opted for a cup of coffee. It was lukewarm and pathetically weak, but at least it was coffee. I'd get another on the road.

Even in daylight, I still couldn't shake the feeling I was being watched. Before I pulled out, I noticed something on the pavement—a pile of sunflower seeds. What are the chances? Could those have been from the kid in the white van? Was it he who installed the GPS tracker in my car?

Enough is enough.

Pimp Yo' Ride was set back in an industrial park amid funky cinderblock buildings and grease-stained pavement. The establishment did it all: tinted car windows, installed car stereos, alarm systems, ignition interlock devices, and even sold sheepskin seat covers. I explained to the lanky attendant the previous owner had installed a GPS device, and I needed to remove it.

"We can do that," he said, scratching his hipster-styled goatee. The scent of *the chronic* was on him—a wake-and-bake candidate, for sure. "When ya need it?"

"I'll wait."

He wiped his runny nose across an overly-tattooed forearm and said, "We'll get right on it then."

I looked for anybody else in the shop and I wondered what he meant by the collective *we*.

He was impressed by my car, called it "bad ass" before he pulled it into the service bay. Less than five minutes later, he had the steering-wheel cowling off and handed me a GPS device. Contact wires protruded from a black plastic casing. I had seen similar battery-powered GPS trackers, but this device was entirely different. It was clearly a model designed for fleet vehicles connected to the ignition. Someone had gone to the trouble of breaking into my car and installing the thing. But who? And how long had it been there?

I thanked him and paid for the work in cash.

"Need a receipt?" he asked.

"No."

He smiled, saying, "Save a tree." No surprise, the cash went into his pocket.

Not far from the industrial park, I pulled into a Pep Boys Auto Parts and bought a motorcycle battery and electrical tape. When I powered the tracking device, a tiny LCD light came on. Using the tape, I strapped the live device to the battery. Then drove around, wondering where I'd plant the thing.

An Allied Moving van was parked outside a home with piles of boxes stacked out on the driveway. I drove around the block and parked.

Nobody ever suspects somebody walking a dog is anything other than a neighbor, so I clipped Suzie to her leash and returned to the house. I waited for the moving guys to go inside before I slipped the GPS tracker attached to the battery rig into one of the cardboard boxes marked "Garage." I had no idea where the moving van was headed, nor did I know long the motorcycle battery would keep the GPS alive, but at least it would be out of my hair.

Suzie and I made our way back to the Chevy and set out for Argonaut. All the while, I kept an eye out for the white van, or anyone else, in my rear-view mirror.

Google Maps estimated about a four-hour drive across California's Central Valley into Eldorado National Forest. On the way, I called Hector to fill him in.

"Bitchin. You got her money?"

"Most of it."

"How?"

"Politely asked."

"Don't bullshit me."

"Nick McClintlock realized the juice wasn't worth the squeeze. I'm heading to Argonaut to hand it over, then heading back."

"You could just mail it."

"Not cash."

"I owe ya. Did you get a receipt from the hotel? How was the Continental breakfast?"

"We'll settle up over the next round of beers."

"You da man Jack," Hector said before we ended the call.

Pulling off the interstate, I reached a curvy, two-lane highway which led to rolling hills and then steep mountains. Google Maps informed me I had reached the town of Argonaut. Beyond the faded Kiwanis sign, there was a tasteful placard which read Bret Harte College.

The small mountain town was a mixture of new and old architecture. There was a quaint main street. A pizza restaurant. Local tavern. General store. I noticed a Placer County Sheriff vehicle parked behind the hardware store with a silhouette of a man in the driver's seat—like a cat hiding in weeds, poised to pounce. Could that be the sheriff who McClintlock had mentioned?

Even though it was cool, with clouds threatening rain, I found a parking structure on campus, shaded, since Suzie would be in the car again.

The campus of Bret Harte College had old-school charm with manicured lawns and Victorian-styled buildings. From a sign on campus, I learned the institution was once the California School of Mines before it was renamed in honor of author Bret Harte, a Gold Rush era contemporary of Mark Twain. I found the building marked Dramatic Arts, where Madeline and I planned to meet.

I made myself known to a student receptionist, who summoned Madeline. I could see a physical resemblance to her brother. She wore hefty black leather work boots in sharp contrast to her flowery dress. Madeline's eyes darted to my scar, like everyone does—human nature. I wondered if Hector had mentioned anything about my near fatal accident.

She escorted me past a few administrator types sitting at desks. A buck-toothed young man in a cable-knit sweater eyed me. I must admit, the scar makes me look suspicious.

We moved to her small office and Madeline closed the door. I handed over the money I'd retrieved from McClintlock, and said, "It's what he had in cash, a little over two grand."

"Amazing," she said, eyes wide.

"We got lucky."

"How much do I owe you?"

"Nothing. Your brother's an old friend."

"I have to pay for your time."

"I told Hector this one's on the house."

"No, I can't—"

"Your brother helped me out when I was down. I'm simply returning a favor."

Her eyes found my scar again. "He said you were in a car accident."

I offered a nod. "And that's when he really stepped up."

"Hector thinks I'm being ridiculous, but he doesn't know. Mike was murdered." She picked up a framed wedding photo and handed it to me. Mike had vibrant red hair and bright blue eyes with a close-shaven beard. They made a great looking couple. She said, "Mike didn't fall into that shaft. He was pushed."

"Who would have reason to do that?"

"I have a few ideas. This place...on the surface it's beautiful, but on the other hand—"

"Where did this happen?"

"Behind the theater," she said, motioning out the window.

"The rains opened up a sinkhole. They claim nobody knew it was there, but that's a lie because there was yellow caution tape around it. One of the maintenance guys heard Mike calling for help. Mountain Search and Rescue rappelled down." She grew emotional, took a moment to collect herself, and continued, "By the time I got there, he was still alive. I told him to hold on, that we'd get him out." She looked away, and took another moment before, "I told him I loved him, and to please hold on. After that..." She swallowed hard. "They pulled him up and did CPR. It wasn't the fall that killed Mike. He drowned. And now everyone's being all weird about it."

"Who?"

"Everybody."

"Tell me about this mineshaft."

"There's a maze of old tunnels below the campus because at one time this place was a gold mine. The school was originally the California School of Mines. There's the Colorado School of Mines near Denver, for engineers. This was California's version."

I told her I'd learned that reading the plaque when I'd entered campus.

"In the thirties," she said, "it became less focused on geo-engineering and more of a liberal arts college. They renamed it after Gold Rush poet Brett Harte. Now the school has gone all high tech, supposedly to feed graduates into Silicon Valley, today's Gold Rush. They're phasing out humanities programs for tech because that's where the money is."

"What did Mike do here?"

"An Assistant Professor in the theater department—tenure track. We were in rehearsals for a production of *Macbeth*. Have you seen it?"

I told her I hadn't.

"That play is cursed," Madeline said.

"Why do you say that?"

"Because it is. Saying *Macbeth* in the theater brings bad luck. We can talk about it here in my office, not a big deal, but in a performance space you must refer to it as *The Scottish Play*."

"Why?"

"Because of the curse," she said gravely.

"Superstition."

"Maybe. Maybe not." Madeline pulled a tattered book of the play from a shelf. "Some claim it's because Shakespeare wrote an actual curse into the text, stuff he'd copied from scribbles found in a witches' coven." Madeline turned to a page and read, *"Double, double toil and trouble; Fire burn and caldron bubble."*

Dismissing that, I asked, "Who do you think may have pushed Mike down the mineshaft?"

"It could have been a lot of people, but I suspect Louis was somehow involved. He teaches in the theater department, too."

"Would he have motive?"

"Louis wanted to replace Mike as the director. Now that Mike is out of the way, he got his wish. Louis is turning the production into a virtual reality movie. You know, where viewers wear goggles and look around."

"So now the play is a movie?"

"A virtual reality movie. I've been cast in the role of Lady MacDuff, a character who appears late in the play. Lord Macbeth has my character and her children killed out of fear, and ultimately faces my husband's vengeance. But let me tell you how our stage play became a movie," she said. "A woman who was a student here many years ago left a trust. She was the widow of some patriarch who made a fortune in San Francisco real estate. In her will, she endowed the theater department to produce at least one work of Shakespeare per year and run it for a minimum of twelve performances. That may be in the trust, but it's totally unrealistic. After opening night, hardly anyone shows up. As you can see," she said, motioning out the window, "this place is in the middle of nowhere, and these tech nerds don't give two shits about Shakespeare. But none of that matters because it's in the trust and can't be altered. For decades, the school has performed to an empty house just to justify the funds drawn from the endowment."

She replaced the book on the shelf. "Last year, Mike directed *Romeo and Juliet,* but set in Japan's Feudal period. He worked his ass off. The sets and costumes were awesome, with traditional Japanese string and flute music, Samurai swords. A critic from the *San Francisco Chronical* came opening weekend. She wrote it up as the best production of *Romeo and Juliet* she'd ever seen. But then..." Madeline shook her head sadly, "they found asbestos in the theater. Nobody can go in there unless they're wearing a space suit or something. But the college wasn't going to leave that money on the table. To fulfill their obligation, they've decided to make the production an independent film. That's when everything changed."

"How so?"

"Louis had directed some films before, but just a bunch of mumblecore."

"What's mumblecore?"

"Super low-budget indies?"

"Indie what?"

"Films. Mostly about twenty-something angst," she said with disdain. "Incredibly boring. You have no idea. His movies are basically vanity projects starring the girls he wants to sleep with. Louis totes these around to film festivals and pretends to be all important. I guess one of them got into Sundance. No...I think it was Slamdance."

"What's the difference?"

"Who the fuck cares?" she said, clearly frustrated. "It's all vanity bullshit. Mike was in rehearsal to make *Macbeth* as a regular movie. Now that he's gone, Louis has taken over and convinced everyone to make it a," quoting with her fingers, "virtual reality experience. Viewers have to wear goggles to see it. So now they've got a bunch of tech students working on the..." again with fingers she made quotes, "VR experience."

"You suspect Louis killed your husband to get him out of the way so he could take over the movie?"

"Behind Mike's back, Louis bitched and moaned *he* was the accomplished filmmaker. Somewhere he's got a participation trophy to prove it," she said with a laugh. "So Louis got his way. He's convinced the college to shoot virtual reality, claiming it will make the movie stand out, different from all the others. But now this production is out of control. They brought in all these crazy Renaissance Faire people. And you know that Medieval Times dinner show?"

I told her I was familiar with it.

"One of those went out of business, so he brought those people in, too. They all showed up with costumes, horses, weapons. There's even these incredibly stupid buhurt dudes."

I asked, "What's buhurt?"

"Medieval battle sport. They bludgeon each other dressed in full armor. The stupidest thing you've ever seen.

"Why is it called buhurt?"

"Who knows? All I know is this thing has gone from Shakespeare to *American Ninja Warrior*."

At that moment, there was a rap on the door.

"Yes?" Madeline called out.

The buck-toothed guy peeked in. "Apologies for interrupting. Chancellor Foster is here."

Madeline clinched her jaw before saying, "Thanks Lawrence." She turned to me, "I'll just be a minute," and made her way out to the hallway. She met a tall, silver-haired man in his sixties. They exchanged a few unheard words before they moved to a conference room.

"Can I get you anything? Bottled water?" Lawrence asked.

"No, thank you."

He smiled and departed.

Alone in Madeline's office, I stood by the window and observed the students milling about in the campus quad below. They seemed different than what I'd remembered when I was in school. Back in my day, we sat around on the lawn, threw Frisbees, kicked around the hackey sack, shared a cigarette or clandestine joint. I hadn't attended college for more than a couple years before I grew bored and dropped out to chase the almighty, ill-gotten dollar. In comparison, these students stood isolated with their noses in their phones, barely interacting with each other. Things have changed.

Madeline returned, a sour note on her face. She had a manila envelope under her arm, closed the door, pulled a document from inside. "Chancellor Foster wants to meet tomorrow to discuss this. It's some kind of contract." Madeline handed it to me and plopped down into her wooden chair. "I knew this was coming. They're going to fire me."

I was vaguely familiar with legalese, but not enough to decipher the language and clauses in the five-page agreement. I advised, "You should have a lawyer look at this."

"Do you know one?

Thinking of Oscar, I told her I knew someone who probably could look it over. I asked if she could copy it into a PDF file and email it to me. She was able to do that at the copy machine down the hall. I forwarded it to Oscar with a note to call after he'd reviewed it.

Seemingly beaten down, Madeline asked, "Will you look into Mike's murder?"

I tried to explain I wasn't qualified for the job. "Investigating a death is not in my wheelhouse."

"Can you at least speak with Louis and see what he has to say?"

"What makes you think he'll talk to me?"

"Mike and Louis were best friends. Competitive, sure, but drinking buddies."

I agreed.

Madeline said, "If you look 'yes man' up in the dictionary, you'll see a picture of Louis, a supreme kiss-ass." She pulled up a photo on her phone. "But I'll save you the trouble."

Louis was a barrel-chested guy with facial hair. Tats. Bravado. Madeline jotted down the location where they were shooting the movie and explained, "They've taken over a Christian summer camp. Built sets. That's where the crazy re-enactors and Medieval Times people are staying. I'll text Louis and let him know you're coming."

I asked, "So Mike and Louis were best friends?"

She nodded.

"Who kills their best friend?"

"In the third act of *Macbeth* the title character does just that, kills Banquo. His best friend."

I didn't know how to reply, so told her I'd be in contact. As I made my way out, I felt the eyes of buck-toothed Lawrence on my back. Something about the guy.

As I walked back to my car, I diverted to the theater building. I needed to check out the scene of the crime.

CHAPTER 11

A portable chain-link fence surrounded the building. The windows and doors of the campus theater were covered in plywood. They stapled a layer of thick plastic at every entrance. Asbestos caution signs were posted in both English and Spanish.

I moved around back.

A garden hose connected to a spigot led up the hill to yellow tape surrounding the cordoned-off sinkhole.

There was a wooden flower planter fashioned as a makeshift memorial of some kind. Stapled on the wooden planter were memorial photos and letters to the deceased. Wilted perennial flowers made it pathetically sad.

Surrounded by a mesh barrier, the mouth of the mineshaft appeared to be about twelve feet in diameter. Discarded medical wrappers were stuck in nearby weeds—evidence a first re-sponse trauma team had worked there.

I peered down into the sinkhole. Daylight illuminated only so much of the cavernous abyss before it dropped into blackness. The thought of falling inside made the hairs on my arms stand on edge.

What didn't make sense was why someone would climb the steep embankment up the hill. Did Mike toss something into the shaft and accidentally slip? Closet-alcoholics hide evidence of booze bottles. Maybe he stepped out of the theater to take a clandestine nip, then went up to toss the empty and lost his footing. Or maybe he heard a noise from down inside and went to investigate.

As I walked to my car, Oscar phoned, "What's this document you sent me?"

I explained the situation; I was helping the sister of a friend investigating her husband's fatal accident.

"Bret Harte College is her employer?"

"She teaches there, yes."

"This is a Covenant Not to Sue, which is an agreement for each party not to litigate. Would the college have any reason to sue her?"

"I don't know."

"If she signs," Oscar said, "and there is a workplace accident of any kind, she would not be able to pursue workman's compensation or a personal injury claim." Oscar is an expert in the slip-and-fall racket, his stock-in-trade. Gotta love him.

"I'll advise her not to sign."

"When are you back in town?"

"Late tonight."

"I've got a job for ya. Need you to start right away. I'll fill you in tomorrow."

"Thanks."

At my car, Suzie was happy to see me. I took her on a short walk. As usual, she spent most of her time sniffing for evidence of other dogs—the canine detective method, olfactory investigation. I often wonder what's going through her mind as Suzie roots around with her nose. What does her mind's eye see?

We returned to my car. I pulled out of town.

The patrol car I'd seen earlier behind the hardware store followed me. I kept a watchful eye in the rearview mirror.

Call it premonition, but you can always tell before you're going to be pulled over.

CHAPTER 12

I drove out of Argonaut and onto the highway. The sheriff followed. I knew he would turn on the lights to pull me over and wondered why he was waiting so long. There was a sign for a turnout just ahead, and finally the flashing lights came on.

I pulled over, killed the engine, and retrieved my license and registration from the glove compartment. The knife I'd used to puncture the tires of the white van was in there. I closed it and rested my arms on the wheel in plain view.

He didn't emerge from the car for a while, so I assumed he was running my plates. Other than crashing into the semi with Mona, I had a spotless driving record. Maybe he was reading about the incident. I had no idea if the Department of Motor Vehicles would have the details if there was a death involved in that accident. I assumed so. Maybe he was reading that.

When he finally stepped out, I could see the sheriff was broad shouldered, tall, in his early forties. He approached my car on the passenger side, so I brought that window down. Surprisingly, he said, "Do you have a weapon in your possession?"

"No," I said, wondering why he asked, thinking about the foldable knife in the glove compartment. Was that a weapon?

"Are you certain?"

"Yes."

"Your license and registration please."

I held them out. As he reached into the car Suzie, who was laying down on the passenger floor, popped her head up. That startled him. He jumped back. His hand went to his sidearm.

"She's friendly," I said.

"Restrain the animal."

I grabbed Suzie by the collar. "She's not aggressive. Gentle as can be."

"What part of restrain your animal do you not understand?" He unsnapped the leather strap which secured the Glock at his side.

I said, "The leash is in the back."

"Leave the dog in the car and step out."

I did so.

"Place your hands on the hood."

I followed his orders.

He came up behind me, pulled my wrists behind me and slapped on handcuffs. He kicked my feet apart, then patted me down. "What's your business in Argonaut?"

"I'm an insurance investigator."

"Doing what?"

"Looking into an accident."

"That bullshit with Mike Ludwig?" Did he know I had met with Madeline? He must have because he asked, "How much life insurance will she get?"

"I have no idea," I said. "My job is to interview the beneficiary and write a report."

"Where's the gun you were waving around?"

"What gun?"

"The weapon I saw you pointing out the window."

I had no idea what he was talking about. I'd left my grandfather's Colt 1903 Pocket Hammerless .32 back in my locked office safe in Los Angeles. That was the only weapon I'd ever owned. "I don't have a gun."

He retrieved something from his boot—a silver compact pistol. I recognized the Jimenez JA-22, a cheap, pathetic, throwaway

Saturday night special.

At that moment, Suzie growled from the passenger seat. She must have sensed my anxiety because her lip curled to reveal fangs.

The sheriff pulled a canister from his belt.

"No!" I said, but it was too late. He doused her face with mace.

Suzie jumped out the side window. He kicked her. But Greyhounds were born to run. That's exactly what she did. Suzie moved like a rocket, zig-zagging and disappearing into the brush as the mist of airborne pepper spray stung my eyes.

He slammed me against the hood. "Resisting arrest. Failure to control a vicious animal. Open carry of an unlicensed firearm."

"That's not mine."

"Then why is it in your car?"

"Because you put it there." I said, "And even if it was mine, how would you know it's unlicensed?"

I'd called his bluff, and that caught him off guard. In retaliation, he punched me in the kidney. He grabbed my shirt and slammed me up against the hood. "Nobody," he said, "comes into my town waving a gun."

It was clear I was being arrested, so said nothing.

"What did Madeline tell you?"

I remained silent. He asked me again, but I said nothing. It was clear that irked him. "I asked you a question."

"Are you arresting me?"

He released his grasp and stepped back. There was a moment of silence before he held out the silver .22 pistol and said, "I'm confiscating this as evidence. Get the hell out of here. If I see you again, you'll regret it."

I nodded. With that, he released me from the cuffs.

I nursed my side where he'd hit me as he returned to his patrol car. The remnants of the pepper spray burned my eyes. He got in, spun a U-turn, and sped back up the hill in a wake of dust.

I called for Suzie.

Nothing.

At first, I heard her whimper. Then finally she emerged from the trees, panting. My dog limped towards me with her tail between legs. I could see her hind leg was quivering, so picked her up and gently carried Suzie to my car. The chemical smell was heavy, so I had to open both doors to air it out.

With bottled water and a hand towel, I cleansed Suzie's face the best I could. Squinty-eyed, clearly in pain, she licked my hand.

I swore that bastard would pay for what he did to my dog.

CHAPTER 13

On my phone I searched Google for the nearest veterinarian outside of Placer County—out of the sheriff's jurisdiction. As luck would have it, there was an animal hospital in El Dorado County in a town named Juniper.

I made my way there with Suzie panting aside me, clearly in pain.

Clay Pigeon Animal Hospital was housed in a double-wide trailer set in front of a restored Victorian farmhouse. I parked and carried Suzie inside to Dr. Lois Reibach, the middle-aged proprietor. She asked me how Suzie encountered pepper spray. I figured I'd avoid mention of the local sheriff and came up with something benign. "From what I could tell, it was a delivery guy dropping off a package. I shouldn't have had my dog off-leash."

"Where?"

"Up near Argonaut. At first, I thought I'd try to get her home, but since she's suffering..."

"Where's home?"

"L.A."

"You did right by bringing her in."

The veterinarian turned her attention to my dog. At first, I wondered why she wasn't doing anything but soon realized she was studying her patient, picking up on signals. I noticed a few plaques on the wall for trap and skeet shooting. There were photos of a teenage Lois posing with trophies and shotguns. "Skeet shooter, huh?"

"Trap and skeet."

In one of the photos, a celebrity I recognized was presenting a trophy to her. I asked, "Is that Robert Stack from *Unsolved Mysteries*?"

"Bob was a Hall of Fame skeet shooter, yeah."

All around the room there were photos of dogs with ducks and pheasants in their mouths. To lighten the mood, I asked, "What do people with pet birds think when they come in and see all this?"

"I tend to an occasional exotic bird, but not often."

Lois gently carried Suzie to a stainless-steel wash station in the corner and proceeded to flush her face with warm water. When Suzie shook herself, as wet dogs do, I stepped back to avoid the spray, but Lois stayed on task. Her polo shirt and khakis were soaked, but she didn't flinch.

After, as Doc Reibach gently dried Suzie with a towel, I explained how my pup had a career on the racetrack before I adopted her from Greyhound Rescue.

She asked, "Do they still race Greyhounds these days?"

"Not so much in the United States, but in Tijuana and the UK...it's still a thing. I didn't rescue her as much as she rescued me."

"You're saying a delivery driver did this?"

It was clear she had the feeling I wasn't telling the entire truth, so I admitted, "Actually, it was a sheriff outside Argonaut."

"Marsh?"

"I didn't get his name."

"If you came across the cop in Argonaut, it was probably Marsh."

I explained how he had pulled me over and went through the motions of arresting me. "Suzie growled at him, so he hit her with pepper spray." I left out the fact he'd planted a gun on me. "I'm an investigator looking into an accident."

"Let me guess, the professor who fell down that mineshaft?" She was one step ahead of me.

"You heard about that?"

"That's the latest scandal. That college has had its share."

"Like what?"

"Oh…" She bit her lip before, "There was a boy from around here, Jimmy…a special needs kid. Very sweet. He loved animals and used to volunteer for me." I picked up a tinge of anger in her tone as she said, "He was crossing the street and killed by a hit-and-run driver. They determined it was a Bret Harte student, some kid from overseas. Sheriff Marsh jailed the boy before the arraignment, but then released him for some unknown reason. He skipped town. There are still a lot of unanswered questions."

"Like what?"

She shrugged, and said, "He was obviously a flight risk, but the kid's parents had given a lot of money to the school, so…" I could tell Dr. Reibach didn't want to go into detail. She turned her attention to Suzie. "Eyes don't appear to be damaged, but Suzie's hind leg has me concerned. I'd like to take an X-ray so I'll need to sedate her. That means keeping her overnight. I won't put her in a crate." Lois thumbed over her shoulder. "She can recover in my home, on a dog bed, so she won't be alone."

"Is that necessary?"

"If her leg is broken, there's the risk of infection, so if it were my dog…"

It made sense, so I agreed.

She assured me, "Don't worry, she'll be fine. Animals are a lot more resilient than we give them credit. These things tend to be a wait-and-see."

I thanked her, signed paperwork, and then bid Suzie goodbye. She looked at me with sad eyes. I was devastated. I stayed at her side as Doc Reibach administered a tranquilizer and she dozed off. "No need to worry. She's going to be fine."

But I was worried.

As Doc Reibach walked me to the door, she said, "Come back

midday tomorrow."

I told her I would, and asked, "What else can you tell me about Sheriff Marsh?"

She scratched her head and considered her answer. "Let's just say he protects the interests of the college. It's a cloistered group up there." She gave me a pamphlet and told me I could call anytime, day or night, to see how Suzie was doing.

I trusted my dog was in good hands, but my plans had to change. There was no way I would head back to L.A. that night.

Returning to my car, the odor of pepper spray remained strong, so I opened the windows and cranked the air conditioner. I tried to figure out my next move. I hadn't eaten anything all day and was starving.

Up ahead, there was a sign for Amarillo Slims BBQ. The scent of white oak wafting from the restaurant's smoker closed the deal. I'd grab something to eat and search on my phone for a place to stay overnight.

Amarillo Slims was housed in a rundown, clapboard building which looked like it was a former filling station. Checking out the menu over the counter, the restaurant offered Texas style BBQ, which is my preference—beef-centric rather than pork, spiced-based rather than vinegar. The walls of the establishment were covered with rusty Texas license plates. There were vintage photos of the restaurant's bolo tied, cowboy hat-wearing namesake—1970s era professional poker player Amarillo Slim. As a lifetime gambler, I knew all about Poker Hall of Famer Thomas Austin Preston Jr. aka Amarillo Slim. My dad pointed him out from his cameo in the old gambling movie *California Split* starring Elliot Gould. This place had a theme.

While a hefty, bearded, biker type worked back in the kitchen, a woman confined to a motorized wheelchair took my order. The counter had been lowered so she could access the cash register and beer taps. A golden retriever in a service animal vest lay at her side. I noticed a chrome Harley-Davidson emblem on her wheelchair as I ordered the brisket sandwich.

The woman asked, "Ice cold beer with that, hon?"

I considered the selection and chose Sierra Nevada; the only craft brew I recognized. She produced a chilled glass, poured me a pint, and gave me a chrome stand with my order number, even though I was the only customer in the place. I thanked her and found a seat outside at one of the tables on the redwood deck. From there, I called Madeline and explained I'd been pulled over on the way to meet with Louis, and been roughed up.

Not surprised, she said, "Sheriff Marsh is an asshole."

"He asked about you."

"He's been harassing Mike and I forever."

"He knew I'd come to meet with you."

"This place...gossip hounds. It's been a feeding frenzy."

I explained the circumstances why I needed to stay overnight since my dog was at the veterinarian. I told her I'd speak with Louis in the morning. That meant I could I'd accompany her to the meeting scheduled with the chancellor.

"Thank you," she said gratefully. "I didn't want to go alone." We made plans to meet on campus the next day.

The biker cook emerged with a caddy of BBQ sauces and a stand for paper towels. The guy had the build of an NFL lineman, but ironically, "Slim" was embroidered on his restaurant apron. I told him, "I smelled the burning oak, and that drew me in."

"Yeah... I burn mostly oak and pecan. Hickory now and again, but everyone smokes that tired ole wood. My wife Sandy wants me to add some vegetarian and vegan options to the menu, but..." Slim shook his head and muttered something under his breath I didn't understand before heading back inside.

A moment later, he returned with a Kaiser roll stacked with a generous portion of thinly sliced brisket, a mustard potato salad on the side. "Just came off the smoker," he said. "Sauces are all homemade, Texarkana Sweetie-pie, Vinegaroon, and Jala-Pecos, which has the Jalapeño kick." The names of each were hand-scribed on the plastic squeeze bottles. "Enjoy," he said and moved on inside.

Authentic Texas barbecue is hard to come by. This guy knew what he was doing. It was incredible. After I'd finished, I brought my empty glass and plate to the counter and asked Sandy, "Can you recommend a hotel?"

"We've got rental cabins here. You're free to take a look." She spun to the wall and pulled a key from a hanging rack. "There's a unit up on the left, number four. Just renovated. Take a gander."

I had in mind a modern chain hotel, like the corporate Best Western Plus back in Santa Rosa. "Dog friendly?"

"Of course," she said, and leaned down to stroke her dog's head. "Got a pup with ya?"

I explained Suzie was staying overnight at the veterinarian.

"Doc Reibach then."

I nodded.

"You're in good hands. She set me up with ole Harley here." The dog perked up at the mention of her name. "Most hotels only set aside a few pet-friendly rooms, and they're always the nasty-ass ones, right? Rank-ass carpet, near the ice machine. Pets are welcome in all our cabins. Go up and take a look. No obligation."

I wasn't entirely convinced, but her charm and persistence won me over.

Emerging from the restaurant, I hadn't noticed the roadside sign for the Panhandle Inn. The restaurant and motel were on the same property. Above Amarillo Slims, tucked beneath the pines, there were a half dozen cabins with handicap accessible ramps. Considering the proprietor, that made sense.

Unit four was sparse yet tasteful. There was a desk, an office chair, and a small kitchenette. The unit had its own router. The clincher was the hubcap hammer-crafted into a dog bowl on the tile floor. I went back to the counter, checked in, and brought my stuff up from the car.

My torso had been aching. It wasn't until I took off my shirt that I saw the purple welt on my side. I cleaned it with warm, soapy water.

I texted Oscar *"call me,"* even though I knew he wouldn't get back to me until the next day. Oscar rarely does business past banker's hours unless it's over cocktails in one of the red-leather upholstered booths at one of the prime rib joints he regularly haunts.

I opened my laptop, connected to the WiFi, and emailed asking if Oscar could look into Placer County Sheriff Deputy Marsh as well as Chancellor Foster of Bret Harte College. As a lawyer, Oscar had access to what's not necessarily public information.

On the Internet, I searched and found plenty of details about Chancellor Foster in academic circles, but nothing about the Sheriff. No surprise. Folks in law enforcement keep their digital footprint to a minimum.

I wondered what I'd gotten myself into.

My phone rang. The number was all too familiar, a surprise call from my father, not part of the regular routine. That happened occasionally. Prisoners barter privileges. He greeted me with, "Christ almighty, my back is killing me."

"Try stretching. Make that a daily routine."

"It sucks getting old."

"Stay positive. You'll be out on the beach with your feet in the sand before you know it."

"Don't bullshit me."

Even though it would be years before my dad would ever be considered for release, I had to keep his hopes up. I make it a point on our phone calls to be positive. No doubt, he got a bum deal. He asked what I was up to.

"Been busy with work." Without going into detail, I explained I was on a new case.

My father didn't understand why I'd changed profession to work for the other side. But he also admitted it put him at ease to know I wasn't following in his same footsteps. "My biggest mistake," he confessed, "was not finding a good woman. You needed a decent mom."

Maybe he was right. Growing up in a single-parent household, if you can call my dad's squalid homes a *household*, there were a string of temporary mother figures in my life. There was some love there between us, but none of that lasted. It was always a sad day when they took me aside to say goodbye. Had my father been legitimately employed, it may have been different. He lived hand-to-mouth and spent money as fast as he made it. Or should I say stole it? The gambling didn't help.

Women need a sense of security. My father couldn't deliver that. He was always looking over new horizons. Unfortunately, that included his love life. There was always a part of my dad that needed to arrive in that shiny new car.

Like father, like son.

Our bi-weekly, twenty-minute phone calls were scheduled Tuesdays and Fridays. He'd often tell stories I'd heard a million times. I humor him by listening—reliving his past. It was a place to go in his mind, a distraction from mundane day-to-day incarceration.

As usual, he was telling a familiar tale when the beeps interrupted us. He ignored them but barely got in his advice to not accept wooden nickels just before we were cut off.

Are nickels or dimes a thing anymore? Weren't there five-and-dime stores not that long ago? Have those become 99 Cent Stores? I don't know.

My plan for the next day was to speak with Louis on the set of the movie, accompany Madeline to the meeting with the chancellor, retrieve my dog Suzie, and head back to L.A.

Best-laid plans. Little did I know.

CHAPTER 14

Three Years Ago
Santa Monica, California

I never expected Mona would show up at my door. She had a swollen black eye, her dark burgundy-velvet dress splotched with dried blood. "Hey," she said, "Remember me?"

"You alright?" I said, concerned.

She shrugged. "I'll survive."

"What happened?"

She avoided that question by saying, "Ya got something to drink?"

At the time, I was leasing a luxury, two-bedroom condominium in the Sea Colony overlooking the Santa Monica Pier. I invited her in, wondering how she discovered where I lived. I retrieved a chilled bottle of water, but she said, "Got an adult beverage?"

I had a bottle of Sauvignon Blanc in the fridge. She chugged the water first before easing herself onto the couch, clearly in pain. I pulled a bag of frozen peas out of the freezer, set it on the coffee table between us, and poured her a glass of wine. "Who hit you?"

"Boyfriend."

"You should call the police."

"Hell no," she said and gulped the wine. Her swollen lip left bloody residue on the rim of the glass.

I asked, "How'd you find me here?"

"You gave me your number."

"Sure, but not an address."

Mona said nothing, wincing as she pressed the bag of frozen peas against her eye. With the other, she looked at me with, "You want me to leave?"

"No. Just curious."

"I tried to call, but you didn't pick up."

I nodded. There was a call. "I didn't recognize the number."

She set the bag of peas down and said, "I didn't text or leave a voicemail because I was afraid you'd turn me away. I ran the number you gave me through a search engine. I wasn't sure if this was the right place," she said, looking around, "but you said you lived by the beach."

My condo wasn't an address you'd come across on Google. All my mail correspondence came through a proxy address at a nearby mailbox center. To find me, Mona would have to have had access to a professional database—a subscription-based tool used by law enforcement, investigative professionals, process servers, and skip tracers. I asked, "What search engine?"

"IRB."

"IRBsearch?"

She nodded, sipped her wine.

I knew it well and was surprised it had my address. "Access to that requires a subscription fee. And that doesn't come cheap."

"I used to work in collections," she said. "My password still works." There was a moment of awkward silence before she asked, "What about that job you mentioned?"

"I can use someone to stuff envelopes."

She nodded, clearly not enthused.

I added. "Real estate opportunities."

"Legit or a hustle?"

"Debatable," I admitted. "It's a lot of cold-calling and follow up. The work can be a grind."

"Cold-calling, huh?" she peeled back her collar and moved the bag of peas to the side of her neck, adjusting a necklace with a silver butterfly as the pendant. I could see purple bruise marks, evidence of strangulation.

"I really think you should call the police."

"No cops."

"You're going to let him get away with that?"

She closed her eyes and said nothing.

I got up, dug out Advil and a first aid kit, and set them on the table. Then I busied myself with making quesadillas. She worked on the bottle of wine, scrolling through her phone until she finally said, "Trevor tried to kill me." She explained how they got into a "knock-down, drag-out fight." She broke away and ran out of their hotel without her purse, credit cards, or wallet. All she had was her phone.

There was a casino junket bus, so she snuck on and hid in the bathroom. After the bus got underway, she learned from one of the passengers it was heading to Koreatown in Los Angeles.

She remembered what I had said about a job prospect, so ran an IRBsearch on her phone. When the bus reached L.A., she jumped the turnstiles of the Expo Line and took the train to Santa Monica.

Mona said, "I looked up halfway houses, you know…for battered women. Looks like there's a decent one near here. But they're going to ask a lot of questions. It'll be best to tell them I have a job, and they'll probably call you to confirm."

"Not a problem."

"Thanks," she said and asked if she could take a shower.

At the time, I had an on-and-off-again girlfriend, Andrea, basically a friend-with-benefits. Andrea was of Vietnamese descent and worked at the Hollywood Park Casino dealing poker. She lived in Garden Grove with her parents and her young son from a failed marriage. Andrea was often busy working or looking after her boy, so it had been over a month since we'd last seen each other. We weren't exclusive, by any means, but she kept some of her clothes in a drawer for when she stayed overnight—loose cotton drawstring pants and a sweatshirt. Some of Andrea's girly shampoo was in the shower, plus a hairbrush, lotion, and light makeup. Mona was grateful.

The hot shower had opened the cut above her eye. Since the mirror in the bathroom was steamed, I blotted the wound, could see it was deep, and said, "You should get this stitched."

"I've had worse."

"It will leave a scar."

The bitter irony was I'd be the one to end up with the facial scar—had I only known then. I did my best to disinfect and bandage the wound. Fortunately, I had a tube of Dermabond medical-grade adhesive, basically Super Glue for human skin. I used a dab on Mona's forehead and that closed the wound.

Mona returned to her wine and called the halfway house. They encouraged her to check into the facility immediately. She reluctantly agreed. After she hung up, Mona said, "Trevor and I had been drinking. A lot. And we were doing lots of blow, which makes him super paranoid."

"Was heroin part of that, too?" I asked.

"What makes you say that?"

"The track marks on your arm," I reminded her. "I saw them back in Vegas."

Instinctively, she pulled the sleeve down. "Those two things go hand-in-hand—the up and down of it."

"I can't hire you unless you're clean."

"Does that include everything?"

"What's that mean?"

"Wine?"

"In moderation."

"Weed okay?"

I shrugged.

She said, "I'll be good. I promise. At the shelter, they'll insist I be sober if I'm going to stay there. Like I said, they're going to ask a lot of questions."

"This isn't the first time your boyfriend hit you, is it?"

"That day in Vegas, when you and I ran into each other, I was trying to get away from him. But he went to my friend Vickie, and she convinced me to come back."

"Why did you?"

"I don't know."

"Not very smart."

That got her angry. She said, "Look, thanks for the wine and for letting me take a shower." Mona stood. "I'll stay at this halfway house until I can find a place of my own. When they call, just tell them I have a job, okay?" Mona swayed a little to keep her balance. The wine had obviously gone straight to her head.

The doorbell rang. That was a surprise. She stopped in her tracks. I brought up the surveillance camera to see who it was.

"That's Trevor," she said with fear.

I told Mona to give me her phone and go to the guest bedroom. She was hesitant until I said, "He tracked you here from your phone. As long as you have it..."

The realization came over her. "Shit," she said, and handed over her phone before ducking out of sight.

I unlatched the chain and answered the door. "Yes?"

"Who are you?" Trevor asked. He had an Australian accent, something I wasn't expecting.

With flamboyance, I replied, "Excuse me, and *you* are...?" enacting an openly gay persona. I'd played the overly-dramatic stock character before, figured it would divert suspicion.

"Where's Mona?"

"Who is Mona?" I said, arms at my sides.

"Don't bullshit me."

"And who buzzed you into my building?" I asked accusingly.

"I know Mona's here."

"I don't know who Mona is or what you're talking about. Did that bitch Clarice put you up to this? It was Clarice, wasn't it? Oh, wait..." I said, snapping my finger as if just remembering, "The phone...that's what brought you here."

Mona's phone was in my back pocket. I ducked out of sight for a second and then opened and closed the drawer of the foyer vanity table, making it sound as if I had put it in there. I returned to the door, clutching the phone, saying, "I found this in the sand off the bike path this afternoon. I was waiting for someone to call."

"That's mine, mate."

I handed it over.

Trevor worked at punching the security code. He appeared to have no luck. "Did you see a blonde?"

"Where?"

"Where you found the phone."

"Throw a stick on the beach, and you'll hit three blondies."

"Who did you see?"

"Nobody. Like I said, I found it beside the bike path."

He stormed off without saying a word. I called out, "You're welcome," and shut the door.

After a moment, Mona timidly emerged from the guestroom.

I went to the window. There was a dark luxury SUV idling on the street below. A tall man in a dark suit was smoking a cigarette. Mona peered out the window too. Trevor and the driver had a few words before the man tossed his cigarette. They climbed into the vehicle and drove off.

Mona said, "That's Rex King. The guy we work with."

"What does he do?"

"Arranges things."

"Like?"

"V.I.P concierge sort of things."

"Drugs?"

"And sex."

"You're part of that?"

"No."

"Why don't I believe you?"

"I'm no whore."

"It sounds like your boyfriend's a pimp."

"Rex is the pimp. I have nothing to do with that shit," she said, angered, and plopped down on the couch. "You know that saying, *what happens in Vegas stays in Vegas*? That's total bullshit. Unless you pay the piper."

"What's that mean?"

Mona pulled a light throw blanket off the edge of the couch for comfort. "Trevor would fish out a prospect, a high roller or big-time exec, stalk the guy. In the meantime, I'd do a deep-dive to find everything I could about him. Trevor can befriend almost anyone—pours on the charm and greases the right palms for access to these kinds of guys. While he's setting up a good time, I'd run a search for their wives, employers, sometimes even the guy's mom."

"Using IRBsearch?"

"That, and other ways. Rex manages a stable of—jailbait is what Trevor calls them. They're hustlers, boys and girls, young. Nubile is the thing. It's about putting the guy in an uncompromising position. Rex is a real pig, brands these kids with his tattoo, like they're cattle or something."

"A tattoo?"

"He gets them wasted, and a guy downtown inks it. Ye Olde King's Throne Tattoo Emporium. He chose that place because his last name is King. I shit you not." She sipped her wine. "The kids are trained to come onto these guys—not to necessarily proposition like an escort, but...other ways. He's even had girls dressed up like hotel maids, knocked on doors, ask for help with something, come on to these dudes. It's all about timing. These guys are not aware of the hidden cameras. Afterward, Trevor confronts the guy and informs him he hooked up with someone underage. He threatens to expose him as a pedophile unless he pays."

I said, "The badger game."

"What's that?"

"It's what the scam is called."

"Why is it called that?"

"Because the mark is badgered to fork over hush money. Blackmailed."

"Hush money. That's right. Hush hush. Most of these pervs deserved what they got. Sometimes they'd resist and threaten to go to the cops. But by then, I'd already mocked up a sexual predator map from their neighborhood back home, and social media posts. Trevor would show them that—"

"Anyone go to the police?"

"Trevor made it clear he'd ruin them, but some did."

"How?

"He had this download link, full of child pornography... called it his Trojan Horse. You know, open it and all sorts of nasty shit corrupts your computer. It doesn't steal bank information but instead infects the hard drive with porno, and there is nothing you can do about it."

"He could do that?"

"Most of these guys would go to the casino cage for a cash advance, or to the bank. When they're back home, Trevor pressures them more. That's what he called a cash cow, pay-ments on a *subscription plan.*"

"And this worked?"

"All depends on what the guys had to lose. If access to cash was a problem, Trevor would walk them through how to stage a burglary at home. We got diamonds, rare gems, engagement rings. Vegas pawn shops don't ask a lot of questions."

"Then why did Trevor try to kill you?"

She fingered the bruise on her neck. "All the marks and how much they paid—all on my phone. A log. I wouldn't give it to him." She swallowed hard. "But now he's got what he wants."

"Look," I said, "I realize you don't know me from Adam, but you can stay in the guest bedroom tonight, if you'd like. That way, you don't have to go to the shelter until tomorrow."

"I didn't plan on staying at the shelter more than a couple nights, anyway."

"It's entirely up to you."

"Thanks."

I had to ask her, "Was Vickie the woman I saw you go to outside the diner?"

"You saw her?"

I nodded.

"Vickie," she said solemnly. Mona's mind went somewhere else for a moment before she asked, "You got another bottle of wine?"

CHAPTER 15

Mona never went to the halfway house for battered women. And like that, I had a stranger as a roommate.

She slept most of the first day and refused alcohol, saying she needed to dry out. Over the next two days, Mona jogged on the beach, spent hours on my exercise bike, and binge-watched hours of sensational true-crime television back in the guest room.

I put her to work, catching up on the correspondence I had active by crafting hundreds of personalized emails. The effort was designed to rope investors into a real estate scheme I was working at the time. I impersonated a high-end real estate broker and listed properties I didn't own. When a sucker came sniffing, I'd give the pitch. The story was always the same—a property near the beach at a price that would not last unless a preemptive bid was made immediately, as a deposit in good faith. Nothing closes better than urgency. After they handed over the money, of course, they'd never hear from me again.

This scam was a scattershot approach. And nibbles were rare. The work was admittedly a grind, but Mona didn't seem to mind that. She was surprisingly good. And having a female voice at my disposal playing the role of the executive secretary gave my business the air of legitimacy.

After a few days, Mona slipped back into drinking. It was only a little at first, but then picked up. My rule was nothing before five o'clock—only when work was finished for the day. She was fine with that, but I sensed her teeth grinding by mid-afternoon.

Andrea, my on-and-off-again girlfriend, called one evening. Her shift at the Hollywood Park Casino had ended, and her parents had taken her son down to San Diego's Legoland for the weekend. Andrea proposed we hang out, which was her shorthand for dinner, drinks, and her usual overnight stay. As I told Andrea it wasn't a good time, Mona motioned for me to mute the phone. I excused myself, put Andrea on hold, and said, "It's not a big deal."

"I'll get out of here," Mona insisted.

"I don't want her to come over. It would only complicate things."

"I'll get a hotel."

I resumed the call and told Andrea I felt like I was coming down with something. Mona seemed disappointed. After I hung up, Mona said, "I don't want to come between you two."

I explained my friends-with-benefits situation, and that neither of us were in love. "We just see each other to scratch an itch."

"Oh, really?" she said, amused, and teased, "And how often does this so-called *itch* come around?"

"Let's not make a big deal out of it. I'll see her some other time. Trust me, her next call will be to some other guy."

"Oh, yeah?"

"Yeah."

She said nothing and went back to watching television.

Up until that day, the daily routine was we'd retreat to our separate bedrooms each night. I'd often hear her watching TV as I drifted off to sleep. That night, she'd gone to bed before me. After I had turned out the light and got into bed to read from the stack of books on my nightstand, there was a light rap on my bedroom door. I asked what she needed.

Mona opened the door wearing Andrea's black silk robe, open

in front. Underneath that, she was naked. She said nothing, just stood there while she ran her fingers down below her belly button.

"Look, I don't think…" I started to get up.

"Shh," she whispered, "stay there. Don't talk."

Mona leaned her weight against the door jamb. Her breathing picked up as she gently pleasured herself.

In silence, I watched. After a minute, her body stiffened before she quivered. Afterward, Mona gently closed the robe and bid me goodnight. I could hear her drift back to her room and close the door.

Was that some kind of overture? I wondered if I should get up and go to her, but decided against it. I didn't know what to do, or how to feel. It took a long time before I could fall asleep.

The next morning, when I got up the nerve to ask what that was all about, Mona echoed what I'd said about Andrea with, "Let's not make a big deal out of it."

I said, "Okay, but—"

"I was scratching an *itch*."

Touché.

Nothing was discussed more. We went about our business. But I caught her looking at me more often than usual.

The next night, I left my door slightly open. Sure enough, Mona appeared in the darkness. This time, she entered my room, slipped off the silky robe, and joined me in bed.

I have no idea where my stamina came from. With Andrea, I would have been done after making love once—roll over and call it a night. But with Mona, I couldn't get enough. Everything about her turned me on. When I thought we were done, and it was time for a break, she had other ideas.

The next morning, we had a lazy breakfast in bed, and Mona opened up about herself for the first time. "My mom and dad both were corporate climbers in the tech world, jumping from startup to startup, jockeying for stock options and greener pastures. All they wanted was that big payday. But they were unhappy, always chained to their work. I didn't want that life. So boring. I found school to be a waste of time. So after graduation, I moved in with friends and found a decent job in collections chasing down deadbeats."

"A collection agency?"

"That was boring too."

I knew how the debt-collection racket worked. After months of unsuccessful attempts, a bank, hospital, or retailer gives up trying to collect what's owed and sells the debt in order to cut their losses and get it off the books. Using aggressive tactics, the collection agency goes after debtors, willing to settle for fifty cents on the dollar. Without necessarily having to put up equity, a collection agency writes a contract to purchase the debt at about twenty-five cents on the dollar. When they collect, it's much more than twenty-five percent, and they keep the difference. It's dirty business, and the racket preys on strong-arming the downtrodden.

Mona said, "I couldn't be that person on the phone hassling people who were broke and down on their luck. My job was to gather information to estimate the assets. If I could find immediate family, that was an angle the agency used. I got really good at digging into people's vulnerabilities," she said, "finding weak spots."

"Through research."

"Yeah. I smoked a lot of weed as a teenager in Marin County. Wake-and-bake computer hackers were my closest friends. I learned a lot from those dudes. If you know what you're doing, and have patience, getting into the backend of a system is not that hard. So, at the agency, I'd write up these reports on the debtors—assessments are what they called them. I called them dossiers, like from a spy movie. Anyway, that's where I met Trevor—at work. He was one of the guys on the phone, pressuring deadbeats to pay up. With his Australian accent, he'd use friendly charm as opposed to threats, and quickly became the ringer. They paid him a bonus tied to how much he could collect."

She finished her latte, licked the foam from her lips, and set the cup on the nightstand. "Trevor and I started seeing each other. Got into trouble. They put up with our shenanigans at first, but then they fired Trevor for cause. *Cause* of what, it's still unclear. I quit out of solidarity, and we went out on our own."

"Out on your own…"

"When I came across you in Vegas, we'd been there for a couple of months, running schemes on pervs, like we did. The problem was, Trevor controlled the money, and the drugs, which he consumed most of. Remember that friend of mine you saw outside the diner? Vickie?"

"Yeah."

With sadness, Mona said, "She OD'd, and it really freaked me out. Coke laced with Fentanyl. That's when I called it quits. No more hard stuff. I didn't want to die. But Trevor didn't quit. He's a fucking fiend, becomes a complete asshole if he doesn't have it around. When we partnered with Rex, business started to pick up."

"How?"

"He's plugged into bigger fish. Corporate guys with fancy titles. Drop crushed benzo in their drink. Blackout. Take off all their clothes, and they don't even have to have sex. It all depended on how much they had at risk. Cancel culture. Blemish on a reputation, that's what we harvested. The day I ran out on Trevor, he refused to give me what I'd earned. I threatened to leave, so he demanded my phone. I wouldn't give it to him. That really pissed him off. He freaked out and tried to kill me. So, I jumped on that bus and ended up here."

I said, "I'm sorry I gave him what he wanted."

"What's that?"

"Your phone."

"Let him have it. I'm not going back. I want to work with you. As equals, which means I've got ownership, a percentage of our take, deposited into my own bank account."

I teased, "By making cold calls?"

"I can do much more than that. Let me prove it."

I could see she was serious.

Mona said, "I want to buy a house, something simple, in a small town with a porch. Have a vegetable garden. Lead a normal life without looking back over my shoulder. I want to be free."

"Freedom."

"What do you say? Equity partners?"

I had no doubt she had great potential. Smart as a whip. Beautiful. "You have a deal." I held out my hand. We shook on it.

That same day, Mona and I drove out to Norwalk, stood in line to obtain a copy of her California birth certificate. Next, we went to the DMV to get a replacement license, stood in long lines there, and then got to the bank minutes before it closed for the day to open her checking account.

From that day forward, we were lovers and partners in crime.

CHAPTER 16

Present Day

The cabin's electric heater did little to warm the morning chill. Clouds were threatening and it looked like rain was inevitable.

There was a wood-burning stove in the corner, but I figured firing that up would be overkill. Instead, I made coffee and warmed my hands on the mug. It felt strange not to have dog Suzie at my side.

Oscar called promptly at nine. I explained how I'd been pulled over and roughed up by a Placer County Sheriff Deputy and how he tried to plant a firearm on me.

"What'd you do?" Oscar asked.

"Nothing. I'm helping a friend's sister with a wrongful death investigation. He must consider me a threat."

"Cops don't like private investigators snooping around."

I tried a different tactic. "At one time, you'd mentioned your firm donates to the campaign of the California Insurance Commissioner."

"We do."

"You also said you were friendly with the elected official."

"He'll take my calls."

"You mentioned the Fraud Division in the Department of Insurance works closely with law enforcement. They probably have access to Marsh's background information."

"What do you want to find out?"

"Who he reports to. His employment history. Anything."

"What does this have to do with the Covenant Not to Sue you sent me?"

"Nothing. Or maybe everything."

There was a pause before Oscar asked, "What the hell are you looking for, Jack?"

"The truth."

"Christ almighty," he said. "I need you back in L.A. I've got a loss management case which needs your immediate attention."

"Loss management?"

"An organized theft ring."

"Where?"

"A retail chain."

I knew what that meant. I'd likely be brought on as an under-cover employee to work shifts on the sales floor or loading dock. "Undercover work?"

"It's a long-term assignment. Steady income."

I could have certainly used the money, but wasn't thrilled with the idea. I said, "I'll deal with that when I get back. In the meantime, can you reach out to your contact at the Department of Insurance?"

"Just wrap up what you're doing and get back to L.A."

"Promise," I said, and thanked him.

Next, I set out to the summer camp film location to talk with Louis. I stayed clear of Argonaut and found an alternative route to the camp on Google Maps. It led me down dirt roads. When I got to the summer camp, the parking lot was cordoned off, so I found a spot amidst assorted vehicles parked haphazardly on the shoulder of the road.

Beyond the woods, I could see the back of plywood structures, flimsy-looking sets secured with wire secured to trees and tent posts. A film crew scurried to and fro. Many of them were in costume. There was a pair of mounted knights on horseback.

A crew guy not in costume, but rather cargo shorts, balanced a contraption rigged with multiple lenses. I assumed it was the virtual reality camera. The guy in shorts shouted, "Rolling." A few seconds later, a voice from a bullhorn called, "Action."

The two knights charged. The business-end of a lance sent one knight flying off his horse. His horse ran on as the fallen performer writhed on the ground, kicking up his feet and moaning as if in great pain.

"Cut," the bullhorn voice sounded.

Assorted crew members emerged from behind a thatched roof shack. Some were applauding. A few helped the fallen knight to his feet. The stuntman removed his helmet and took a bow to cheers and applause. He was obviously one of the Medieval Times performers.

I assumed Louis the director must be the guy with the bullhorn in his hand. He announced, "Great. We'll turn around for the reactions of the peasants." A whirl of activity followed his order—equipment and personnel set in motion.

I approached. "Excuse me, Louis. I believe Madeline texted you. I'm Jack O'Shea. Can you spare a second?"

He glanced away with, "I'm kind of busy right now." Louis obviously didn't want to be bothered.

I said, "I'm following up on Mike's accident for the life insurance claim. It's just a formality, won't take but a minute."

Louis was clearly reluctant. "Can't you see I'm in the middle of something here?"

"I see that."

He gave in, saying, "Okay," and led me out of earshot of the others.

"I understand you and Mike were good friends."

He nodded, "Yeah."

"Were you with him the night of the accident?"

Annoyed, he said, "I've told everyone what happened a thousand times."

"I understand, but for the record, please tell me what happened?"

"We were rehearsing. I was there, videotaping the auditions."

"In the theater?"

"Not in the theater. We were in a classroom. Mike split but never came back. I tried to call him. Nothing. He didn't say anything. It was weird."

"Us?"

"Me, Jim and Kathy." He pointed to the pair of actors seated near set. "Figured he'd gone out for a smoke. I went to look for him, thought maybe he went to the student center, or something. Didn't see him anywhere."

"Mike smoked? "

"Vaped. He was checking out a text or something on his phone then cut out all of a sudden."

"When you were looking for him, did you ask anyone if they'd seen him?"

"No."

"Did you speak to anyone at the student center?"

"Nope."

"Did anyone see or acknowledge you?"

"I don't know."

"You don't remember, or you don't know?"

He folded his arms and said nothing.

I continued, "Just creating the timeline," and asked, "Since that sinkhole is thirty feet or so up the hill, and off the back of the theater, why do you think he'd go all the way up there?"

"Who knows?"

"What did you do when you couldn't find Mike?"

Louis let out a sigh. "I returned to Kathy and Jim. We called it a night. Later, some maintenance guy heard Mike calling from down in the mineshaft.

"Where were you at that point?"

"I was home, half asleep, watching TV. Madeline called me. By the time I came back, the firemen had a rescue guy down in the mine. They pulled Mike up in a basket. The paramedics tried to revive him with CPR and stuff, then a...what do you call those shock things? Defibrillator." Louis took a moment before adding, "Madeline was a wreck."

"Was Mike in any conflict you were aware of?"

Louis softened, shifted his weight before, "His mind seemed somewhere else."

"Meaning?"

"I don't know. He wasn't...present."

At that point, it started to rain. Louis looked to the heavens and cursed. As the cast and crew moved for cover, a young, take-charge Asian woman marched up holding her clipboard over her head to shield the onslaught. "Rain delay," she said. "Won't match what we already shot. What do we do now?"

"Wait it out," Louis said, not happy.

Before he moved on, I asked, "So Mike didn't mention anything to you that might explain why he wasn't himself that day?"

"We were busy working. Like I said, I've already told everyone everything."

The rain came down even harder. I could tell I'd get nothing more out of Louis, so said, "Thank you for your time."

In a lowered voice, he said, "Mike told me Madeline was expecting. Maybe that's what had him so freaked out."

"Pregnant?"

"Yeah. Losing Mike was hard on her. That's probably why she had the miscarriage. Bad luck on top of bad luck, insult to injury."

That came as a surprise. Madeline had not told me anything about being pregnant, nor that she'd had a miscarriage. I thanked Louis, and he went back to work. The rain began to fall even harder as I avoided puddles on the way back to my car.

CHAPTER 17

I took the chance, driving the main highway back to Argonaut. I figured if Marsh saw me, I could rely on the Chevy *Secret Sauce* and outrun him in the pouring rain. Thankfully, he wasn't lying in wait behind the hardware store.

I met Madeline outside the Dramatic Arts building. She wore a navy pea coat and was carrying a jumbo-sized golf umbrella. We shared it on our walk to the chancellor's office. I explained what I'd learned from Louis. "He went looking for Mike after he left the classroom."

"Yeah."

"And he doesn't appear to have an alibi."

She asked, "What's your gut tell you?"

I didn't know how to respond, so said, "Hard to say. He told me you were pregnant, and after Mike's death, you had a miscarriage."

Madeline bit her lip. "Yeah. I was in my second trimester. We've been trying to have a baby for years. Mike and I couldn't afford in vitro, not on the pittance they pay us here. Then all of a sudden it happened. I had a dream our baby was going to be a boy." She grew emotional as the sound of rain pelted the umbrella above our heads. "I lost both my husband *and* a baby. Please don't tell Hector. That's why I didn't tell you. I never let my mom know. She'd been hounding me for grandchildren since we got married. I wanted to be further along before I said anything, not to get her hopes up. She was devastated enough after my dad died, and then with Mike gone…"

I said, "You have my discretion."

"One of these days, I'll tell Hector. When I'm ready. I'll probably never tell my mom."

The campus administration office was a turn-of-the-century Victorian building with ornate, arched windows. Madeline shook the rain off the umbrella, closed it, and left it hanging among the others on the railing outside.

From the signs on the doors, I could see the Admissions, Financial Aid, and International Student Center on the bottom floor. Behind frosted glass partitions, twenty-somethings wearing headsets sat in front of computer monitors. It reminded me of a call center boiler room.

The office of the chancellor was at the top of the grand staircase. An attractive receptionist woman guided us to a small conference room. The decor celebrated the Gold Rush era from California history. Black and white photographs of miners and Turn of the Century San Francisco architecture adorned the vintage-styled wallpaper.

Madeline and I found a seat. After a moment, Chancellor Foster entered the room flanked by a put-together woman I gauged to be in her forties. She wore a dark business suit who had a leather-bound folder in her hands. Both seemed surprised to see me. Using my real name, I introduced myself as Madeline's "representative." I'm no attorney but calling myself her rep was technically true.

The woman introduced herself as Christine and pulled an embossed business card out from her folder. She was a lawyer. I noted her last name was Foster, same as the chancellor—apparently a husband-and-wife team. I estimated Christine Foster to be about twenty years younger than her husband, her coifed hairstyle in contrast to the chancellor's trimmed gray beard and salt-and-pepper mane. Her look reminded me of the

1920s silent movie star Louise Brooks—sleek, close-sheared bob and straight-cut bangs of glossily reflective jet-black hair. Her style made a statement.

They took seats across from us, and we started with small talk about the weather before Chancellor Foster turned to Madeline and asked in a soothing tone, "Madeline…how are *you* doing?"

Madeline said nothing, eyes downcast.

He added, "If there's anything you need, please don't hesitate to ask. We're here for you."

Christine piped in. "Mike was a gifted instructor and a great asset to our faculty team. So giving and charismatic. He'll be deeply missed."

Madeline barely lifted her eyes off the mahogany tabletop and said, "Everyone loved Mike."

Christine said, "I can't imagine what you're going through. Our deepest condolences."

Madeline uttered, "Thank you."

Christine opened her leather-bound folder, pulled out a sheet of paper and slid it towards Madeline. I could see it was a check made out to fifty thousand dollars. "Nothing can make up for your loss," Christine said, "but we'd like to help with your transition."

Madeline finally looked up. "Transition?"

"Yes."

"You want me to quit?"

Chancellor Foster cleared his throat before, "Not quitting, but advancing your career in an environment where you're not surrounded with the constant memory of the tragic accident."

With ice in her eyes, Madeline said, "It was no accident."

To break the uncomfortable silence, I asked, "The Covenant Not to Sue?"

Christine offered me a Saccharin smile. "Upon signature, this gift is hers." She turned to Madeline, saying, "I understand you're upset. Denial is part of the grieving process, and—"

"—I'm not in denial."

Christine nodded. Clinically, she said, "The stages of grief are how one manages to live with loss. Denial, anger, bargaining, and depression are all milestones on the path to acceptance."

Madeline said, "You want me to," and made quotes with her fingers, "*accept* Mike's death was an accident?"

"No," Christine said, "we want to help you."

"Then help me figure out who killed him. Somebody pushed Mike down that shaft."

There was a painful moment of silence. And then, in what I perceived to be an overly calm tone of voice, Christine offered, "Madeline, I feel we're being very generous. This is in your best interest."

I asked, "Why are you asking her to sign a Covenant Not to Sue?"

Christine replied, "It's an agreement for both parties to move on."

I asked, "Is there a liability here? Why would Madeline have reason to seek damages against her employer?"

There was even more uncomfortable silence.

I continued, "If you'll allow me to consult with my client, we'll get back to you."

Without a reply, Christine reached for the check and carefully placed it back into her folder. To me, she said, "Do you have a card, Mister O'Shea? How can I reach you?"

"Not with me," I said. It was a lie. I had one in my wallet, but I felt it wasn't a good time to give up I was a private investigator and not an attorney. "But I have yours."

I could see that irked her.

To Madeline, Christine said, "You have until end of day, or our offer is off the table. Don't make us regret this gesture." There was clearly a dash of anger in her tone.

Foster gave his wife a shake of the head to indicate *Don't go there.*

With that, they thanked us for our time, and Christine and Chancellor Foster departed.

I said, "Well, I think—"

Madeline shushed me, saying in a whisper, "They're listening." She pointed to the door, motioning we should leave.

We were deathly silent as we walked past the receptionist and down the stairs. As we made our way to the door, a guy was entering and shaking off the rain from his Patagonia jacket. Madeline stiffened. The guy was in his late thirties, sported a hipster-Fu Manchu goatee and styled-moustache, attired in expensive-looking outdoor men's fashion. He greeted, "Hey Madeline."

"Paul."

He stared at me as we made our way out the door.

Outside, thunder sounded in the distance.

Madeline said under her breath, "I'm willing to bet that conference room is bugged. They *know* things. And I think they've bugged our home."

"Why do you say that?"

She grabbed her umbrella and said, "Something's rotten in the state of Denmark," quoting *Hamlet*. "Mike wasn't stupid. He wouldn't have climbed up that hill for no reason. Someone killed Mike to silence him. And I'm sure they've been listening."

I'd remembered Hector mentioning he thought Madeline was paranoid. At that moment, I began to question her perception of reality.

I felt eyes on my back and turned to see Paul at the window, watching us. Madeline followed my gaze, and I asked, "Who's that?"

"Paul runs the International Student Center. Mike made fun of him, called him lumbersexual. He puts on the act like he's all outdoorsy and rugged, but it's just a facade. Drives his vintage Range Rover around. Posts pretentious Apre Ski photos. Paul's a yes man, like Louis. They're both so lame."

As we made our way in the pouring rain, I admitted, "I really don't know if I'm the best man for this job. We were lucky enough to get your retainer back, but like I said, I'm no homicide detective. I can help you find someone who can—."

"Thank you for everything you've done," she said, cutting me off. "There's more I need to tell you—not here. And we can't go to my home because it's bugged. And not with termites. Microphones."

Since I needed to pick up Suzie from Dr. Reibach's office, I suggested we meet at Amarillo Slims.

"I know that place," she said.

We agreed to meet there. She kept the umbrella, so I walked to my car in the pouring rain.

Pulling out of the campus parking structure, I saw the Sheriff's vehicle pass going in the other direction. In my rear-view mirror, I could see him making a U-turn. As I sped to the outskirts of town, emergency lights flashed in the reflection of the wet pavement.

Once clear of Argonaut, I put the Chevy to the test, racing in the rain.

The Chevy's manual transmission combined with all that mighty horsepower—the sheriff didn't stand a chance.

I'd lost him for the time being, but then again, Marsh knew I hadn't left town.

CHAPTER 18

I parked behind Amarillo Slims and draped my canvas car cover over the Chevy as a precaution in case Marsh trolled El Dorado County.

Sandy was behind the counter reading a paperback. She greeted me as I peeled off my wet jacket. "Some fine weather we're having."

"And I'm not dressed for it."

There was a repetitive thump on the counter. The source of the noise was Sandy's dog, wagging her tail. Sandy said, "Ole Harley, she doesn't like thunder and lightning. That's one of the reasons she washed out of her service dog program. Doesn't like loud noises."

"So she's not a service dog?" I asked.

"Harley was in training but didn't make the cut. Doc Reibach made a few phone calls, and we adopted her. I got a service dog vest on Amazon to keep the county health inspector from hassling when they come around, since dogs aren't allowed in restaurants." When Sandy went down to comfort Harley, a black holster fell from the wheelchair. The wooden grip of a pistol stuck out of the leather pouch. She leaned down and picked it up, tucked it back under the blanket.

"That for the health inspector, too?" I teased.

"Pay that six-shooter no mind. Slim insists I keep it for protection. I told him I don't want it, but he says I have no choice in the matter." Sandy resumed petting her dog. "Ole Harley isn't gun steady either."

"Gun steady?"

"Like hunting dogs…won't flinch when guns go off. Harley's not like that, but she's good at retrieving things and keeping me company. That's all that matters."

Madeline arrived moments later, and Sandy poured coffees. We took them to a booth. After we settled in, Madeline asked, "How much do you know about my family? Did Hector tell you we were born in Mexico?"

"Yeah. And he said you guys grew up in West Covina."

"Our parents came to California, from Baja, as migrant workers when Hector and I were little ones. We lived in a double-wide trailer outside Coalinga in the San Joaquin Valley. That temporary mobile home wasn't anything fancy, but it was *so* much better than what we had back in Mexico. While my parents were out in the fields, Hector and I learned English in a schoolhouse trailer. They worked the seasons for a couple years until my folks found better jobs in L.A.—my mom a seamstress, and my dad as an independent gardener."

I remembered some of that. "Your brother said your father built his business out of the back of a Toyota pickup."

"Exactly. Hector and I helped him after school and on weekends. Our parents worked their asses off to send us to private school. Why? Because the public schools where we lived were for shit. Educating their children was our parents' top priority. Any extra money they made went to immigration lawyers to gain our citizenship. By the time Hector and I were in high school, we all had become naturalized at a ceremony in downtown L.A. That was a great day," she said with a glimmer in her eye. "My parents did it by-the-book. Legally. They jumped through all the right hoops—paid the fees and played by the rules."

"The American Dream."

She nodded. "I was inspired by some really good teachers, so I pursued a career in acting, and education. Hector became a writer. I'm so proud of him, writing TV shows like he does."

"Your brother's a great guy."

"For both of us, it was all about making our parents proud. I was offered a job at Bret Harte. And that's where I met Mike. We were married a year later. Professors in love, that's what we were. But as time went by, we began to have doubts about Bret Harte. Now it's clear it's nothing more than a visa mill."

"What's that?"

"Overseas kids from rich families enroll to get a student visa as an entry into the United States. Many of the students aren't even on campus. They're loaned out to," she made quotes with her fingers, "*internships* which boil down to cheap labor for tech startups, mostly in the Bay Area."

"How does that work?"

"Say a student applies to Bret Harte. First thing admissions does is determine if the family can afford the tuition. If not, they're rejected. If there are means, they're accepted, but only after establishing that they can pay, and a hefty deposit is made. The admissions office arranges all the travel and F-1 student visa. Tuition may be expensive, but it's the price of entry into the United States, and better yet, California."

I asked, "The school is selling student visas?"

"And making a fortune. The government looks the other way. And no politician cares. Some migrants save for years to pay a coyote and risk their lives crossing the border, but Bret Harte *is* the coyote—for the rich. The business of international students is a forty-five-billion-dollar industry, and California is the destination of choice. Counselors who steer kids to Bret Harte get a kick-back. Money in their pocket."

I said, "But it's not permanent, right? I mean, there must be a time limit before the student visa expires."

"There's supposed to be, but it's bullshit. The school extends the stay for years, even decades, claiming the student is working on their thesis or serving as a teaching assistant. And for the girls…" She let that hang there for a moment before continuing. "Let's just say there's always the option of an anchor baby. Birth tourism. A child born in the U.S. becomes a citizen. They won't deport the mother."

"How is this connected to Mike?"

"The more we looked into it, the more we questioned whether we should be working for what's essentially a scam. Don't get me wrong. The students that come work hard. Most of them, anyway." She took a moment to sip her coffee before, "Mike and I did the math, sketched out how much students pay in tuition compared to the salaries and benefits the professors are paid. It's criminal how much money is collected, per unit, compared to the professor compensation. We're paid less than barista wages. Who knows where all that money goes? Not to the people doing the work. And the housing around campus is all owned by the college. On paper, it's made to look like a separate entity, but it's not. Our landlord is just a shell company, and Argonaut is not much different now from over a hundred years ago, when everything was owned by the oppressive mining company."

"Company town with a company store."

"Exactly," she said. "Mike started talking about this and that's when everything got weird. People started asking us about personal things nobody would have known unless they were listening in."

"Like what?"

"Stuff from conversations at home. That guy Paul, who said hi to me as we were leaving the meeting. He's the Director of International Studies. He started chumming up, all fake. Schmoozing. Buying drinks and dinner. Mike thought he was trying to seduce me. And then he started asking questions about things Mike and I had only talked about at home.

"So you think your house is bugged."

"It must be."

Thanks to Nick McClintlock, I had a bug detector in the trunk of my car, and said, "I can sweep your place for surveillance, but that's it. I can't stick around to investigate further. You're going to need a detective experienced in homicide investigations. Did Mike have life insurance?"

"I wish. The college's health plan is bottom-of-the-barrel—one of those HMO bronze plans. Flimsy. Made of tin. Bare minimum. And that fifty thousand dollars offer to go away...that's their Pontious Pilate move. Wash the hands." She looked out the window and took a deep breath. "Can we at least go to my place to see if it's been bugged?"

"Now?"

"I won't be able to sleep there till I know."

I'd fulfill one last request before heading back to L.A., so agreed.

CHAPTER 19

As I followed Madeline's Honda Civic to her home, Oscar called. He said, "Here's the skinny. Edwin Foster has been the chancellor of Bret Harte College for over twenty years. He's also the chairman of the board of trustees and controls the endowments. Before that, he was in the disposal and recycling business."

That seemed strange, so I asked, "How does someone go from disposal and recycling to collegiate academia?"

"It's a family business founded by his dad. His brother runs it now. The company handles industrial waste. A few years ago, Foster was charged with money laundering, a case brought on by the Major Economic Crimes Bureau of the Manhattan District Attorney's Office. Supposedly, a bank lent Bret Harte millions for high-capacity computer servers, which were never purchased. The DA's office tracked the funds to bank accounts controlled by Foster, but the case was dropped. I suspect because he retained Clive Saxon."

"Should I know him?"

"Saxon is a white-collar criminal defense attorney, and he doesn't come cheap. His firm countered for lack of evidence, and the case was dropped. Since the DA office is in the business of pursuing cases they're certain they can win, I can only assume Saxon's team overwhelmed them.

I asked, "What do you think the money laundering was all about?"

"Let's just say it's getting more and more difficult to avoid the IRS, but college endowments have long been a favored tax shelter. Colleges and universities, even top ones like Harvard, keep financial details away from public scrutiny."

I asked, "Could the money laundering be tied to F-1 student visas?"

"Hard to say."

"Did you find anything on Marsh?"

"About two years ago, he was placed on administrative leave. There was a lawsuit involved. Officer involved shooting, but the details are not clear. That's all I've got."

I told him my plan was to head back to L.A. later that night and followed Madeline as she turned into a driveway. Hers was a single-story bungalow in desperate need of paint and repair. I parked behind Madeline's Honda and retrieved the bug detector from the trunk. On the porch, I asked, "Has Marsh ever been here?"

Madeline put her finger to her lips to signal silence and led me inside.

The home had eclectic art, theatrical posters, and antique weapons on the walls. The vintage arsenal included crossbows, throwing stars, and a samurai sword perched over the mantel.

Once I turned the device on, the bug sweeper buzzed in my hand. It signaled near a light switch, then directed us to what appeared to be a smoke detector on the ceiling in the living room.

Madeline stood devastated. She buried her head in her hands.

We moved to the kitchen. The scanner lit up near another smoke detector positioned high on the wall. Upon closer inspection, a tiny lens was visible.

Lastly, we scanned the bedroom. Sure enough, there was another smoke detector with a mini spy device.

White as a ghost, Madeline looked like she was going to be sick. She backed out of the house. Outside, she put her hands on her knees. Assuming there may be a device out on the porch, I moved us out to my car. She covered her mouth and ran out into the trees. I heard retching.

Moments later, Madeline joined me, and we slid inside the car. "Holy shit," she said, slamming the passenger door, "Those fucking bastards! There's a camera in our bedroom!"

"When were those smoke detectors installed?"

"Over a year ago. Some guys came by and said it was because of the fire code. That was just after the hit-and-run."

"What hit-and-run?"

"A special-needs kid was run over by a student. His Mercedes was found covered in blood, so they arrested the guy. But before the arraignment, he flew the coup and caught a flight back to Saudi Arabia. Mike was certain Marsh and the college helped the kid get out of the country."

I told her Doc Reibach had mentioned something about that.

"The kid's mother was a wreck. The boy was all she had, and committed suicide afterward. Mike became obsessed with the injustice of it all. He had been in contact with a reporter from the *San Francisco Chronicle*. They spoke and emailed each other, but nothing ever happened. I overheard them talking about both that, and the closed theater. And now Mike's laptop is gone. I think someone broke in and took it."

"Do you know this reporter he was in contact with?"

"I heard her on the phone, but Mike never told me who she was. Everything was on that laptop of his."

"Can you access his emails?"

"I tried, but I don't have the password."

I heard tires on gravel behind me. In the rear-view mirror, Marsh was coming up the driveway.

Madeline slid down in the passenger seat. "They saw us."

CHAPTER 20

Marsh pulled up and got out of his car. I weighed the options. Let him arrest me, or get the hell out of there? I didn't feel like getting roughed up again, nor spending the night in jail, but most importantly, I needed to pick up my dog.

I cranked the ignition, spun the wheel, popped the clutch, and maneuvered the Chevy around him. There was a look of surprise on the sheriff's face. He'd drawn his gun as I pulled away.

"Holy shit," Madeline said, turned back.

In the rear-view mirror, I could see Marsh running back to his car. Once on the pavement, the Chevy SS was able to gain traction, and accelerate. "Hold on," I said, and worked the clutch and gearbox.

Madeline hunched low, her boots on the dash. I said to her, "Best put your seatbelt on." She sat up, managed to wrestle the strap over her shoulder and secure it. I could feel the slip of the tires on the wet pavement, probably due to residual sand on the mountain road from snow maintenance. The two-lane highway was curvy, and I lost sight of Marsh, but I knew he was not far behind—and likely radioing ahead. I figured I'd get off the highway and looked for the first opportunity.

I found an intersecting dirt road up ahead which looked promising. I downshifted to slow the car without using the brakes, the engine revving, and made a hard right turn. There was a cluster of trees that offered cover. I came to a sliding halt, banked a U turn, and readied the Chevy in position to gun past in case the sheriff turned onto the dirt road. The move was only possible because of the torrential rain. If I'd been on this dirt road when dry the dust would have given me away.

Seconds later, Sheriff Marsh blew past on the highway. The ruse worked. He missed us.

I gave it a moment before I cautiously crept back and then turned left—the opposite direction. As we headed back to Madeline's house, I suggested she collect some things and move in with a friend for a while.

She said, "I need to get rid of those cameras."

"Not yet. If you disable them now, whoever is spying will know we are aware of them. It's better to play dumb."

She got it.

I said, "Do you have a friend you can stay with?"

"I don't know. Probably Laura."

"Does she work at the college?"

"No. She's an artist, and bartender at the Eureka Tavern."

"Good." I considered my next question. "Do you know who went down into the mineshaft to retrieve Mike?"

"Some guy from Search and Rescue."

I waited for her to elaborate.

"When hikers or skiers get lost, volunteers with mountaineering experience help. It was one of those guys."

"Did you get a name?"

"No."

I told her I was going to try to find who the volunteer was, to get his perspective. Madeline was one step ahead of me. "In case Mike said something down there. I hadn't thought of that."

I dropped her off back at her home and said, "Get your stuff, and get out quick, before Marsh comes back."

After she got out my car, she turned back, and asked, "Then you're going to help me find Mike's killer after all?"

Non-committal, I replied, "We'll see what I can do."

Something told me I wouldn't be heading back to L.A. anytime soon.

CHAPTER 21

I got back on the road. While keeping an eye out for Marsh, I called to learn the Placer County Sheriff Department organized the Mountain Search & Rescue Team in the town of Auburn. I didn't want Marsh to know I was snooping, so I impersonated a British television producer, Nigel, a stock character I'd used a few times before.

I said to the woman on the phone, "Love, we're preparing a documentary with the BBC on volunteer efforts. Who can I speak to regarding the brave men and women in the Mountain Search & Rescue Brigade?" I knew their team wouldn't be called a "brigade," but figured that's how a Brit would phrase it.

As luck would have it, she connected me with Deputy Netro who organizes the rescue volunteers. I poured on the continental charm; told him I was looking for a local volunteer with mountaineering experience to feature in a television segment. I said, "We Brits are fascinated by the rugged wilds of North America. The plan is to shoot B roll of him rappelling down the side of a cliff...and whatnot. And then have an interview. Wasn't there a bloke who fell in a mine not long ago? Who assisted there?"

Deputy Netro was hesitant to give information, but he admitted there was a guy by the name of Tyson Stark who had assisted the department in the past. He mentioned he worked as a ski instructor at the Palisades Tahoe Resort. I thanked him for his time.

Tyson Stark was a unique name, so I searched on my phone and learned he was the proprietor of a mountain bike and cross-country ski shop in Truckee, California. With a name so unique it had to be the same guy, so I phoned. Keeping up the Nigel persona, I asked, "Mister Stark, what can you tell me about your volunteer adventures?"

"Call me Ty," he said, and explained he assisted with lost cross-country skiers. I asked if he had helped pull, as I put it, "that poor professor from the mineshaft at the University."

"I did. Look, I'm in the middle of something, so—"

"Brilliant," I said. "I'd like to interview you about that, and other efforts."

There was a long pause before he regretfully said, "But that dude didn't make it."

"I'm quite aware. The segment can't be all jammy, can it?" I'd heard the term *jammy* years ago from a Londoner, and it stuck with me. It's supposedly British slang for something good—most likely a metaphor harkened to fruit preserves since jam, biscuits, and tea are celebrated across the pond. I said, "That story will be the pathos of the segment—a wee bit of *pull-the-heartstrings*, if you will. Tragic indeed, but heroic nonetheless."

Ty suggested I come to his bike shop, so we made plans for that afternoon. I immediately set out for Truckee.

It was about a two-hour drive east on Interstate 80 over Donner Pass. While other vehicles labored over the mountain incline, the Chevy SS climbed with ease thanks to the horsepower of the muscle car.

I reached Truckee as an Amtrak passenger train pulled in. I found parking on the main drag while the ringing bell of a railroad crossing echoed off the brick. The town felt historic. I imagined a time when steam locomotives stopped for fuel and water before chugging over the Sierras. I felt as if the ghosts of soot-covered railroad workers haunted the town's rugged brick and mortar.

Around back of one of the buildings off the main drag, I found the *Keep on Truckin' Bike Works*. The sign featured the iconic cartoon character Mr. Natural. I recognized him as the R Crumb bearded character associated with Grateful Dead artwork. Upon closer inspection, Mr. Natural's front-forward foot was on the pedal of a mountain bike—appropriate in a town called Truckee.

Ty was in his mid-thirties with a face weathered from sun exposure. He wore baggy jeans, a sports-fleece top, and a knit cap. I suggested I'd buy lunch, so he left a scrawny teenage employee in charge of the shop and led me to the Bar of America, a tavern on Donner Pass Road overlooking the railroad tracks.

We sat against the window with a view of the passing train. Ty explained he had joined the Placer County Search and Rescue Team a few years ago. "The EMS guys don't have a lot of mountaineering experience, so they use us volunteers when needed."

As Nigel, I began with the same spiel I'd given Deputy Netro, how the British people are fascinated by the rugged individualism of the American West.

Ty sipped his beer and said, "Unfortunately, everything around here is named after the Donners—Donner Pass, Donner Lake, Donner Memorial State Park."

"Why is that unfortunate?"

"Because it glorifies incompetence," he said. "There's not another place named after men of such inadequacy."

"Oh?"

"The Donner brothers were ego-driven entrepreneurs. They made one stupid decision after another, which led to starvation and cannibalism." Ty explained how George and Jacob Donner, alongside James Reed, led a band of pioneers from Independence, Missouri. "Motivated by greed, not religious freedom. California wasn't in the Gold Rush yet, but there was plenty of land to be taken. The Donners were not poor, not like the dust bowl Okies who came during the depression. They had resources, outfitted themselves with fancy wagons and oxen, hired teamsters, scouts, and cooks. Their first mistake was leaving Missouri way too late in the Spring. Their second was trying to take a shortcut. Instead of following the trail up through Idaho, they second-guessed and listened to a rat by the name of Lansford Hastings, who convinced them to go through Utah."

I wasn't expecting a history lesson, but Ty was on a roll. I encouraged him with, "Fascinating."

"After they finally got over the Wasatch range, they struggled to cross the Salt Flats. There was no fresh water. Oxen died from thirst or broke free and ran off." With the mention of thirst, Ty sipped his beer and licked his lips. "By the time they reached the border of California, it was already too late to cross over the Sierras. They had no choice but to wait out the winter." He paused in dramatic effect, lowered the tone of his voice, "Forty people died, many of them children, all because of the incompetence of the Donner brothers. Now everything around here is named Donner this, Donner that. They weren't heroes. They were fuckups. Don't get me started."

"I won't," I said, steering him back. "How were you chosen to go down the mineshaft?"

"I teach spelunking."

I was somewhat familiar with the term, but wanted to hear his take, and I asked, "Beg your pardon, spelunking?"

"Cave exploring."

"Indeed. Walk me through what happened."

"I harnessed up. Was given a radio. Went down."

"What did you see?"

"That shaft isn't a straight shot. It curves, especially towards the bottom." Ty demonstrated the jig-jag of the descent. "I saw claw marks on the walls, so it looked like that poor bastard bounced off the sides going down, trying to grab onto things. There's a pool of water at the bottom, like a well. Rank as hell. Smells like kerosene. From the light on my helmet, I could see his body just below the surface."

"Was he alive?"

"I pulled him up, but...nothing. They lowered the stretcher."

"So, he didn't say anything?"

"He looked like he was dead. I strapped him onto the stretcher, and they pulled him out. As I waited for my turn, I could see what it was like down there, like the inside of a pipe. Slick walls. Nothing to hold on to. I figured he'd waded as long as he could."

"I understand that area is full of abandoned shafts and tunnels."

Ty nodded. "Five or six leading to the shaft. And oil drums."

"Oil drums?"

"In the tunnels. When I was being pulled back up, I saw there was a tarp covering one of them."

"What kind of tarp?"

"Black plastic. The kind you'd drape over a leaky roof. Near the top. Figured it was all part of that asbestos removal they're doing."

I said, "I'm impressed by your bravery."

Ty shrugged. "All in a day's work." After reading a text on his phone, he apologized he had to go, "Put out a fire."

I thanked him for his time and said I'd get back to him to schedule the video interview. There'd be no actual interview, but I had to keep up the façade.

Ty headed out, and I settled the bill and got back on the road. As I drove out of Truckee, a black Ford Explorer followed me onto Interstate 80. Was there another GPS tracker in my car? I concluded either somewhere in Truckee, or along the way, I'd passed an infrared license plate reader. When Marsh pulled me over in Argonaut, he would have entered my license plate into the system. Maybe I'd been tagged by an algorithm. With today's technology, the deck is always stacked against you.

The SUV was on my tail.

CHAPTER 22

I drove the speed limit as the Ford Explorer followed me up towards Donner Pass. Checking Google Maps, there was an exit ahead, Soda Springs Road, so I pulled off.

I drove past the Royal Gorge Cross-Country Ski Resort as the SUV followed. It was near a development of mountain homes. It wasn't winter or ski season, so most of the homes were not occupied. I cut through the quiet neighborhood. The SUV followed.

From there, I engaged the Super Sport's special ability, down-shifting through turns and accelerating. The Ford Explorer tried to keep up.

I made a high-speed turn. In the rear-view mirror, I saw the SUV take the corner fast. It slid off the pavement before settling into a drainage ditch.

After a few more turns, I made my way back to Interstate 80. It was past time to get my dog.

Hector called. He'd just spoken to Madeline. She'd told him her house was bugged, and he said, "My sister is crazy, always been that way."

I explained there were hidden cameras in her home. "I have a bug sweeper and the thing lit up like a Christmas tree. She thinks it's her employer. Apparently, Mike dug up dirt. Someone wanted to find out how much."

"Madeline said they offered her money, some sort of sever-ance."

"They did."

"She should take it and come home."

I explained the condition comes with the stipulation she sign a Covenant Not To Sue, a release of liability, and said, "That suggests they're trying to hide something."

There was a moment of silence before Hector said, "You know, my sister's got this idea everything in life has got to be fair. She's naïve that way. The world is not in balance. She needs to accept that. There is no such thing as karma. Only chaos theory. You don't have to do this, you know. You've gotten her money back. That's enough. Don't believe everything she says."

"Why shouldn't I?"

"All that drama...she lives in a fantasy world."

"You're a screenwriter," I said. "You write drama."

"I don't live it."

I said, "They're covering something up. Bluffing. She's right about that."

"What makes you think so?"

"My gut."

"So what are you gonna do?"

"I haven't figured that out yet. Let's see where the cards land."

CHAPTER 23

In Doc Reibach's office, Suzie was happy to see me, tail wagging. But it pained me to see the Velcro splint around her leg. As she licked my hand, I caught myself getting emotional, didn't know where that came from.

Doc Reibach said, "She's going to be fine," and motioned to the X-Ray on a monitor. "No broken bones, fortunately. It appears she pulled the palmar carpal ligament. Nothing we can do other than splint her leg to let it heal." She placed a bottle on the counter. "These are nonsteroidal anti-inflammatory chews to reduce the swelling. Give her three a day. Doesn't have to be with food."

"Torn ligament?"

"That's right."

I'd torn a ligament in my knee from a collision on the soccer field in high school. It had taken me out of the season my senior year. Even though that was many years ago, the injury still flared from time to time.

Doc Reibach said, "She probably won't win any more races, but she's strong and resilient. Very sweet and affectionate."

"Affection is the reward for winning races," I said, what I'd learned from the greyhound rescue agency.

"How so?" she asked.

"In training, dogs from the kennel will race against each other.

The losers are leashed to look on as the winner receives affection, and food. Dogs that lost are sent to the pens hungry. It doesn't take long before the greyhounds learn winning means dinner and a belly rub."

"There's never enough affection to go around."

How true, I thought. Mona's affection was one of the most memorable and loving things about her. The occasional hand on my back. A stolen kiss. Her touch. I hadn't known any of that growing up in my dad's household. With me, a little goes a long way.

Reibach said, "If she tries to chew on the splint, you're going to have to put this Elizabethan collar on her, what I call the Cone of Shame." She showed me the white plastic cone and how it fit around Suzie's neck.

"For how long?"

"Three weeks or so."

The thought of my dog with the plastic collar was heartbreaking, but I trusted her expertise. I settled the bill and Doc Reibach sent us on our way.

I returned to Amarillo Slims and weighed whether I should extend my stay or head back home. Maybe Hector was right. My former self would have said "sayonara" but there were things left to do.

I carried Suzie into the cabin and made an impromptu dog bed with the terry cloth guest robe I found hanging in the closet. Thankfully Suzie did not nibble at the Velcro splint. After she dozed off into a light snore, I figured I'd get something to eat and figure out what to do next.

I had a canvas cover in the trunk of my car, so I draped it over the Chevy SS as a precaution.

Down at the restaurant, I bellied up to the counter. Slim poured a Sierra Nevada for me. "How's our accommodations working out for ya?"

"Very comfortable."

"Saw you carried in a dog."

"She needed to stay over at the vet."

"Doc Reibach is a good lady. Got a good heart. I just pulled a rack off the smoker. Interested?"

"Sounds good."

As he worked on preparing the order behind the counter, Slim said, "That's one hell of a ride ya got there. Didn't they put a Corvette V-8 in that thing?"

"You know your cars."

"Sound of the engine gives it away."

As much as I tried to disguise the Chevy Super Sport, Slim was right. The rumble of a high compression engine is not something that can be easily disguised. Slim brought me a basket of dry-rub pork ribs. The meat was lean and savory. "You know what the hell you're doing on the grill."

"Smoker," he corrected.

"What do you know about the Bret Harte college? Had any dealings with them?"

"Catered a few events," he said. "Alumni fundraisers, and whatnot. But I just dropped off the trays."

"Ever go inside the theater?"

"Why do you ask?"

"I understand they found asbestos."

"You some kind of ambulance-chasing Mesothelioma lawyer?"

"I'm a private investigator. My client is the wife of the professor who fell into the mineshaft."

"A private eye, huh? Like Magnum? That explains the car. All you P.I.s have super cool rides. Didn't Magnum drive a Ferrari?"

"I suppose."

He snapped his fingers, reached under the counter, dug around, and came up with a bottle of Four Roses. "And private eyes favor bourbon, am I right?" Slim explained the restaurant only has a beer and wine license, so he keeps the whiskey out of sight.

He produced a mini mason jar and poured. I couldn't refuse. He apologized he couldn't join me, confessed he'd, "drank my fill over the years so gave it all up." I thanked him for the hospitality, and he said, "Those college folks stay among themselves."

I said, "Doc Reibach mentioned there had been some problems."

"Seems like there's always something."

"Have any dealings with the sheriff?"

From his reaction, I could see I'd hit a nerve. "If you're talking about Marsh...he threw me in lockup, impounded my bike, claimed I had a warrant out for my arrest. All bullshit. I reckon he saw I had priors. I sat in jail for a few days before they let me go. Sandy was beside herself."

I told him what happened, and how Suzie tried to protect me before Marsh doused her with pepper spray.

"That's the reason Doc Reibach tended to your pup?

I nodded.

Slim cursed under his breath. "Marsh considered you a threat. Same as me. I may have been an outlaw at one time, but that's all behind me now." I didn't tell him I also had a criminal past. Slim went on. "Years ago, I rode with the Cossacks out of Texas. Ever hear of them?"

I told him I hadn't.

"There was an incident, what on the news they called the Waco Biker Shooting. A lot of good men died. Some not so good, too. I had to make myself scarce after that. Then one day, after coming off a bender, I ran into Sandy on a Sunday morning. I was in a state, like the Kris Kristofferson tune *Sunday Morning Coming Down*."

"Great song."

He nodded. "Sandy is an angel sent from heaven. She restored me—saved my life. If I'd stayed in that biker club, I'd be a dead man now, for sure." He stroked his beard. "That was about a year before she and I had the spill south of Dallas. I broke my leg in three places, and it put Sandy in the chair." His tone simmered. "Some dumbshit in a pickup cut right in front of us, but the insurance company claimed I was partly at fault. After all was said and done, it was Sandy's idea to come home and fix up this old place she'd inherited from her old man. I built the paths and ramps to make everything handicap accessible, since many of our guests are folks with physical disabilities. I tease Sandy we're in the *Green Book* for gimps."

"That explains how dog-friendly you've made the place."

"To accommodate the service animals, that's right."

I could see we were kindred spirits, but I didn't say anything about my accident and Mona. I certainly understood his shame and guilt.

"I see you covered up your car."

I explained a mysterious Ford Explorer had followed me from Truckee and I'd outrun both that and Marsh earlier in the day.

"And I thought I was the outlaw," he teased. "Sounds like they've got you tagged as trouble."

"Trouble is my middle name," I said as a joke.

"Born to be bad, I reckon. I've got an idea. Follow me."

There was a sagging, wooden Tuff Shed behind the cabins, a structure you'd expect for housing mowing or snow removal equipment. Slim unlocked the door, cleared cobwebs, and turned on an overhead lamp to reveal a pair of Harley-Davidsons collecting dust. One had authentic Texas longhorns on the front handlebars, as if it were a masthead. "I'm still rebuilding mine. Waiting on a few parts," he said, then pointed out the other motorcycle. "But this one is Sandy's...I mean, *was* Sandy's. Feel free to borrow her to get around, long as you need."

"That's not necessary."

"It's better to run these bad boys than to let 'em sit, so you'd be doing me a favor."

"I, uh, don't have a lot of experience on bikes."

"Ever ride before?"

"Dirt bikes as a kid."

He waited for me to elaborate.

"An old Yamaha DT250. We'd jump mounds of dirt on the edge of town."

He wriggled his pinkie finger into the lobe of his ear for a moment in consideration. "What's that old saying? *'It's like riding a bike.'* No worries. I've got an extra helmet." He pulled a black helmet down from a shelf. "Tons of weekend warriors ride through these hills. You'll blend in, and Marsh will have no idea it's you."

I thanked him.

Slim said, "Don't push your luck in Argonaut. Sandy says that town has bad energy. Tons of folks lost their lives digging those tunnels. You won't find much of that in the history books. There were cave ins, mishaps with dynamite, cholera, and tuberculosis. Lotta ghosts in those hills."

I asked, "So you think it's haunted?"

"Don't believe in ghosts…just saying that place has bad juju, if you know what I mean."

CHAPTER 24

Three Years Ago

With Mona's help, my real estate schemes picked up. She had a knack for digging up personal details of those who came sniffing the bait. Mona dove deep into social media, explained, "Moneyed men don't necessarily post, but their wives do."

Mona had done this style of research working at the debt collection agency and later perfected it in the badger game. She said men of wealth fear their wives most. An ugly divorce means they could lose half of their worth.

I kept an account in an offshore bank in Georgia—that's Georgia north of Istanbul, nowhere near Atlanta. I had to admire the boutique bank tailormade for fraudsters and tax cheats like me. From the institution's website, it appeared to be based in the State of Georgia, primarily because it had a logo featuring what looked like a peach. Upon closer inspection, it wasn't a peach at all, but rather a pomegranate, the agricultural symbol of Georgia nestled between the Black and Caspian Seas.

If someone scrutinized the routing number and BIC/SWIFT code, they'd see the wire transfer does not land in the United States. Some of my marks picked up on that, but it was surprising how many didn't.

The real estate schemes took a lot of back-and-forth. Incorporating her graphic design skills, Mona created fake real estate listings, which wasn't something I could have done myself. They looked legitimate.

We weren't selling anything more than the story of how the property was liquidating, and the mark needed to move fast or lose the opportunity. My scores weren't big, maybe ten thousand dollars or so, but get a few of those a month and you're doing alright.

One morning, Mona got out of bed early, made coffee, and dug her nose into her laptop. I went out to take care of a few errands. When I returned, she proposed her caper.

Mona said she'd previously looked into Kenneth Coleman, a savvy investor, and Wall Street wizard. She came across him when he'd traveled through Vegas to auction off some of his wine collection. She and Trevor weren't able to put him into an uncompromising position at the time, but Mona always felt Kenneth was the fish that got away.

"I know a bit about wine," she said, "and not just because I drink it. In high school, I had a summer job working in Napa Valley. My best friend's dad was a wholesaler, but also a broker of collectable wine. I remember limos pulling up to his warehouse delivering businessmen from Tokyo and Hong Kong. They'd buy cases, sometimes pallets of the stuff. The cabernets these guys bought in California sold for ten times as much back home."

Mona said, and told me about the shipwrecked 1907 Heidsieck & Co. Monopole Diamant Bleu Cuvée. The wine has a great story. In 1916, a Swedish freighter was attacked by a German U-boat. The submarine fired a single torpedo; an easy shot, like shooting fish in a barrel. The ship sank within minutes. The manifest included French champagne destined for the court of Czar Nicholas II of Russia. It never got there. The Bolsheviks would eventually exile the Romanovs to Siberia and assassinate the entire royal family, the end of a dynasty.

For over a hundred years, the champagne sat at the bottom of the Baltic Sea. Treasure hunters found the shipwreck. The salvaged bottles became all the rage at auction.

She showed me an online blurb of how a Russian oligarch had purchased one of the bottles for a quarter of a million dollars. Surrounded by supermodels in a St. Petersburg nightclub, he opened the champagne. Since he was Russian, the irony was not lost how the sunken WWI freighter was delivering the champagne to the Imperial Court of the Romanovs.

Mona said, "A noted sommelier and wine blogger was in that St. Petersburg nightclub that night and offered a glass. He wrote a glowing description about how rich and complex the champagne was, called it a 'sensory time capsule.'" Mona explained there were other shipwrecked wines, but the vast majority of those bottles had turned into vinegar. What made this champagne so special was the bottles sat undisturbed at the perfect temperature at an ocean depth which mimicked the pressure inside the bottles—well preserved for over a hundred years.

She said, "At first, a Swiss-based auction house sold them for what turned out to be a bargain, about five thousand dollars a bottle, before experts sampled the wine and wrote about how fantastic it was. The auction price surged like crazy."

I had to admit, that was a good story, and asked, "What makes you think this Kenneth Coleman wants one?"

She showed me another source. "I hacked into the Christie's auction site. One of the bottles sold a few months back. Kenneth was in the running, but outbid, so that tells me he's looking. I wonder how hard it would be to fake a bottle?"

That surprised me. "Really?"

"Before Trevor and I went to Vegas, we did all sorts of crazy shit, including dumpster diving outside five-star restaurants for empties. We'd refill them with Trader Joe's Two-Buck Chuck, fake the cork, and I'd sell them to another restaurant, or a boutique liquor store."

"Seriously?"

"We wouldn't use actual Trader Joe's Two-Buck Chuck, but

you get the idea."

I was impressed. "You really re-corked bottles?"

Mona nodded. "Trevor did. It's all about the label, but that won't be an issue here because these bottles were underwater. The labels all dissolved."

"Okay," I said, "even if we could create a fake bottle, what about authentication?"

"Let me worry about that," she said. "I've seen the paperwork. Fabricating one would be easy. But for this to work, we'd first have to get close to Kenneth and build his trust."

"How do you propose we do that?"

Mona was one step ahead of me. She clicked another tab to reveal a beautiful woman dressed in equestrian attire. "We start with the fiancée, Rebecca Olsen, an heiress to a coal fortune." Mona scanned through assorted photos of Rebecca and Kenneth together attending social events. "Rebecca competes in equestrian dressage. Rich girl sport. Horse and rider perform a series of predetermined routines. She's going to be in Lexington, Kentucky competing in nationals at the end of the month, a leg to qualify for the Olympic team. It's a big deal. If Kenneth truly loves her, he'll be there."

I was impressed by her homework but had obvious concerns. "There is still the hurdle of creating a counterfeit bottle."

"We'll need to find a Heidsick bottle from 1907. Maybe that's possible. Can you help me?"

The challenge set, we both spent the next few hours researching the obscure field known as bottle morphology. Resources included both the Federation of Historical Bottle Collectors and the Society of Historical Archaeology. We learned champagne bottles in 1907 were hand-blown and made of heavy, olive-green glass. For champagne, there is a finish at the top of the rim the wire of the cork grabs onto, so they are unique.

Searching the Internet, I found a retired aerospace engineer in Oregon whose hobby was the forensics of vintage glass. His website was a treasure-trove of information with images of everything from obscure liquor flasks to apothecary containers.

I came up with a story. Using my stock Nigel persona, I got him on the phone and inquired about obtaining "turn of the Century Heidsieck Champagne bottles to be used in a museum exhibit featuring the work of Paul Cézanne, the father of Post-Impressionism."

Hearing the accent I used, Mona couldn't control her laughter. I had to shoo her away.

It was just enough bullshit to get the guy talking. He didn't have the bottles himself but referred me to collectors who might. The glass expert said, "A hidden cellar was discovered in Saratoga Springs, New York. A contractor working on an old home and came across a false wall in the basement—a hidden vault built during Prohibition full of wine, beer, and liquor bottles, some still intact. The homeowners have been auctioning it off." He gave me their contact information.

After Mona's laughter subsided, I called and got the home-owner on the phone.

As luck would have it, there were two empty Heidsieck bottles, pre-1920, in good condition. Had we found a sealed bottle, it would have been perfect, but that was not the case. I had them shipped priority from upstate New York.

When the bottles arrived, they were carefully bubble-wrapped. Both had labels, so we needed to soak those off. As they bathed in buckets of salt water, the next step was to find a way to fabricate the cork and wire.

I learned Heidsieck's corks had not changed in over a hundred years; they'd only really updated in the late eighties when Piper-Heidseck became part of the corporate Remy Cointreau Wine and Spirits Group. Although the Piper-Heidsieck logo was branded into the inside of the cork—it did not matter because the inside of the cork wouldn't be visible unless someone opened the wine.

We still needed the real deal, an authentic cork.

While Mona searched, I purchased bottles of common champagne to practice removing and then reinserting the cork. It wasn't easy. Once a cork is removed, it expands, especially for champagne. Using plastic PVC pipe, I fashioned a clamp to keep the diameter of the cork at a compressed circumference when pulled to not blossom into the mushroom shape.

Mona found all of this very amusing, hanging over my shoulder as I practiced.

For the cork and wire, she came across fifty-year-old Heidsieck Champagne bottles from a wine collector in Newport Beach. The plan was to buy those, extract the cork and salvage the cap and wire to complete our counterfeit bottles.

That afternoon, we made plans to head out to Newport Beach, about an hour's drive south. We gathered our things and went downstairs.

A big surprise—Trevor was leaning against my car.

CHAPTER 25

Trevor stepped forward and asked Mona, "Who's the old poofter?"

I understood the "poofter" part. I'd put on the flamboyantly gay persona when Trevor came to my front door. How did mid-thirties make me *old*?

"Fuck you!" she said defiantly.

Trevor turned to me and said, "You had me fooled, mate. I completely bought the bullshit you'd found her phone." He turned to Mona, and said, "Did you really think I wouldn't find you?"

He'd come armed. I could see the black handle of a pistol holstered inside his jacket. I sensed someone behind me and turned. It was Rex.

Trevor said, "Mona," tilting his head, "time to go, love."

"You tried to kill me," she said.

"I didn't mean to hurt you, babe. Come on, we've got work to do."

"I'm done with your bullshit."

"I was drunk, babe. Sorry, it won't happen again. We'll talk about how I'm going to make it up to you."

"Hell no," Mona took me by the arm.

Trevor cackled. "You can't be serious. This guy?"

"Get the fuck out of here," I said, standing my ground.

Trevor stepped forward. "This is none of your business, mate."

I was holding my car keys in my right hand. Even though he had a gun, I considered a sucker punch, the key protruding from my fist.

To Mona, Trevor said, "Let's you and I have a little chat."

"There's nothing to talk about," she snapped back.

At that moment, a pair of Santa Monica bike cops came pedaling up the street. In New York City's Central Park, NYPD rides horses. In Santa Monica, beach cops ride mountain bikes.

Mona yelled, "He has a gun!" pointing to Trevor.

The cops jumped from their bikes and drew weapons. "Hands up!" one barked.

"Everyone on your knees," commanded the other.

I slowly raised my hands above my head. Trevor and Rex followed. "You too!" one of the cops yelled to Mona. Her hands went up as well.

Guns trained, they instructed us to lock our fingers behind our heads and drop down to our knees. Once we'd done that, they asked Mona who had the weapon.

She nodded to Trevor, "He does." Then to Rex, she said, "And probably this guy too."

"Are you carrying a weapon?" the cop asked Trevor.

"Yes," he admitted. "In my holster."

"You?" he asked Rex.

"No, sir," said Rex, all business.

"Anyone else have a weapon?" asked the other cop. That was followed by silence. While one kept his gun trained, the other frisked us.

From Trevor, he retrieved the handgun. He then pressed him down against the pavement, knee on his back, and handcuffed him.

Rex next, he said, "I'll ask again, do you have a weapon?"

"I do not."

He frisked Rex before bounding his wrist with a zip-tie.

I told them I did not have a weapon, but they frisked me anyway. I, too, was zip-tied. Only after the three of us were face down, with our hands bound behind our backs, did they start with questions.

Mona told them, "He threatened us with a gun."

"She's my ex-girlfriend," Trevor replied.

More cops arrived. They pulled our IDs and separated us all for questioning. I told the cop exactly what happened. "I live here. That guy threatened us with a gun."

"You all know each other?"

"Mona knows them."

"What reason would he have to threaten you?"

"He's her ex."

The cop shot a look to Mona and nodded to himself. We waited for what seemed like an eternity as they ran our IDs for what I assumed were background checks. I knew mine would be clear. I could have had plenty of priors, but didn't, in part thanks to blind luck and my dad.

Trevor's gun was confiscated. He was taken into custody and placed into a police cruiser. They asked Mona lots of questions. Because we were separated, I couldn't hear what she was saying.

One of the cops took the handcuffs off Rex and escorted him away. From what I could tell, it didn't look like he was going to be arrested.

Mona agreed to press charges. One of the cops instructed her to consider getting a restraining order. Under his breath, he said, "And I'd suggest you find somewhere else to stay for the night."

She asked, "Aren't you taking them to jail?"

Thumbing to Trevor sitting in the patrol car, the cop said, "Unless there's an outstanding warrant, he probably won't be held overnight."

"But he had a gun."

"Without additional factors, carrying of a loaded weapon without a permit is a misdemeanor. And with the zero-bail policy..." The cop leaned forward in a lowered tone. "I see a lot of domestic disturbance calls. I suggest you look into alternate living arrangements until things cool down."

Next, we were driven to the Santa Monica Police Department, where Mona formally filed charges.

When we returned to the condo, Mona went out on the balcony to make sure Rex was nowhere in sight. "Trevor's coming back," she said. "He won't let this go."

Maybe she was right.

I knew the manager at the Terranea Resort in nearby Rancho Palos Verdes. I called him and was able to get a decent room rate. We packed a few things and headed out. All the while, Mona kept an eye out for Rex.

The sun was setting by the time we got to the Palos Verdes luxury hotel property. We checked in and settled into a private bungalow. I ordered room service and a bottle of wine.

Mona couldn't stop pacing. "Trevor's going to kill me."

"Why do you think so?"

"Because he's killed before."

I said, "You never told me—"

"I know, I know. I didn't tell you everything."

"Sit down and give me the details." We sat on the balcony as the sun set over the Pacific. It would have been a tranquil setting had it not been for the subject at hand. I asked, "Who did he kill?"

"Jonas was his name," Mona said. "Trevor had a sex tape."

"And?"

"The guy refused to pay. We learned he'd gone to the cops. Trevor and Rex went to the guy's hotel room, injected him with fentanyl-laced heroin, and left behind evidence to make it look like he was an addict."

"What makes you think Trevor wants to kill you?"

Fingers to her throat, she said, "If there's anyone who can put Trevor away, it's me. He's scared shitless of going to jail." She swallowed hard and gulped her wine.

"I can set you up with a new identity. He won't be able to find you."

Her eyes showed a glimmer of hope. "How?"

"Arrange an alias. I'm just renting in Santa Monica. We could move somewhere else."

Mona asked, "Where?"

"How about here in the South Bay?" I said, waving a hand to the sparkling ocean. "As long as I'm near the ocean, I don't care. I have to be near sun and sand."

She lit up with a smile. "You can take the boy out of Florida, but you can't take Florida out of the boy."

"Yeah."

"If he somehow gets me," she said. "Promise me you'll avenge my death."

"He won't."

"But if he does. Make it painful."

The thought of killing someone had never crossed my mind, but at that moment I said, "I promise." And I meant it.

CHAPTER 26

At the Terranea Resort over the following days, Mona split her time between morning dips in the ocean and collecting information about Kenneth Coleman. She also dug into his fiancée, Rebecca Olsen.

Meanwhile, I found ocean-view properties in the cities of Newport Beach, Rancho Palos Verdes, Redondo, and Hermosa Beach. Mona wanted outdoor space—more than just a balcony—so I put a rental deposit on a townhome in Hermosa Beach. It was not as upscale as my furnished Santa Monica condo, but we had a postage stamp-sized backyard and a partial ocean view.

In the event Trevor was watching my place, I made trips in the middle of the night to move out of the Santa Monica Sea Colony condominium. If anyone was following me, the speed of the Chevy on the 405 Freeway was insurance I wasn't being followed.

When we moved in, Mona insisted she pay half the rent as partners—so we split it down the middle. We made the townhome's second bedroom our business office. Mona and I made a great team. We spent hours assembling furniture kits. Since the custom mattress had yet to be delivered, we slept curled up on the couch. Finally, it arrived.

As the U.S. Dressage Finals approached, in the back of my mind, I thought Mona's scheme was a longshot. But since she had put so much effort into the caper, I respectfully did not second guess any of her decisions. "If we're going to present ourselves as legitimate wine brokers," Mona said, "we'll need something to get Kenneth's attention."

"What are you thinking?"

"A really good bottle. Something he'd recognize."

As I made enchiladas, Mona got on her laptop and hacked into the Christie's wine auction site—the same source that had the record of Kenneth's lost bid of the shipwrecked champagne. She said. "Last year, he bid on a case of 2016 Domaine de la Roma-nee-Conti La Tache." She pulled up a photo of the wooden crate containing the wine. There appeared to be a lot number branded on the side of the box. "He won the bid, but buying the wine in its original case means it was probably purchased as an investment. He wouldn't necessarily open the crate unless he planned on drinking all of it, because that would diminish the value."

I finished her thought, "But if we were to have a bottle with us..."

"It doesn't have to be that same vintage, but..." Mona pulled up images of the equestrian venue. "We can't bring alcohol inside the Alltech Arena, so we're going to have to find another opportunity to socialize and strike up a conversation."

It seemed like a lot of hoops to jump through, but I wasn't going to be critical. Instead, I asked, "So you think we should buy a bottle?"

"As bait."

"If things don't go as planned, and we don't find the opportunity to elbow up next to him, do we need to open it?"

"Nah. Burgundy is a tad heavy for my taste," She slid up behind me as I prepared dinner, hands around my waist. "I'm more of a chardonnay shakedown artist."

"How does that work?"

"Oh...charm some guy to buy me a drink and then order the most expensive pour."

I turned to her, "Then what?"

"Play it by ear," she said with a seductive look in her eye.

"You really like this stuff, don't you?"

"What stuff?"

"The inside of a caper. Admit it."

"You do, too."

I carried her to our bedroom, and we christened the new mattress.

Afterward, as we lay post-coital, I began to tell her how much I loved her. I said I'd never felt so close to anyone before. But the moment was interrupted when the smoke alarm went off. I'd forgotten about the enchiladas. They were burnt to a crisp.

To this day, I regret I never got to tell Mona fully how much I truly was in love with her. I never again found the spontaneity. I was afraid to talk about my feelings. It seems there was always something we were doing, something brewing, or something in the oven. I regret I'd never get the chance again.

CHAPTER 27

Present Day

Madeline called at the crack of dawn, said, "The Chancellor has been texting me. Christine is leaving all these voicemails. They want me to take that money."

"For now," I said, "reply you're having your lawyer look over the agreement."

"Why not just say *no*?"

"Because it will buy us time." I suggested she not to go campus and lie low for a few days.

"But I've got to teach my classes."

"Can you do that online or something?"

"Hell no. And they're shooting my scene in a couple of days.

"What scene?"

"The movie," she reminded me. "I play Lady Macduff. She dies in the play."

"Who dies?"

"My character. Macbeth considers her husband a threat, and orders Lady Macduff and her children killed. Ironic, isn't it? Considering?"

"If you think if you're in danger then you should go stay with your mom."

"I'm not going anywhere," she said.

I asked her when asbestos was discovered in the theater.

"Shit, I don't know," Madeline said. "Less than a year ago."

"Has there been any work done there?"

"Like what?"

"Demolition."

"Haven't seen any."

"No workers in protective gear going in and out?"

"Not that I've seen."

I asked, "Did Mike ever talk about the asbestos?"

"Mike complained about a weird smell in the theater giving him a headache. For all the hours we both spent in there, in rehearsals, late nights painting sets…"

"What kind of smell?"

"Chemical."

I told her to be careful. "Business as usual. And call me if you feel threatened in any way."

Before we ended the call, Madeline thanked me.

I had to clear my head so took Suzie for a short walk. It surprised me how well she got around with the plastic splint on her leg. My dog seemed more interested in sniffing the foliage at the edge of the walkways more than anything else. I assumed she could detect dogs which had been there previously, likely service dogs considering what Slim had told me about his place.

Above the cabins, Slim had pulled the Harley out of the shed. A black leather jacket in hand, and said, "Bike's good to go."

I was hesitant, my mind on the hot cup of coffee I haven't had yet, and said, "Going to take some time to get used to."

"Take it easy, and you'll do fine." He handed me a worn leather jacket. Painted on the back was a leggy calendar-girl, a Texas flag, and an armadillo smoking a cigarette. I imagined if the bomber jacket sat in a vintage clothing store on L.A.'s trendy Melrose Avenue hipsters would've paid a fortune for it.

A Ford F-150 pickup truck drove past with a friendly honk of the horn. I recognized Dr. Reibach. Slim offered a friendly wave before she continued on her way. I asked him, "Doc Reibach told me about a hit and run, a special needs boy, the driver skipped out."

Slim said, "she'd practically adopted that kid." That explained the tinge of emotion Reibach held back telling me about the incident. "Jimmy loved animals and would hang around her office just to help out and be around them. She helped him establish a dog walking business. He was walking a pup on the side of the road when he was hit, and Sandy suspects Marsh arranged to get the driver out of the country."

"Why does she think that?"

"She saw the kid in his squad car the day he disappeared. You'd have to ask her about it." He held up the leather jacket, "try this on." It was a size too large, but better than being too small.

Without a chance to have morning coffee, I donned the helmet and kick-started the motorcycle. Slim wished me luck. I pulled out onto the pavement and wristed the bike throttle on the handlebar. I'd forgotten the torque a motorcycle is capable of. And Harleys are loud.

Riding up and down the highway, I rode back-and-forth to get used to toeing the gears and handling the brakes. After a couple of minutes, I felt confident enough and made my way to Argonaut. I have to admit gliding up the mountain roads was exhilarating.

Reaching Argonaut, it surprised me to see that familiar white van pulled over on the side of the road. *Was it the same van?* I doubled back to make sure.

The hood was propped up and the Polynesian kid who attacked me with nunchucks at the gas station outside L.A. was pouring antifreeze into the radiator.

I ran through the possibilities of why he was in Argonaut. I wondered if the Chevy SS had another GPS tracker hidden inside. But if that was the case, he would have been hovering near my Chevy SS at Amarillo Slims, and not in Argonaut. I circled back, shut the bike down, and rested it on the kickstand on the side of the road. I was determined to find out who this kid was, and who he was working for.

Steam was drifting from under the hood. I couldn't help but notice the rear tires of the van, due to my handiwork, were brand new. They still had the manufacturer stickers still on the side-walls.

I hid back in the cover of trees and watched.

As he screwed on the radiator cap, the boy burned himself and cursed. He closed the hood and went to the van's side door, dug into a cooler and came up with ice. He sat on the van's sideboard and held the ice cube to his palm to cool the burn. Then he pulled out his phone to scroll. Behind him, inside the van, I could make out a camping stove and ratty cot.

After he finished checking his phone, the boy went to the bushes to take a leak. That's when I moved in.

The kid returned, slammed the van's sliding door, and climbed into the driver's seat. He was surprised to find me sitting in the passenger seat, and his eyes went wide.

I calmy said, "We need to talk."

He swung his fist. It caught me in the jaw.

I grabbed him by the collar. "Who are you working for?"

He snarled and bit my forearm. That hurt, so I punched him.

The kid snarled and bit harder.

I kept punching.

He yelped and sprung between the seats and into the back of the van. I could see he was going for the nunchucks. I dove after and we crashed through a rack of electronic equipment. After I landed a few more punches, the kid gave in. "Okay, okay...don't hit me," he pleaded.

"Who are you working for?"

"I don't reveal my clients."

I threatened my fist.

"It's confidential."

As opposed to punching him, I twisted his arm behind his back. He squirmed and kicked. "Okay, okay, brah...Some dude in Vegas."

"Who?"

"A guy named Trevor. I don't know his last name."

Trevor? That is not a common name. I asked, "Trevor Dunn?"

"I just know the dude as Trevor," he said.

It had to be him. I hadn't seen Trevor since the day he was arrested outside my Santa Monica condo. After Mona and I moved away, I assumed I'd never see him again. I asked, "How long have you been tailing me?"

"I don't know," he sniffled.

I cranked his arm.

He cursed and said, "Like…two months or something."

I released him from my grasp. "What's your name?"

"Alexandro," he said, rubbing his shoulder.

I examined the bite mark on my hand. There was blood and broken skin. I showed it to him. "Let's hope you don't have rabies."

"Gingivitis for sure. Herpes probably."

"Herpes?"

"Skanky bitches, brah," he said with a smile.

"Where are you from?"

He said nothing.

"L.A.?"

"Southgate."

"You Hawaiian?"

"Filipino *and* Hawaiian."

"Why aren't you in school?"

Alexandro scoffed and said, "No money to be made there. Total waste of my time."

"Get a high school diploma, and it may work in your favor."

"School is for chumps."

"What do your parents think of that?"

"My mom lives in Kona, and I never knew my dad, so I guess that makes me a bastard." He forced a smile displaying yellowed teeth.

"A rat bastard," I replied. "Let's hope you don't have rabies."

"That's me."

"I bet your mom wants you in school."

"I don't care what she thinks."

I never knew my mother. I wished I had maternal love at his age, and said, "You should be in school."

I'd given Alexandro enough of the stick, so next I tried the carrot. Considering the funky smell in the van, it was clear the vehicle was his home. I proposed, "I'll pay you back for the tires, but first you've got to tell me everything."

Alexandro eyed me with distrust. "You're gonna pay me for those tires you slashed?"

"Only if you're honest."

"That bullshit cost me over four hundred bucks."

"I'll make good. And then some."

He leered at me. "Look, I don't normally follow people around. Boring as shit, dude. This is my side-hustle. I'm a photojournalist by trade," he said proudly, motioning to his photo and video equipment splayed on the carpet. "Paparazzi, and stringer."

"Why is Trevor tailing me?"

"Like I said, brah, I don't know. I just do it, then send updates, texts and video."

"What video?"

"Like you driving around, and shit...going in and out of plac-es."

"Did you put that GPS tracker in my car?"

"Trevor did that. He said he hired some Black Cat guy, then sent me the link so I could follow you."

"Black Cat?" I asked.

"Or maybe it was Black Cube."

"Black Cube or Black Cat?"

"I forget."

"Black Cat is a firecracker."

"I know," he said. "Bad ass."

"Black Cube is an intelligence agency."

I could see that meant nothing to him. He scratched the side of his head.

I asked, "Where was my car when the tracker was installed?"

"The garage of your apartment."

"You've been there?"

"Culver City. Yeah."

"When?"

"A few times. But I didn't put that thing in your car." Trevor said, "Black...whoever did it."

"Was it Black Cube or Black Cat?"

Exasperated, the teenager said, "I don't fucking remember."

It seemed odd, but it made sense. Black Cube is an elite agency run by former officers of the Israeli Mossad. Very secretive. Very expensive. The firm claims to be in the risk assessment business, but in reality, they're corporate spies.

Alexandro continued, "I don't know how you moved that GPS thing into that moving van, but..." He shook his head in dismay. "I was halfway to Arizona before I figured that shit out."

"How'd you find me here?"

"Trevor told me."

"How'd he know?"

"He didn't tell me."

"You're lying."

"Seriously. He just texted me and said go poke around." He looked out to the trees. "Dude pays, so I do what I'm told."

I wondered if it was Black Cube that had followed me from Truckee, and not an undercover vehicle from the Placer County Sheriff's Department. If Trevor had hired Black Cube, they too would have access to the automated license plate reader database. What I couldn't wrap my mind around was why Trevor would follow me after all this time. And for what? I asked Alexandro, "How did Trevor end up hiring you?"

He explained he'd built a reputation as a celebrity paparazzi in Hollywood and Vegas. "Most guys use long lenses from a distance. I get hidden cameras up close."

"You help Trevor make sex tapes?"

"I hook him up with tiny cameras and shit. Whatever he does with the video is none of my business."

"Did you know Mona?"

"Who?"

"His partner."

"Who's Mona?"

"How long have you been working for him?"

"Just over a year."

I asked again, "Why do you think he hired you to follow me?"

"Like I said, brah, *I don't know*. He doesn't tell me shit."

"How much is he paying you?"

"Five bills a day."

"Five hundred?"

"Yeah."

"How does he pay you?"

"Cash. That's how he does it. There's a bar in Lake Las Vegas. We meet there."

I was vaguely familiar with Lake Las Vegas, a suburb east of Sin City with gated communities and plush golf courses. Maybe Trevor chose the restaurant as a meeting place because he lived near there. I asked, "When are you scheduled to meet him next?"

"I was gonna head there from here. He owes me for over a month by now."

"Why doesn't he wire you money?"

"That's how he wants to do it. No complaints from me."

"I'll double what he pays. You can stay on Trevor's payroll at the same time."

His eyes lit up. "A grand?"

"One thousand a day. Trevor keeps paying you, so you clear fifteen hundred a day."

I could see the idea greatly intrigued him. "Legit?"

"You'll be a double agent."

"Like...from a spy movie?"

"I'll need Trevor's phone number and email address. But first, I need you to find out why he's following me."

"I have his number, but that's it."

"We'll start there."

Alexandro thought about it for a moment before, "So, like...I'll be getting paid from both sides?"

"That's what being a double agent means."

He blinked twice, stroked his chin, and said, "Legit."

CHAPTER 28

On Slim's motorcycle, I followed Alexandro's van through downtown Argonaut, steam trailing from under the hood. Thankfully, I wasn't in my car because Marsh had parked in his usual perch beside the hardware store, like a cat waiting to pounce.

Alexandro pulled over at an ATM. I felt confident I could take off the helmet, but still kept an eye out for Marsh, anyway. The maximum I could withdraw was eight hundred dollars. That covered the cost of replacing the van's rear tires, and then some. Next, I wired Alexandro a three-thousand-dollar retainer. Once he confirmed he received the payment, Alexandro gave me what information he had—which was simply Trevor's cell phone number.

"How often does he contact you?"

He showed me his phone. "Late last night he texted me about you being up here, so I hit the road."

"How did he know I was here?"

"I don't know," Alexandro said.

"Find out for me."

"What if he doesn't tell me?"

"Ask. See what he says."

He shrugged, "Whatever."

Next, we took his van to a mechanic at the edge of town to

have the radiator looked at. The diagnosis was a leaky hose. That was good news because it was something which could be fixed immediately without waiting for a part. As the mechanic made the repair, Alexandro said, "I'll need to get some video of you going in and out of stores and shit. So Trevor can see I'm doing my job."

He had a point. I hadn't thought of how to handle Trevor's expectations. He knew I was in the mountains, but did he know why? If Trevor was aware I was investigating a death, it could complicate the case. I wasn't going to tell Alexandro about that because I was not entirely sure if I could trust him. Instead, I told him about the production of *Macbeth* being filmed at the summer camp, how I was representing an investor financing the independent film, overlooking the production.

"Who's in it?" he wanted to know.

"Students mostly."

"No stars?"

"It's low budget. Virtual reality."

That news disappointed the teenage paparazzo.

I said, "Capture video of me on set, and send that to Trevor. Ask him when you're going to be paid."

Thinking it over, I tried to remember any activity over the last couple of months that would interest Trevor. Most of the work I'd done was investigating disability fraudsters, penny-ante stuff. What was Trevor looking for?

I settled the bill with the mechanic, and had Alexandro follow me to the summer camp. Passing the hardware store, Sheriff Marsh was no longer there.

CHAPTER 29

At the summer camp location, Alexandro and I parked amongst a cluster of assorted vehicles. The haunting music of bagpipes echoed from somewhere beyond the trees. The distinctive, ceremonial drone made me remember Madeline had called it *The Scottish Play*.

As we made our way to the camp, the scent of marijuana was wafting from two college-aged girls dressed in Elizabethan costumes seated in foldable camping chairs shaded under the awning of a dilapidated Winnebago. Alexandro greeted the girls with a playful, "Good day, me ladies," and gave them a bow. They giggled, eyeing us as we walked past. One of them took a selfie.

The sound of power tools blared as a ragtag construction crew built a façade which resembled a castle. As we passed, I could see a bearded young man in overalls mixing sand and crumbled Styrofoam into a bucket of dark grey paint. Another guy applied the mixture to the plywood. I could see from the dried sections the process gave the surface a texture that vaguely resembled stone. One long-haired painter wore suspenders and a "Get Medieval" T-shirt.

Down in the meadow, it appeared as if they were shooting a battle scene.

We passed a falconer with a bird perched upon his leather-gloved hand. There were trumpet players and maidens in bustier corsets carrying baskets.

Background extras dressed as soldiers and squires held an assortment of prop swords, longbows, and battle axes. The bagpipes kicked in. I heard Louis's voice shout "action," and the performers clashed.

Alexandro gawked at it all, bug-eyed. "Bitchin'," he said aloud.

Aside I could see the actors playing Macbeth and Lady Macbeth, Kathy and Jim, sitting in the shade, not part of the scene on camera. I said to Alexandro, "Hang back. Try not to be obvious. Unauthorized video not allowed."

"Not my first rodeo," he said before slinking off.

Kathy, the actress playing Lady Macbeth, had long, curly auburn hair and sat engrossed reading a novel. At first, I thought she wore a costume wig but then could see it was her natural fire red mane. I apologized for interrupting and introduced myself using the same story I'd told Marsh—I was an insurance investigator following up before the company signed off on Mike's life insurance.

From the look on her face, I assumed my scar made her suspicious. "Insurance agent in colors?" Kathy questioned, indicating the leather biker jacket I was wearing.

"Since I was coming up to the mountains, I figured I'd take the bike. Always looking for an excuse to get her on the road."

She squinted into the sun and asked, "Weren't you here the other day talking with Louis?"

"That's right. He suggested I speak with you. I promise this won't take long."

"Okay then," she said, and Kathy summoned her colleague.

Jim was a tall guy with an oversized Adam's apple. He too eyed me with distrust. Jim had a unique look; dominant cheek bones and a protruding forehead. I explained I was helping Madeline. That seemed to put him at ease. We found a picnic table to sit away from the others.

"Apologies," I said. "I realize you've been questioned about this a million times."

Kathy said, "Not really, but glad to help."

I started in with, "If you don't mind...walk me through that night."

"We were in a classroom, rehearsing act two, scene two."

Jim nodded to confirm.

"Which classroom?"

"Quartz, I think."

Jim said, "The classrooms are named after minerals."

"Where's Quartz?"

"In the Computer Science Building," he said.

"Where is that in relation to the theater?"

"Near," Kathy said.

I said, "Madeline mentioned Mike had noticed a chemical odor within the theater building."

Jim said, "We all did. And then we were kicked out."

"Tell me what happened the night of Mike's accident."

Kathy started in, "We were going through a scene, and Mike got a text. He said he'd be right back. We waited for a while. Like...a long time. We got concerned and called, but Mike's phone went to voicemail. Louis went out looking for him."

Jim motioned to Louis out in the meadow directing the scene, and explained, "Louis was shooting the rehearsals."

"That's right," Kathy said. "Once they decided to make it a movie, Mike brought in Louis to videotape rehearsals. After Mike, uhm..." she searched to find the right word, "had the accident...they decided Louis would direct because he's a filmmaker and was shooting the rehearsals, anyway."

"Who is 'they?'"

"Chancellor Foster," Jim said.

I asked, "How is Louis doing?"

They gave each other a knowing look before Kathy said, "Alright." She didn't sound convincing.

Jim said, "With all these re-enactors and everything, Louis needs to learn what's important is not these big action scenes," he said, motioning to the crew out working on set, "but instead the performance of the actors, and Shakespeare's language. Mike knew that. Louis is trying to make this a 3D version of *Braveheart*. And this crazy three-sixty view virtual reality camera takes forever to set up. Even the crew has to be in costume because the camera might pick them up."

I sensed resentment. "I understand Louis has made a few films."

Jim scoffed, "If you call an improv exercise shot with a handheld camcorder a film, then yes, he has."

Kathy said, "But this is entirely different. You can't improvise Shakespeare."

It was clear neither were happy with the captain of the ship. I asked, "Did Mike say where he was going that night?"

Kathy shook her head. "No. He seemed concerned about something, though. Most of the time, Mike was super chill and joked around. He made the work fun. But that night, his mind was somewhere else."

"So, you assume the text he got is what prompted Mike to excuse himself?"

"It was obvious," she said. "He'd been stressed by a lot of things."

"Like what?"

Jim said, "Mike was really pissed off about how it all went down when Special Eddie got hit."

Kathy punched Jim on the shoulder.

"What?" he said to her.

She explained to me, "There was a boy born with Down's Syndrome, a really sweet kid, killed by a hit-and-run driver. People called him Special Ed—a cruel nickname." She glared at Jim, then returned her attention to me. "He suffered a concussion and died in the hospital. Nobody witnessed it, but they found the guy who did it—a student. There was damage on the grill of his jeep."

Jim said, "Not only damage. Blood and bone on the grill. And it wasn't a jeep. It was a Mercedes G 350. Luxury SUV. The driver was an international student. Rich kid. They arrested him but let him go." Shaking his head, Jim added, "A week later, the guy's back in Dubai, posting photos with his homies in a hookah lounge."

I asked, "How was Mike involved?"

Kathy said, "He wasn't, but he suspected the administration helped get the kid out of the country."

"Did he mention that the night of his accident?"

"No," Kathy said.

"Is there anyone you can think of who would have had any reason to harm Mike?"

Kathy said. "Not really. Everyone loved the guy."

"In your own opinion, what do you think happened that night?"

Kathy ventured a guess. "It was dark. Maybe he was looking down at his phone while walking around and didn't see the mineshaft."

Jim said, "Or maybe he was up there in the trees taking a piss or something. Maybe he got spooked by something in the dark, ran, and didn't see the pit in front of him."

"What would have spooked him?"

"A bear or a mountain lion. We have wild boars, too."

At that moment, another actor joined them. He carried a few extra pounds and had facial hair that gave him an aristocratic look. Kathy introduced him as Ricardo, playing the role of Lord Macduff. Madeline had mentioned her role was Lady Macduff. He and Jim spoke briefly about a swordfight scene scheduled for later in the day.

Getting back to business, I asked, "Are you guys aware of any tunnels which could be connected to the mineshaft?

Kathy said, "There's a tunnel in the basement of the Eureka Tavern. They say it was used during Prohibition. But it only goes so far before it's caved in."

"You've seen it?"

Jim nodded. "One night, we shimmied in there and went exploring."

Kathy added, "Creepy in there."

The take-charge assistant director came up. She said to the actors, "We need you on set, please."

Kathy said to me, "I feel bad for Madeline. Give her my condolences." With that, they followed the assistant director.

I was waiting beside Alexandro's van when he emerged from behind the trees. He held his camera and gave me the thumbs up. "Got you talking to those peeps."

"Send the video to Trevor. Say you've learned I'm overseeing the production and will be here a while. Insist you meet him in Vegas to get paid ASAP."

"I'll try, but it may take a day or two for him to get back to me."

"Where do you plan to stay?"

"I sleep in my van."

I suggested he consider parking overnight at the summer camp. He'd easily blend in since so many working on the production seemed to be doing the same. Alexandro checked out the girls under the shade of the RV awning, and said, "Bitchin'."

Just beyond us, a sleek Range Rover pulled into the parking lot. Chancellor Foster stepped out, followed by Christine. As opposed to her business attire, she wore tight capri pants and a stylish satin top. The Chancellor donned his usual sports jacket. Of course, they reeked of money.

Louis came up and greeted them with forced enthusiasm. He began what appeared to be a tour, displaying the sets equipment.

Madeline had mentioned Louis was a kiss-ass. I saw proof as the Chancellor and his wife soaked up the attention.

Before I set out, I texted Madeline. *Meet me at the Eureka Tavern.*

CHAPTER 30

Except for an old-timer hunched over a Bloody Mary, the woodsy Eureka Tavern was empty. The place felt timeless. Shuffleboard table. A dusty Olympia Brewing Company neon sign. Mining implements decorated the walls. I bellied up and ordered a beer. Laura, the bartender, a lanky cowgirl in worn overalls, hair in braids, poured.

Minutes later, Madeline joined us. As I suspected, Laura was the one Madeline was staying with. She introduced me. "Jack is a friend of my brother. He's the private investigator helping me sort everything out."

"Investigation consultant," I corrected.

"Welcome," Laura said and got Madeline a cup of coffee. "Want that Irish?" she asked with one hand on the neck of a bottle of Jameson.

"I wish, but I've got a class to teach."

As Laura tended to the old guy at the end of the bar, I explained to Madeline what Jim and Kathy had said—Mike's text that night.

"Nobody ever told me that."

"Who took their statements?"

"Sheriff Marsh. Who else?"

"When Mike was pulled out of the mineshaft, was his phone on him?"

"I don't know. I mean, I never got it back. I guess we all figured it was at the bottom of the shaft." Saddened by the thought, she added, "A couple days later, they gave me his watch and wedding band."

"Contact your cell phone provider and request the correspondence from that night."

"How do I do that?"

"Who opened the account?"

"Mike."

"Is it in your name?"

"I forget. Probably not. He had it before we were married, handled most of the bills and stuff like that."

"You should be able to get that info. Did you text Mike that night?"

"No."

Laura was flipping through sports channels on the TV. I said to her, "I understand there's a tunnel in the basement here."

"Who told you that?"

"Jim and Kathy."

Laura laughed. "Yeah, well...that figures. We don't advertise it, but there is a crawlspace downstairs. It goes maybe a hundred feet or so."

I said to Madeline, "I'm wondering if Mike could have fallen into the mineshaft from an interconnecting tunnel, as opposed to from the sinkhole above."

"A tunnel?"

"I met with the first responder who retrieved Mike. He said there are interconnecting tunnels leading to the shaft." I turned to Laura and asked, "Do you know of any other entrances to the mine, other than downstairs?"

She shot a knowing look to Madeline before Laura said, "There is an entrance at the old mill. A bunch of us went exploring once. I asked Mike and Madeline if they wanted to come, but..."

"There was *no* way I was going into some nasty tunnel," Madeline said. "I'm claustrophobic."

Laura teased, "Plus, spiders freak you out, right?"

Madeline said, "Arachnophobia, acrophobia, nyctophobia. I've got all the phobias."

"How about coulrophobia?"

Madeline asked, "What's that?"

"Fear of clowns," Laura said. "I suffer from that. Big time. A lot of them here at closing time."

The sound of Madeline's laugh reminded me of her brother Hector's.

Laura went on, "Wikipedia says twelve percent of adults suffer from fear of clowns." She poured a shot of Jameson for herself. "I definitely have that," she said, then downed the shot of whiskey. Laura shook with a shudder, then added, "Don't judge me. That was medicinal."

Madeline laughed more and teased her friend, "Didn't you say your ex-husband was a clown?"

Laura cringed, "Rodeo clown. That's where it all started. Good riddance."

I asked Laura, "So you've been in these tunnels?"

"Yeah. We made a party out of it, gathered lanterns, helmets and climbing gear...went down to the old sawmill where there's a blocked off entrance. We were able to get past that with a little bit of ingenuity," she said with a smile. "Inside it's a like a maze. Narrow. We did the Hansel and Gretel thing by leaving electric tea lights behind so we could navigate our way back. Didn't see much other than oil drums."

"Acid," the old timer at the end of the bar said. He'd obviously overheard our conversation.

Laura asked the guy, "Why do you think it's acid, Bill?"

"Cause I've seen 'em."

"What kind of acid?" she asked, egging him on.

"Hell if I know. Nuclear acid. Nasty. You can tell by the stickers on the barrels. Skeleton skull and crossbones," he said with a spooky voice.

Madeline said, "Isn't that the symbol for poison?"

"Suppose so," the old-timer said. "There's also the test tube liquid burning some poor bastard's hand. That means corrosive."

"Like my ex-husband," Laura joked, and poured herself another shot.

Bill raised his empty glass. "Going to need another one of these, if you please."

Laura went about fixing Bill the Bloody Mary, and I asked her, "Did anyone take photos?"

She said, "I don't remember. After a while, we got bored and followed our Hansel and Gretel trail back out."

Madeline checked her watch and said, "Damn. I've got to get to class."

I reminded her to call her phone company to access Mike's phone records. She said she would, and thanked me. After Madeline departed, a few customers came in and seated themselves in one of the booths by the window. Laura retrieved menus and attended to them.

Bill eyed me before saying, "I can get you in that mine if you want to see it." I moved to the barstool next to him, and he introduced himself as, "Bill, but everyone around here calls me Two-Dollar Bill."

"Nice to meet you. How'd you get that nickname?"

"Cause that's how I tip," he said, picking up a two-dollar bill from his money set on the bar. "I get these from the bank. Our third President, Thomas Jefferson on the front," he said, and turned the bill over, "and the signing of the Declaration of Independence on the back."

"Why go to the trouble?" I asked.

"So people remember me," as if it was obvious. "Unfortunately, there's not a lot of two-dollar bills in circulation these days. Or Susan B. Anthony dollar coins, for that matter, but that's because folks confused them with quarters." In a lowered voice, he said, "Say...I work on campus and know of a special, secret entrance. I can show you, but you've got to promise to keep it on the down-low. It's not a secret if everyone knows about it."

"Scout's honor."

"The deal is…we'd need to stop for provisions."

"Whatever you say."

After he finished his drink, I thanked Laura and followed Two-Dollar Bill from the tavern.

He squinted into the afternoon sun, looked at the threatening clouds, cursed to himself, and then motioned me to follow him into the town's general store.

Inside, he filled the handbasket with exactly what he had in mind—a bottle of Popov Vodka, cans of spicy V8, and a handful of Slim Jim meat sticks. I was a little hungry so found a combination platter of cheese, salami, and dried fruit which looked promising and added that to the handbasket. Since I was in no mood for vodka, I found a tallboy can of light beer.

At the register, Bill added two packs of Marlboro Reds and a plastic container of Tums Antacid. I paid for it all before we set off for campus. He lit a smoke on the way, and I asked, "What do you do for the college?"

"Whatever needs to be done. Mow lawns, take out rubbish, clean up after the kids and maintain my sanity—you name it."

"What's it like working here?"

Two-dollar Bill shrugged.

We made our way to the maintenance yard past lawn mowing equipment and assorted service vehicles to a nondescript cinderblock building. I asked, "Were you on duty when the professor fell down the mineshaft?"

"I was the one who heard him calling from down in there."

"What happened?"

"Heard him panicking. Told him to hold on and called 911. Lost a lot of sleep thinking about what went down that night."

"What was the worst part?"

"That he was alive…and then he wasn't."

Inside the maintenance building, he led me past a break room with lockers to a dimly lit stairway. Down the flight, below the garage level, there was a storage space lit by flickering, yellowed fluorescent lights. Shelves were stacked with old tools and what appeared to be industrial fluids.

In the corner atop an oriental rug there was a worn, crushed-velvet couch. A frayed Denver Broncos blanket and matching pillow were placed near, proof it also served as a bed. Bill set the grocery on the mini fridge and pulled out its contents. He produced a pair of red Solo cups and began to make the drinks. I said, "I'm good with the beer."

"Suit yourself." He pocketed a few Slim Jims and tossed me the cheese and fruit snack.

"I got this for both of us," I said.

"Thanks, but I have reason to *not* to eat cheese," he said.

"Lactose intolerant?"

"Political reasons."

From the fridge, Bill grabbed ice and mixed a healthy pour of the Popov vodka with a splash of V8. He pulled out a celery stick and then fingered olives from a jar, followed by pepperoncini peppers from another. He doused his drink with a bottle of Crystal Hot Sauce. Lastly, Bill topped off his craft-cocktail with black pepper from a tall, wooden grinder like you'd see at an old school steakhouse. The process was so precise, like a chemistry lab. "Down here," he said, "is my man cave. I sleep here when I'm in the doghouse with the old lady, ya know? When wife kicks me out of the house." I noticed a gold wedding band on his hand as he sampled his drink. "You get to be my age..."

"Appears to be nice and private," I said.

"Got that right," Bill said, seemingly satisfied with his drink before he led me over to a darkened corner of the room. There, he carefully set his drink down and pushed a shelving unit aside to reveal a metal door. Bill opened that. There was another door secured by a hefty lock. From the overstuffed keychain on his belt, he unlocked the final barrier to reveal a dark, concrete-walled tunnel. Bill said, "This here entrance is connected to the mine. Only a few of us know about it, so like I said, don't say anything to anybody. Got me?"

"Promise."

"Last thing I need is people messing with my stuff down here." Grease-stained hardhats hung on hooks on the wall. He gave me one. Each had a battery powered light above the visor. He turned his on, and I did the same.

It was cool and damp inside. As the tunnel descended, the concrete floor transitioned to a loose gravel surface. Between slurps of his drink, Bill said, "They say they pulled a shitload of gold out of these hills back in the day. All they had were pickaxes and shovels." He pointed to scars in the rock wall. "Dynamite, too."

There were splintered wooden support-beams above our heads. Some had fallen in. Others rested on oil drums stacked upon each other. We stepped around drums toppled over or half buried in dirt.

Bats hung from the ceiling. Bill advised me to give their droppings a wide berth, and not disturb them. He said an airborne fungus could cause a condition known as histoplasmosis that, "Makes ya bat shit crazy."

After descending further, we came across a cavern with stone shapes in what appeared to be massive white fangs. Bill explained, "Stalactites and stalagmites, formed over thousands of years. Words sound so alike and the only way to remember which is one is which is by saying, 'when mights go up...tights come down,'" He laughed at his own joke.

We moved farther into the cave.

More oil drums were piled haphazardly, and there was a pungent chemical odor in the air. "This is what I was talking about," he said, "all these drums stored down here."

I asked, "How'd they get these in here?"

"From the entrance at the sawmill, the one Laura talked about..."

"When was that?"

"Long ago. I can't remember. They sealed off the entrance with concrete for good."

I examined the faded labels on the barrels. One denoted sodium cyanide. Many contained trichloroethylene. The metal surfaces of the drums had a residue seeping out, some of it crystalized. I pulled out my phone and Bill said, "What are you doing?"

"Okay if I get a few shots?"

"Of this shit?"

"It may have something to do with Mike's accident."

He sipped his drink before saying, "Alright then...but no selfies or anything of me."

I snapped a few photos of the labels.

Bill sifted through his pack for the snacks we'd brought, and said, "The reason I don't eat cheese...you're probably too young to remember, but back during the seventies the Carter administration subsidized the dairy industry by buying up excess milk and cheese, helped keep dairy farms afloat during the recession. They stored it in caves like this one. Became known as *government cheese*. Ever hear of that?"

I told him I was vaguely familiar with the phrase, but I didn't know what it meant. "Why caves?" I asked.

"Cold storage ain't cheap. It takes a constant source of electricity. So some bureaucrat comes up with the idea to store all the excess cheese in caves where it's naturally cool, mostly out in Kansas. Federal government stockpiling cheese seems crazy, but they did it. After Reagan was elected, they decided to give the cheese away to the poor, but it also went to prisons and public schools. Well...I was doing a stint in the slammer back then, for some shit I did when I was young. For those years in lockup, it seemed like every goddamn meal was made with that government cheese. Why spend tax dollars to feed prisoners when there's free cheese to be had? That's why I don't eat cheese—not once since I did my time."

I said, "I think there's crackers, salami and dried fruit in that kit, too."

"I'm good with my Jims." Bill produced a Slim Jim, peeled back the plastic wrapper, and took a big bite off on the end. He motioned, "This way, but watch your step. Treacherous footing, and probably more bat shit."

As we shimmied through narrow openings, sand and small rock sprinkled my hardhat. I tried not to dwell on the thought how if there was a cave in, we'd be trapped forever.

The chemical smell gave way to something different. It was unclear at first, but then I recognized the scent of decay, assumed it was decomposed rats or something. The tunnel ended at a dark silo.

"Careful at the edge there," Bill warned.

The light from my hard hat illuminated the vertical mineshaft. I went to the edge to look down, but with the loose rock at my feet, I hesitated.

Bill said, "Think of this as the elevator shaft back then. They brought in rock and ore from the tunnels and lifted it out from here. There must have been some sort of steam or mule powered lift of some kind."

"How many tunnels intersect this thing?"

"I haven't been in, so hard to say."

The circumference was larger than what I'd imagined, twenty feet or so. I picked up a pebble and tossed it, and then I heard it knocking off the edge of the shaft before there was the sound of a splash below.

Bill asked, "Seen enough?"

I thanked him, and as we headed back, the scent of decay made me cough.

As we made our way back, Bill said, "The night they pulled Mike out, I was standing next to Madeline when she realized her husband was a goner." He shook his head. "Losing a loved one like that...change ya forever."

That hit home. Mona was the love of my life, and I'd lost her in an instant. The emotional toil I lived with was beyond description. I rarely ever talked about it, even to my dad. I said, "All one can do is press on."

Bill said, "Suppose it's about time I mosey on back home and apologize to the old lady for being so stupid and whatnot. Nothing's more important than having love in life. If I lose that, then where'd I'd be?"

"True wisdom," I said.

We retraced our steps and returned the hard hats to the hooks. Bill locked the entrance. He held his finger to his lips. "Mum's the word cause I'll get in trouble for showing you, but I had to do it. For Madeline's sake."

I thanked him.

Outside, as we emerged from the maintenance yard, I asked about the asbestos abatement in the theater.

"They haven't done much other than put up those OSHA signs. I keep asking what's going on, but apparently I'm on a need-to-know basis. Which means nobody tells me shit."

Back on main street, he gave me a salute. "Give my best to Madeline. She's always been kind to me. A kind heart."

I said, "We'll figure out what happened that night," but, honestly, I wasn't entirely sure.

"Thanks for the provisions." He handed back the snack pack containing the cheese. "You take the government cheese. No need for that." Two Dollar Bill lit a cigarette and waddled on.

As I made my way to the Harley, I noticed buck-toothed Lawrence, the guy I'd seen in Madeline's office, in a campus security uniform. Did he wear two hats, one as an administrator, and another as a campus security? I got the feeling he recognized me. After I mounted the bike and pulled on the helmet, he reached for his phone.

Keeping my eye out for Sheriff Marsh on the ride back to Amarillo Slims, a thought occurred to me. I wondered if the chemical fumes I'd experienced in the tunnels had seeped into the theater. Could the asbestos abatement be a ruse to hide a toxic dump? Maybe Mike discovered that, threatened to expose the truth, and was silenced forever. It wasn't until I was back in my cabin feeding Suzie I decided to break into the theater to snoop around.

CHAPTER 31

Three Years Ago

Mona came up with our fictitious business—purchasing wine from estates after a death in the family. Widows and children of the deceased do not necessarily realize the cellar value. According to the directive in the last will and testament, heirs generally account for possessions such as real estate, stocks, bonds, jewelry, and collectibles. But the wine cellar is often neglected. Undervalued.

She assigned our aliases. As Leslie, Mona appraised the collections. As Richard, my job was handling the business side, and negotiations.

Mona jumped on the computer and started to build a website. Her skill was impressive. By midnight, she'd published the *Eagle Fine Wine & Spirits Exchange* site, and we were in business.

I booked our flights to Cincinnati. The plan was to drive to Lexington, Kentucky from there, about a ninety-minute drive. I told Mona I was familiar with the area since my father, and I, had traveled to Kentucky years ago. He had put together a business plan to establish a thoroughbred farm on the island of Guam. There would be no actual farm, but every "investment opportunity" needs a story.

I told her how thoroughbred racing in Japan and Hong Kong is wildly popular, and the purse money has grown to be massive compared to the UK and United States.

Many of the world's top stallions, including Triple Crown winners, breed out of Australia. Due to the proximity to all that Asian money, my father tried to convince a gullible investor there'd be a massive return-on-investment getting in on the bottom floor of a thoroughbred farm in the U.S. territory of Guam. Why? Simply because it's far easier to fly a mare into the U.S. territory of Guam as opposed to Australia which has extremely stringent, expensive, and time-consuming quarantine restrictions. Daunting for any thoroughbred owner. My dad had the guy committed but, as original as the story was, he could never get the mark to pull the trigger.

Mona and I caught a flight out of LAX. She slept most of the way. It was approaching sunset by the time we descended into Cincinnati. From the window on the plane, I could make out the Ohio River down below—the border between Ohio and Kentucky. You'd think the Cincinnati International Airport was in Ohio, but it's in Kentucky, near the border, perched on a bluff above the river.

At the airport, I stopped to admire the museum-quality miniatures of notorious steamboats. I explained to Mona the historic significance of river commerce, riverboats built in Cincinnati, and expansion of the game of poker up from New Orleans. Riverboat gambling history. Mona showed little interest.

We rented a luxury sedan at the airport and made our way to Lexington.

Having grown up on Florida's Gulf Coast, I knew Interstate 75. From Cincinnati, the highway weaves southward through Knoxville, Chattanooga, Atlanta, and then finally makes its way down Florida's Gulf Coast. When it reaches the tip, the route makes a hard left to connect with Miami.

Freight-hauling semis dominated the southbound interstate. At that time, I had no fear of them.

I explained to Mona how three things were key to this region: horses, bourbon, and college basketball. "The bourbon and horse part," I said, "all stems from the limestone." I pointed out exposed layers of sediment visible from highway excavation. "At one time, all of this was underwater. Ancient life accumulated at the bottom of the sea, fish bones. Continents moved around, and the sea went away, leaving a soil rich in calcium and minerals."

She stared out the window and said nothing.

I continued, "Young horses eat the blue grass which is super high in protein, like spinach or kale, but better, and full minerals for strong bone and muscle. Combine that with a long tradition of equestrian professionals, and that's why the fastest horses in the world are raised right here."

Mona considered horses frolicking in the field and said, "So it's the dirt. Sort of like with wine."

"Exactly."

"What about the bourbon?"

"The spring water which bubbles up through the limestone—that mineral-rich water—also makes for great whiskey. It's similar in Scotland for scotch. The circle of life from thousands of years builds the essence."

"And basketball?"

"Great college programs here. Has nothing to do with the dirt."

"Okay Professor O'Shea," Mona teased, "am I going to be quizzed on all your mansplaining?"

"A pop quiz when you least expect it."

"Look," she said, "when it comes to talking about wine, let me handle that. You bubbas may know a thing or two about riverboats, bourbon, and racehorses, but we NoCal girls know *the grape*."

"You consider me a bubba?"

"You're from Florida. That makes you a bubba."

I didn't know if I should be offended or laugh.

She said, "You play the silent type. The numbers guy. Maybe Kenneth knows something about bourbon, horse breeding, or

March Madness. You guys can talk about that…but let me handle the wine."

Mona *so* amazed me. I leaned over and kissed her.

We checked into the Griffin Gate Hotel and Resort, where Kenneth was supposedly booked, and christened the crisp hotel bed sheets making love. Mona was on fire. Like me, she was truly alive. Because there was a fish on the line.

After a brief, blissful nap, we ordered room service and watched a romantic comedy. With Mona asleep in my arms, lightly snoring, my worries kept me awake. Our scheme to defraud Kenneth Coleman had so many moving parts, and that worried me. If one thing didn't fall into place, the house of cards would come crumbling down. But Mona was navigating this riverboat, and I was not going to second-guess. At the very least, the Kentucky trip would be a welcome vacation.

The next morning, we had a light breakfast delivered to the room before dressing the part: khakis and a polo shirt for me, Mona in a western-style sundress. She put her hair back in a ponytail, claimed it was her, "horsey-girl look."

I thought she looked great.

Outside the hotel, was hotter, and more humid, than either of us had bargained for. Stopping at a market, we put together an impromptu picnic basket in the unlikely event we found an opportunity to open the bottle of Domaine de la Romanee-Conti La Tache, our bait, outside the venue since we couldn't bring it in. I figured it was a longshot, but it was better to be prepared. We set out to the Kentucky Horse Park.

Inside the massive acreage, past assorted barns, museums, and administrative buildings, we found the Alltech Arena, a venue which appeared to be about the size of a minor league hockey arena. Inside, banners of equestrian products lined the ring. There were private VIP boxes. I wondered if Kenneth would sit in one of those.

We wandered around for a while until Mona spotted him. "There he is."

In the distance, Kenneth Coleman chatted with a few middle-aged women before all went to their seats. Thankfully they were not in a private box. We positioned above them with a clear view of the arena.

The event began. I found the sport incredibly boring, but Mona was captivated.

When Rebecca Olsen was finally announced, she emerged from the tunnel mounted on a tall chestnut mare. Kenneth and his entourage stood in ovation. Once horse and rider were set, they went through a series of canter pirouettes. I had no idea what was going on.

Rebecca finished her routine to applause, and Kenneth and his entourage stood from their seats. We followed at a distance.

Backstage, Kenneth congratulated his fiancée, and they kissed.

From the exchange within her entourage, I determined which of the women was her coach since she was the one offering pointers. They all hugged and seemed happy with Rebecca's routine. Handlers escorted the horse away, and they conversed some before returning to their seats.

More of the same. Riders guided horses. I couldn't tell how one performance differed from any other, but Mona seemed to understand it all. Back in L.A. she had studied YouTube links—done her homework.

After the event wrapped up, we followed Kenneth and Rebecca to their car before they departed.

On the road, we tailed them to the Griffin Gate Resort & Spa, not far from the Kentucky Horse Park. After they parked, Mona retrieved the wine from the backseat, and then froze in fear. She muttered, "Shit."

"What's the matter?"

"It's too warm." She handed me the bottle. "Why did we leave it in the car? I should have known."

Mona perceived this as a major crisis. I didn't understand why.

CHAPTER 32

Mona said, "We have to find a way to cool it."

It felt like the bottle wasn't necessarily hot, but rather warm. I said, "Who knows if we're even going to open it?"

Meanwhile we could see Kenneth and Rebecca gather their things and head towards the hotel.

"How could I have been so stupid?" Mona lamented, pacing, a panic attack. I hadn't seen her in this state since Trevor came to my condo.

I gave her a gentle hug "Relax. We've got this." I could feel her release tension. What she needed was a boost of confidence. "You're doing great," I said.

Mona pulled away, nodded. This caper meant so much to her. She was proving herself.

I said, "Roll with it."

"Okay," she said, and bit her lip.

We followed Kenneth and Rebecca into the hotel.

Inside, they went straight to the elevators. I suggested we roll the dice and plant ourselves at the bar, assuming there's a chance they come down for a celebratory drink. We found seats at the corner, a position to allow full view of the lobby. Those entering the bar would need to walk directly behind our padded barstools.

Mona flagged the bartender and asked for ice. When it came,

she took two cloth napkins from a tabletop and wrapped the bottle in one, ice cubes in the other. She set the bottle in her lap and covered it with the impromptu icepack.

I explained to the young male bartender that we'd brought a celebratory bottle of wine and willing to pay the corkage fee. He stroked his beard and said, "That's fine, but you'll need to order something to eat." He handed me a bar menu. "It doesn't have to be an entrée. Any appetizer will suffice." Mona suggested a charcuterie board since that would accompany the red wine. The attentive bartender brought us two wine glasses. After a little more time in the ice wrap, Mona handed over the bottle.

The bartender took great care opening it, and carefully poured it like a pro. Afterward, Mona positioned the bottle between us, with the label facing outward.

"Here's to nothing," I said, "A toast?"

Mona nosed her glass before tasting the wine. She shook her head, frustrated. "It's *way* too warm."

"It's not the end of the world. We're drinking it, not Kenneth."

As if on cue, Kenneth appeared in the lobby and crossed into the bar. Luckily, he chose a seat near us. As the bartender went to serve him, Mona gave me a smile and turned the label in the direction so Kenneth could see.

I overheard him order bourbon. "Blanton Old Fashioned."

"Good choice," replied the bartender, and got to work on it.

Mona began an impromptu, one-sided conversation directed at me, throwing around words like "vintage," "provenance" and "estate." Buzz words, I assumed. I forced myself not to look at Kenneth, assuming he'd eavesdrop.

When the charcuterie board arrived, I went about plating the appetizer. Kenneth had taken notice. He said to us, "DRC? Is that on the wine list here?"

"No," Mona said. "We acquired it this morning. We're in the wine business, and Richard and I treat ourselves with a perk whenever we make a purchase. Chalk it off as handling charges." I could see Kenneth's interest was piqued. Mona continued, "We probably should have decanted first, but there's plenty more where this came from."

"Oh?"

Mona introduced us as "Richard" and "Leslie." The narrative quickly unspooled—how we'd come to Lexington to purchase wine from an estate sale. "We did good today," she said, turning to me for affirmation.

"Appears so," I replied and sipped the wine. If it was too warm, I didn't care. I gave her a smile and pretended to be busy with messages on my phone.

The ball was in Mona's court.

To Kenneth, she elaborated our business is purchasing wine and spirits at estate sales. Our story was an old woman in Lexington had passed away and the heirs were selling assets, which included the farm and horse stables which had been in the family for generations. The estate sale included artwork, real estate, breeding rights to racehorses, but not necessarily the contents of a cellar. "In their heyday, she and her husband hosted elaborate parties."

Kenneth admitted he too collected wine, and he'd recently acquired a case of what we were drinking, Domaine de la Romanee-Conti, at auction.

Thanks to Mona's research, we were aware, but played along as if it was a coincidence. I sat on the sidelines observing as Mona expertly played the hand. She asked, "What brings you to Lexington?" even though we knew.

Kenneth explained his fiancée had competed in the U.S. Dressage Finals. Mona said, "I see you're enjoying bourbon, but can we offer you a glass?"

Kenneth accepted the hospitality, and she asked the bartender for another glass. As Mona poured, she said, "Apologies, but the bottle got a little warm in the car. Not quite cellar temperature."

Kenneth was grateful, nosed the glass and sampled the wine. When he closed his eyes to concentrate on the experience, Mona and I shared a smile.

"Thank you," Kenneth said, seemingly pleased. "There's good reason DRC is so coveted." This was the second time he'd referenced that. I wasn't sure what it meant until I realized it was simply an acronym. DRC. Domaine Romanee-Conti.

Mona and Kenneth compared notes of assorted California vineyards I knew nothing about. Talk of bourbon, horse racing, or college basketball never came up.

Showered and dressed for dinner, Rebecca joined us. Without acknowledging either of us, she asked Kenneth, "When do they get here?"

"I'll text them we're ready. What are you having?"

"Just water."

Kenneth introduced us to Rebecca and thumbed at his phone. From their conversation, it was clear they had dinner plans, possibly with the equestrian group we'd seen earlier. In Rebecca's presence, Kenneth was far less attentive to us. When Mona and Kenneth spoke a little more about wine, it seemed to irk Rebecca since his attention was not entirely devoted to her.

A few minutes passed before Kenneth's phone buzzed. He glanced at it and said to Rebecca, "They're pulling up."

Mona asked Kenneth, "Can we send our catalogue?"

"That would be great, especially if there's more of this," he said, lifting his glass. "Do you have a card?"

We'd just invented our personas, so there had been no time to print business cards. But I bluffed, digging into my wallet, apparently searching for mine, and said, "I think I have one..." Kenneth's phone buzzed again.

"You ready?" Rebecca said, impatient.

He finished his wine in one gulp and signed the check for his bourbon, with most of the whiskey still in the glass. Mona asked, "Where can we reach you?"

Kenneth handed over his business card.

Bingo.

"Thank you for sharing the DRC," he said. "Cheers."

We bid them goodbye before they glided across the lobby and departed through the hotel's sliding glass doors.

In triumph, Mona waved Kenneth's business card under my nose. I was impressed at how she handled herself, and said, "You're *so* good."

"What a total *bitch* that Rebecca is," Mona said. "She's got like…a major case of RBF."

"Enough with all these acronyms. DRC. RBF."

"Resting Bitch Face," she said, as if I should have known.

"Oh," I said, "Or maybe she's simply a bitch."

"Appears so." Mona raised her glass to toast in affirmation. She asked, "What's he see in her?"

"Kenneth is nouveau riche. Rebecca offers prestige and pedigree—the stuff money can't buy. We've baited the hook," I said, the analogy my father used to say. "Now we wait for the nibble."

Mona exhaled, finally at ease. Post adrenaline rush, she was basking in a glow. The bartender cleared Kenneth's half-finished bourbon and topped off our water glasses. Mona sampled a bite of the prosciutto and asked, "So what do we now?"

I held up my wineglass. "Celebrate by finishing this three-thousand-dollar bottle of wine."

Mona raised hers. "Absolutely."

Success. We toasted as partners in crime.

CHAPTER 33

Present Day

I awoke in the mountain cabin with plans to explore the theater on campus. I had to determine if the cordoned off building was due to asbestos, or what lies beneath.

The scent of burning charcoal drew me to the cabin window. Slim was at the smoker and at work. He prepared with a wire brush, adjusted vents, and with a large fork dug out rubbed briskets from a plastic bin. Each was laid out with great care. I had to admire the man's dedication. Making something exceptional takes time. I wished I had that kind of patience.

Slim then went to work on the redwood deck of one of the cabins. Thinking about it, I couldn't remember a moment when he was not moving forward, *on task*.

Oscar called promptly at nine. "Foster, this chancellor you had me look into," he said. "I've made a few calls."

"And?"

"He's an officer at San Francisco's Bohemian Club. They maintain an exclusive clubhouse and hold an annual retreat at their camp in Sonoma County, essentially a getaway for power brokers. Conspiracy nuts claim it's part of the Illuminati, a secret-society scheming world domination. I see it as an excuse to get away from wives, get drunk, and play cards."

I brought him up to speed about the oil drums of chemicals I'd seen in the abandoned mine.

"If that's industrial waste," Oscar said, "it probably has something to do with Foster's family business."

"Hazardous waste disposal," I remembered. "His academic career window-dressing. Gives him a cloak of legitimacy."

"I'd have to look into that more."

Anything on Marsh?"

"Not really. I suggest you stay clear. This is not your problem, Jack. What's that saying? Curiosity kills the cat?" He stressed that I needed to return to Los Angeles. Oscar was right. None of it was my problem. But there were unanswered questions. If I didn't follow through, who would?

I sifted through the photos I'd taken of the oil drums. On my laptop, I found the site for the Environmental Protection Agency Criminal Investigations Division. They had a whistleblower contact. I composed a brief description of what I'd seen, kept it vague, and uploaded a few of the photos.

While sitting on the porch, Slim came up the path. He greeted me with, "Sandy had an idea, thought companionship would do the doggies good. We're wondering if your pup is on the mend enough to hang out with ours, Harley. Doggy play date is what Sandy called it."

I thought it was a good idea and brought Suzie down to the restaurant. Our pups did get along. Dogs will be dogs.

Sitting in a booth over coffee, I called Madeline. We needed to compare notes. I suggested we meet at the mineshaft, the scene of the crime.

"I planned to go there to fix the memorial."

"What memorial?"

"Mike's. I'm told someone kicked over the flower box."

"Who would do that?"

"I wish I knew. Maybe it was a wild animal rooting around."

I said, "I've been thinking about this and wondering if the asbestos abatement is a cover up."

There was a moment of silence before she said, "That would explain the chemical odor. Weird."

We agreed to meet in an hour.

I asked Slim if I could borrow the motorcycle again. He was agreeable, so I rode to Argonaut, parked near campus, and headed up to the mineshaft. Something felt different. I couldn't figure out what it was. The flower box memorial had been vandalized, laying on its side. It didn't look like an animal had disturbed it, but what did I know. I turned it upright and tried my best to salvage the spilled topsoil and dried flowers.

Waiting for Madeline, I saw Alexandro had texted, so gave him a call.

Alexandro said, "Trevor called. I told the dude I needed to get paid. He said I'd have to meet him in Vegas."

"Where?"

"Lake Las Vegas."

I said, "Collect what he owes. I'll follow him afterward."

"He can't know I'm working with you."

"He'll have no idea. We'll drive separately."

"I don't know, Brah..." I could tell Alexandro was nervous about the idea.

I said, "You'll get paid and go on your way. I'll follow Trevor to see where he lives. Unless you can get me that information now."

"I told you, all I have is his phone number."

"Then this is how we'll do it."

Alexandro reluctantly agreed. We made plans to meet at the filming location and drive to Vegas from there.

I finished the call as Madeline climbed up the hill carrying potted flowers and garden hoses draped over her shoulder. The bulky black boots she always wore finally made sense to me. Living in the mountains, thick-soled footwear is essential. Far better than my leather dress shoes I'd been running around in which were cracked, caked in mud, and worse for wear. They would have to be professionally refurbished or thrown out altogether.

She was saddened to see the state of the memorial. She held up what she'd brought, and said, "I'll make it better than before." Madeline went about connecting sections of the garden hose to a spigot down behind the theater. I helped her unspool the hose and lay out the drip system.

She knelt at the flower box, potted the flowers, and said, "I had a dream about Mike and saw white lilies. They're the flowers of resurrection, you know."

As Madeline busied herself with the project, I told her about the oil drums, showed her photos, and said, "I suspect the theater is connected to this shaft, and I wonder if the college is hiding the fact they're sitting on hazardous waste."

She stopped her work to consider.

I added, "And I'm curious if the asbestos abatement is a ruse to keep the dump a secret. Maybe there's no asbestos." I pointed to the portable chain link fencing surrounding the building. "And all these posted warnings are just to keep people away."

She stared at the yellow caution tape fluttering in the wind for a moment before, "Why would there be toxic stuff stored down in the mine?"

"When I was a kid living in Florida," I said, "organized crime was dumping toxic waste in The Everglades. The same thing happened in the Meadowlands of New Jersey. The handling of hazardous waste is big business. Instead of storing it in designated areas, in containers to keep the chemicals from seeping into groundwater, dumping it out the back of a truck off the New Jersey Turnpike is a far cheaper option."

Madeline nodded silently. I could see there was something on her mind.

I went on, "Rusty oil drums sitting abandoned in a field might draw attention. But nobody sees them if they're underground. Could Mike have discovered the dump and brought it to someone's attention?"

Madeline's eyes glassed over. "One day, he told me to stop drinking the tap water. Said it might harm our unborn baby. I asked why he thought that, but he wouldn't tell me...probably didn't want me to worry. After that day, Mike brought home jugs of water."

I told her what I'd learned from Oscar, how Foster had ties in the waste disposal business. I said, "We need to know who texted Mike that night."

"I called my cell phone provider, finally got someone on the phone. They just gave me the run-around because I don't have his security code."

"We'll need to subpoena the records."

"How do I do that?"

I forwarded her Oscar's contact info and explained she should email him all the information she had, the cellular provider, account number, and even the copy of the death certificate.

She said, "I'll do that when I get home."

Then, I told Madeline I needed to take care of some personal business.

"Going back to L.A.?"

"Las Vegas. Won't take long."

"Another case?"

"That's right." I wasn't going to get into the fact that I was being followed. She understood, went back to the garden box, then said, "Mike is still with us. I can feel it."

"Madeline," a voice called from below. It was the guy who had greeted us on campus after the meeting with Chancellor Foster and Christine. He was making his way up the hill.

Madeline said, "That's Paul. He oversees the International Student Center."

Paul reached us, said, "Beautiful flowers. A thoughtful memorial, like from a roadside accident."

Madeline snapped, "It was no accident!"

Paul raised his hands defensive. "Sorry. So very sorry. Didn't mean it that way." He extended his hand to me. "Paul Sutton."

I introduced myself, "Jack O'Shea." His palm was clammy.

"It's my understanding," Paul said, "that you're investigating this…uhm…unfortunate incident." He turned to Madeline. "I think it's because you're leaving no stone unturned. Good for you. Please let me know if I can help."

I could tell Paul annoyed her. With nothing to lose, I tested the waters and said, "I understand you handle the recruitment of students."

"That's one of my responsibilities."

"And this place is a visa mill, disguised as a college."

He blinked, offended. "Excuse me?"

I eyed him to see how that landed, said, "I'm looking into the legitimacy of the nonprofit status, academic accreditation, and endowment funding sources." It was all a bluff, and about gauging his reaction. "What can you tell me about the recruitment process?"

"What do you mean?"

I fished even more with, "I'm curious what the finder's fee is for advisors and counselors who steer a student who is ultimately enrolled here. Is it a percentage of the tuition?

"I don't know what you're talking about."

I pivoted to, "Can someone corroborate your whereabouts the night of the murder?"

He scowled at me before turning to Madeline. "Who is this guy, Maddie?"

"Only my friends call me Maddie."

Paul stood speechless. He shot me a nervous look before he returned his eyes to her and said, "I'm sorry you feel that way."

"Face it," she said, "You're a spineless prick, will sell your mother's soul for the right price."

He sneered, spun on his heels, and trotted back down the hill. Before he was out of earshot, Madeline voiced aloud, "Such a kiss ass. I'm tired of being nice."

After Paul was gone, she returned her attention to the flowers.

Afterward, as we made our way down to her Honda, Madeline said, "I'm scheduled to shoot my scene tomorrow. After that, I need to get away from this place. I'm going to stay with my mom for a while."

"I think that's a good idea," I said, and offered, "I'll escort you back to L.A. We'll drive in tandem."

Madeline was grateful. She said her plan was to pack her car that night so she could leave immediately after they'd shot her scene. She estimated she'd be wrapped by mid-afternoon. That meant we'd drive back to Los Angeles tomorrow into the evening, so my timeline was getting shorter. I still needed to follow Alexandro to Vegas and determine where Trevor was living. I figured I'd return to the mountains for Suzie, and then escort Madeline back to Southern California. Back home in Culver City, I'd devote myself to finding out more about Trevor, why he was following me, and plan countersurveillance.

What's that saying? *Best laid plans of mice and men.*

CHAPTER 34

Back to Amarillo Slims, I grabbed a few things and informed Slim and Sandy I'd be gone for the night, asked if they would continue to look after my dog. They were happy to oblige. Buttermilk Suzie seemed to be in good hands.

Having been followed by the mysterious SUV from Truckee, I'd learned my lesson. Not to risk the license plate-analyzing software tracking my movements again, the solution was simple—a bike rack. I pulled the cover off the Chevy SS and hit the road.

As luck would have it, there was a bike store nearby. I found a rack which looked like it would work, strapped it on in the parking lot, and adjusted it to cover the rear license plate. I had no bike, but that didn't matter. The rack served its sole purpose—covering the plate to disguise me.

Approaching the film location, smoke was bellowing from the pine trees. Initially, I thought there was a fire, but nobody appeared to be in panic.

I parked near Alexandro's van on the side of the road. From there, the mystery was solved. I could see a special effects technician working on some kind of smoke machine. Downwind, the plywood castle I'd seen them building earlier was finished, and they were filming a scene out front. The wafting theatrical smoke made the castle appear as if it was cloaked in a misty fog.

Movie magic.

As I approached, I heard a voice over the radio. A twenty-something production assistant held up his hand to keep me back, out of view of the camera. He whispered the camera takes in a 360-degree view so anyone not yet in costume needs to stay hidden.

I could see Alexandro in the pasture among the background extras. He was dressed as a soldier, complete with a kilt and cloaked in what looked like an animal hide. As the performers waited for their cue, Alexandro twirled his prop spear much like he'd done with his trusty nunchucks.

"Action!" was called through a bullhorn. I recognized it as Louis's voice, but he was nowhere in sight. Alexandro and the others marched through the scene as Jim and Kathy engaged in dialogue near the camera. I could not hear them, but I probably would not have understood the Shakespeare old English anyway.

Louis called, "Cut!" He emerged from behind the plywood castle and had a conference with the actors.

Alexandro spotted me and came up. "Isn't this shit rad?"

"I see you've gotten into the act."

"Hell yeah," he said, looking to the others. "Catering makes awesome breakfast burritos."

"I'm glad you've eaten," I said. "We've gotta go."

"Now?"

"It's a long drive, and I have to get back here tomorrow morning."

Disappointed, Alexandro climbed out of costume, bid farewell to his newfound friends, and we set out for Lake Las Vegas.

I followed Alexandro's van east over Donner Pass and through Reno before we transitioned onto Interstate 580 heading south. The road was a barren two-lane blacktop. Nevada is an odd state. The federal government controls eighty-four percent of the land, most of it by the Bureau of Land Management. It had been the nation's open air nuclear test-kitchen before they moved aboveground atomic blasts to the Marshall Islands in the Pacific,

Underground blasts continued for decades. Area 51 is in Nevada. The phrase "Battle Born" on Nevada's flag is attributed to the fact the state joined the Union during the Civil War. The state may have been born in a time of battle, but no actual blood from the Civil War was spilled on the land.

We reached a railroad crossing in the small town of Schurz, and Alexandro pulled over to a tin warehouse hailed as Big Chief Fireworks. I pulled over beside him, rolled down the window, and asked, "What are you doing?"

"Getting fireworks."

"Why?"

"Because these are the *real* ones."

"What's that mean?"

"Rockets and mortars. Roman candles. Firecrackers and cool shit like that," he said before heading inside. The cash I'd given him was clearly burning a hole in his pocket. I parked and followed him in passing a massive no smoking sign.

The space smelled of sulphur which is a key ingredient of flash powder. Shelves were stacked high with assorted fireworks of all shapes and sizes.

Alexandro was like a kid in a candy store. As he filled a shopping cart, he came across Black Cat Firecrackers. He held up the brick-sized package up for my benefit. "Black Cat, dude."

"Black Cube," I reminded him.

"Whatever. Bad ass."

After spending what appeared to be most of the cash I'd given him, he wheeled boxes full of fireworks out in a shopping cart and stacked them in the back of his van. "Whatever you do," I pleaded, "Don't shoot off any of that anywhere in the mountains. California has enough wildfires."

"I'm not stupid. This shit's not for me. I'm selling it."

"To who?"

"Homeys back in L.A."

"Why?"

"Triple my money, brah. Easy peasey. Quadruple even. Cash

money. I take Venmo too. My side-hustle." He lifted the last carton of the fireworks into the back of his van and covered it with a ratty blanket.

"Don't smoke in there," I said.

"I vape."

"Of course you do," I said.

"Want a taste? I got the chronic."

"Not today."

We got back on the road, continued south, and passed Walker Lake, a large body of water perched between hills and the high desert.

I received a call from a number I did not recognize and let it go to voicemail. Listening back, the message was from a woman who introduced herself as Agent Williams from the Environmental Protection Agency Criminal Investigations Division. She said, "This is regarding the photos you posted on the EPA portal. If you can give me a call at your convenience, I'd really appreciate it."

By the time we reached the outskirts of Vegas, it was getting dark, and city lights illuminated a cobalt blue sky. I couldn't help but think of the day I met Mona when she tried to pick my pocket.

CHAPTER 35

Lake Las Vegas is a shallow, man-made body of water surrounded by a residential development in the suburb of Henderson. The golf courses are private. There is no public beach. It reminded me of the exclusive gated communities in Palm Springs.

I followed Alexandro's van to the parking lot of an Italian architecture-themed outdoor mall next to luxury condos and a resort hotel. We parked, and Alexandro led me through the outdoor mall to Sunrise Cantina, a restaurant in the plaza with a view of the lake. The establishment felt like one of those chain Mexican food restaurants where they serve fish-bowl-sized margaritas and deep-fried Chimichangas.

Alexandro said, "I texted Trevor that I'm here, so I'll hang out eating chips and salsa till he shows up. Last time it took him a while. He gets here when he gets here."

"How long?"

His reply was a shrug.

"What time does this place close?"

"Shit if I know."

I could see from the sign on the glass door the restaurant shuttered weekdays at ten. That seemed early for Vegas, but probably not in this bedroom community. "If he doesn't show up by nine," I said, "text him the restaurant closes in an hour."

Alexandro gave the thumbs up, said, "I gotta pee" and slipped inside.

The outdoor mall had benches with a view of the restaurant entrance. I found a spot in a dark corner to observe. A warm breeze blew litter around the plaza, and the sound of water in a fountain echoed through the corridors. Most of the guests who came and went appeared to be retirees, but there was a younger set as well. From the ski boats I'd seen in the parking lot, they were likely the wakeboard and waterski crowd.

After about a half an hour, I saw Trevor approach. He wore sunglasses at night, brightly colored linen slacks, and a tight-fitting black polo shirt. He carried a manila envelope under his arm, and ducked into the restaurant like he owned the place.

I moved in for a closer look.

Through the window, I could see Alexandro seated at a high-top table near the bar. Trevor was pointing a finger into his chest, spewing angrily about something. After Trevor said his piece, he placed the envelope on the table, had a few last words, and then headed out. I ducked for cover.

Trevor emerged from the restaurant, and I followed from a distance.

In the parking structure, Trevor climbed into a black Mer-cedes. I dashed to my Chevy, concerned by the time I pulled out I'd lose him. Luckily, he was forced to stop at a traffic light up ahead, so I pulled up behind. The light turned, and I followed, careful not to get too close.

About a mile or so down the road, he pulled into a gated community. There was a guard shack with two entrances, one for guests and the other for visitors. He went through what I assumed was the homeowner gate. The guard on duty waved at him.

I pulled up to the guard shack visitor entrance and nodded to the old guy holding a clipboard, saying, "Uber Eats."

"Where ya going?"

"Let me see…" I pretended to search for the address on my phone, punching the screen as if searching. "Just following

Google Maps. Give me a sec." I cursed and said I'd lost my connection.

In the meantime, he went to the back of my car and jotted down my license plate on his clipboard. When he came back, the old guy said, "That bike rack doesn't look like it's on correctly. Better check that." He was right. The only purpose was to block my license plate.

"Thanks," I said.

A security vehicle pulled up to the other side of the guard shack. The old guy went to have a few words with his colleague, a younger guy wearing the same team uniform. I could see the pistol holstered in the small of the old timer's back. These guys were serious. Engaged with the other guard, he finally lost patience with me and buzzed me in. The gate lifted.

At first, I'd thought I'd lost Trevor. But then, in the distance, I saw the illumination of a garage door. I shut off my headlights and drove in to get a closer look.

The two-story mansion was on an island surrounded by water. A thin strip of land served as the driveway. The lights of the lavish home gleamed off the water. I wondered how Trevor came to live in such a place. When Mona left him, they were living in an off-the-strip casino hotel. Between then and now, I wondered how he'd come into such money. If this indeed was his residence, that explained how Trevor could afford to hire the Black Cube agency.

I could see the lights of the private security vehicle in my rear-view mirror. It slowed. The security team was obviously checking up on me, so started the car and spun around. As I drove out of the gate, the old guy inside the shack gave me the evil eye. They must have determined I hadn't delivered anything. Once clear of the guard shack, I determined the best way to get a closer look at Trevor's home would be from the water.

I pulled over and checked my phone. There was a sporting goods store close in Henderson. I sped and got there minutes before they closed.

Sports + and More was a retail superstore. They seemed to have everything, including golf, tennis, and an array of guns and hunting supplies. I found what I was looking for—a one-man kayak. Above me, mounted deer and elk stared down at me as I paid for it at the cash register.

The assistant manager, an acne-faced kid no older than twenty, wheeled the kayak out on a four-wheeled dolly. He had twine and a pair of scissors. Together, we tied the hard-plastic boat to the top of the Chevy. He also noted my bike rack wasn't correctly fastened and volunteered to help me secure it. I told him I was in a hurry, tipped him ten bucks, and returned to the Lake Las Vegas gated community.

About a quarter mile from the entrance, the guard shack in the distance, I eased to a halt on the shoulder of the road, using the emergency brake to avoid illuminating the car's taillights.

On the sandy shoulder, in darkness, I cut the kayak loose from the roof of my car and carried it to the concrete wall surrounding the development. I pushed the boat over the edge, tossed over the oar, and then scaled the eight-foot-high barrier. A dog barked in the distance, obviously sensing an intruder in the darkness.

Dragging the boat, I crossed a golf course green as the dog continued to bark. I thought about my own dog, Suzie, who rarely barks. I wondered how she was faring without me back at Amarillo Slims.

At a clearing, between a pair of luxury homes nowhere as massive as Trevor's, I set the boat at the water's edge. Trevor's mansion would be around the bend. I took off my shoes and socks, set them in the kayak, rolled up my pant legs and stepped into the warm water. Settling into the boat, I got my bearings and oared out into the channel.

The only experience I'd ever had kayaking was while on vacation in Hawaii. But like riding the motorcycle, it came back to me. The trick was to stay low and centered. I silently made my way into the middle of the channel, then followed it around the bend. The dog in the distance had stopped barking as I glided through the watery darkness. Stars dotted the sky above.

I came upon Trevor's lavish home and illuminated grounds. There was an array of modern outdoor furniture, a private pool, pickleball court, and a strip of sandy beach. I could see Trevor through the floor-to-ceiling glass doors. He and a leggy brunette appeared to be having some sort of argument.

Then it got physical.

She was trying to get away, but he grabbed the woman and slapped her. That made me cringe. She tried again to get away. That only made it worse for her. Trevor pulled her arm around her back, then dragged her to the sectional couch. He yanked her tight-knit dress up and unbuckled his belt, intentions clear.

I'd promised Alexandro I wouldn't approach Trevor, but I could not stand by and do nothing while this young woman was assaulted.

I beached the boat and jumped out. My presence must have set off motion detectors because security lights lit up. Trevor didn't seem to notice. His back was to me as he wrestled the woman on the couch.

I shouted, "Hey!"

Trevor turned back, surprised. "What the...?" I saw in his eyes he recognized me.

The young girl scurried off the sofa. I could see Trevor was trying to piece together how I'd crashed his party. Then a pit bull emerged from the kitchen, growling at me.

To make matters worse, the girl had a long barrel revolver in her hands and pointed at me. The weapon must have been buried in the cushions of the couch. Only then did I see how young she was.

Trevor said nothing, eyes glued.

I said, "Just like with Mona, your fist does the talking."

Trevor said, "How the fuck did you get in here, mate?"

I ignored that and asked, "Why are you having me followed?"

There was a long silence before the girl asked Trevor, "Who's Mona?"

"Shut the fuck up. Give me that."

She sheepishly handed over the long-barreled revolver.

I asked him again, "Why are you following me?"

"Did that paparazzi kid lead you here?"

Not to compromise my source, I said, "What kid?"

"The lad from the restaurant."

"I don't know of any lads," I said. "I found you from metadata tied to the tracking device you put in my car." It was all fiction. I bet he didn't know that. Again, I asked, "Why are you following me?"

Trevor took a deep breath. "My plan was to approach you in Los Angeles, but you've been out of town, haven't you?"

"You'd know."

"And here you are. I didn't expect to see you here."

"I'll ask one more time," I said. "Why are you following me?"

Trevor licked his lips. "To be honest, I need your assistance. Both from you...and your father."

The mention of my father came as a complete surprise.

Trevor motioned to the outdoor furniture. "Have a seat, mate. Let's have a drink." He turned to the girl, "Can't you see we have a guest? Make yourself useful." He zipped up his trousers to make a point.

Trevor turned back to me and asked, "What's your poison, Jack?"

CHAPTER 36

We sat across from each other at a fire pit. Trevor passed the long-barreled silver pistol from one hand to the other, toying with me. He said, "Englewood Federal Correctional. You know what I'm talking about."

"My dad."

"Yes. Patrick O'Shea."

The girl brought Trevor a three-finger pour of scotch and set a bottle of Corona in front of me. I'd asked for a beer because, if necessary, I could break the bottle and use a shard of glass as a weapon.

The girl's mascara was smeared, and it looked like a black eye was forming. I noticed a tattoo on the inside of her wrist—a pair of three-pronged crowns side-by-side. Mona had mentioned Rex branding his stable of escorts. Was this the "Rex King" tattoo? Rex means king in Latin, his last name being King. A double crown to brand them like cattle.

The girl realized my eyes were on her tattoo and she pulled away.

Trevor took a long drag from his whisky before saying, "It's a small world. Incredibly small. When I learned your reckless driving killed my beloved Mona...I have to admit I was heartbroken. That bird may have left me, but I still had great affection for her. Much of this..." he said, motioning to the surroundings, "is the result of how brilliant Mona was."

"You beat her. Just like what I saw here tonight."

He eyed me before saying, "You and I both know how head-strong she could be."

"Men don't hit women."

He scoffed.

"Period," I added.

Trevor turned his palms upward and wiggled his thumbs as if searching for the right words. "You don't understand, mate. Mona was disobedient. Insolent. And ungrateful. She stepped out of line."

"This girl," I said, motioning to the brunette seated inside at the kitchen counter, "does she step out of line?"

"Daniela?" Trevor said, "needs the occasional spanking."

"You're pathetic."

"Realize as you laid there in that hospital bed, all decrepit," he said, his fingers on his face to indicate my bandages, "wrapped up like a nasty burn victim, I planned to kill you. Was all set to pull the trigger, too. Had arranged to have someone slip a little something into your intravenous catheter. Medical errors are the third-leading cause of death, you know. I was about to do it before I learned you were the son of Patrick O'Shea."

"What's he have to do with anything?"

"Well, at his age, your old man will likely die behind bars. You know it. I know it. I can make his extended-stay a little more...palatable."

"You've got a sex tape of the warden?"

"No," he laughed, "But trust me, I can make your father's life considerably more unpleasant."

"That a threat?"

He sipped his scotch. "I'm simply asking for assistance. I need your dear old dad to deliver a message."

"To who?"

"A fellow inmate and former client of mine by the name of Garret Luth. You'll send your father a message with instructions to pass it on to Garret. They are inmates in the same ward."

"What's he in for?"

"Possession of child pornography is a crime. Distribution is entirely a different matter. Garret was convicted on both counts."

I considered the underage girl, and said, "A perv like you."

Trevor chose to ignore that, instead said, "In Garret's case, he was foolish enough to share his collection with like-minded enthusiasts."

"Pedophiles."

"A harsh label for someone viewing artistic photos, but yes. When the FBI seized his laptop, the district attorney had everything."

"So that's it. You've got a black book, incriminating video of rich and powerful men, much like that freak Jeffrey Epstein." I motioned to the opulent surroundings. "To afford all this, you must have a few well-heeled clients."

He said nothing, studied me.

I added, "What's any of that have to do with my dad?'

"I don't know if you're aware, but in federal lockup correspondence is screened. The prison keeps a log of emails, letters, recorded phone calls, and visits. Algorithms scrub it all, and people are watching. That being the case, my message can't be sent to Garret directly."

"What message?"

"To keep his mouth shut."

I remembered Mona had mentioned Trevor's paranoia and asked, "What are you so afraid of?"

"Garret's got a parole hearing on the docket. Intel from his lawyer suggests he is willing to spill the beans to possibly take a few years off his sentence. So, you see, this has a bit of urgency."

"What makes you think I'll do this?"

"Because I can make your father's life a living hell. Maybe arrange a special roommate, if you know what I mean."

"I don't believe you have that kind of influence."

"Don't test me. I'm not asking for much. Explain the situation to your old man and leave the details to me. I understand you two chat a few times a week."

"What makes you think my father will agree?"

"Because you'll ask him," Trevor said, as if it was obvious. He finished his drink. "I've written it as a story, the message as a piece of fiction." He ordered Daniela to bring him his briefcase, and produced a seven-page, double-spaced document. It was a short story titled *Rat Terrier*. My name was on the title page as the author. Trevor said, "You'll write a letter which will accompany this story. You're simply informing your father it is going to be published in *Ellery Queen Mystery Magazine*. And then when you speak to him, stress he needs to pass the pages on to Garret. Make that very clear."

"What's this about?"

"This is based on a true story. I'm not sure if you're aware, but New York City has a significant rat problem. Volunteer dog owners come together in the middle of night with their pet Rat Terriers and make sport out of hunting the vermin. The dogs don't necessarily eat the rodents," he said, "but rather shake the bastards violently from side to side, snapping their necks. Fascinating."

"I don't get it."

"Garret will recognize the names of the characters. The narrative serves as a metaphor. Read it now."

The story was told from the point of view of the doomed rat. Cornered by the Terriers, the rat tries to negotiate freedom by telling the dogs where the other rats have hidden. It doesn't end well for him. A paragraph of a considerable column-length was devoted to the rat's gruesome death, including grim details about how the dog's fangs punctured the rat's soft underbelly, and clenching jaws crushed the skull.

I asked, "So this going to be published?"

"I may have influence," Trevor said, "but not necessarily among New York's literary circles. Although I have submitted the story in your name. Because you have pedigree of a published writer...maybe it will rise above the slush pile. But it doesn't have to be published for Garret to get the message."

"What makes you sure he'll read it?"

"That's where your old man comes in. Englewood Federal Correctional distributes mail twice a week. A parole board interview has been scheduled, so the story needs to get to him by this weekend. You'll need to explain to your old man what he needs to do. Is that clear?"

"Sounds like a lot of moving parts."

"That's why you can't fuck this up, mate. Your father calls are scheduled Fridays, Tuesdays, so tomorrow you'll explain what he has to do."

I couldn't help but wonder how long Trevor had been monitoring me. "How do you know when our calls are scheduled?"

"I have people."

I wondered if he was referring to the Black Cube agency. "What if he doesn't call me?"

"It's your routine, so I'm sure he will."

He was right. My dad rarely missed the opportunity. Our calls broke up his monotony. I was the only connection he had to the outside world.

Trevor had an overnight envelope already printed. The return address was my office in Culver City. He handed me a pen and paper. "Write your father the letter by hand. Take your time. Make it legible."

I wrote the one-page letter and kept it brief. As instructed, I ended the letter by urging him share it with Garret.

Upon Trevor's approval, the letter went into the envelope with the manuscript. Seemingly satisfied, Trevor scribbled a phone number on an index card. "This is my cell. Call me after you've spoken with your old man."

I noticed it was a different phone number from what Alexandro had given me, but recognized the same 702 area code—Las Vegas. "So this is why you've been following me?"

"If Garret keeps his trap shut, then you'll likely not hear from me again. But if he squeals I'll have to escalate the matter."

"As in?"

"Have him killed."

"I don't believe you can arrange that in lockup."

"I trust you won't be a liability, Jack. If I have to go to the trouble of killing Garret, then adding your father can also be arranged."

A black Ford Explorer came up the driveway. It came to a stop on Trevor's concrete patio. I recognized the vehicle. It was the same Explorer that followed me from Truckee, the SUV I'd outrun at the top of Donner Pass.

Rex stepped out. He had a gun in his hand.

Trevor said to Rex. "We're going to escort Jack to his car."

Both kept their pistols on me as we made our way to Rex's Ford Explorer. My shoes were in the kayak, but they didn't let me retrieve them.

Inside, Rex's vehicle reeked of marijuana and sweet perfume. It wasn't necessarily the scent of a recent burn, but rather an odor which had permeated into the upholstery over time. I assumed the perfume was from the girls who worked for him.

On the drive, Rex studied me in the rear-view mirror as we made our way past the guard gate. His beady eyes gave me a chill.

Outside of the community, I directed them to my car. Trevor asked me, "What are you doing up in the mountains, Jack?"

"You know about that?" I said, acting surprised, even though I knew he'd been tipped off by Alexandro.

"I know everything."

"I'm consulting on a movie project," I said, which was the story I'd instructed Alexandro to pass on.

"Who are you working for?"

"A client who has financial interest."

"Let me guess, a tax scheme?"

"Why do you say that?"

"Aren't most independent films financed that way?"

I said, "Let's just say the camera isn't hidden in this film."

He and Rex exchanged a laugh before Trevor said, "What I said about you becoming a liability…I meant it. I can make your father's life miserable, or end it all-together," he punctuated the point by raising his pistol. "The same goes for you, mate. I have no qualms."

As Rex pulled up to my car, Trevor said, "Call me at that number I gave you after you've spoken with your old man. Is that understood?"

"If he calls."

"Oh, he will, mate. That I know."

They hadn't let me get my shoes out of the kayak. I climbed out and walked through the sandy gravel on the side of the road. They waited as I got into my car and drove off, barefoot.

Rex flashed the high beams as a parting gesture.

The first thing I did was call Alexandro. The call went to voicemail.

Beyond Lake Las Vegas, I sped through the night, heading back to northern California. Back to Madeline. Back to my dog.

CHAPTER 37

Three Years Ago

After Mona and I returned from Kentucky, she embarked on deep research. Combing through social media posts, she found the country club Kenneth was a member of in Greenwich, Connecticut. As opposed to golf, tennis was Kenneth's game. Over the years, he'd attended Wimbledon, the U.S. Open, and recently the PNB Paribas Open in Indian Wells, California. With that information, she scoured sports news to learn everything she could about the top ranked contenders. Common ground is what she was trying to establish.

To echo her enthusiasm, I went about making the champagne bottles appear as authentic as possible. My first task was to figure out a way to age the bottles as if they'd been in salt water for over a hundred years. Searching auction sites online, I found high-resolution photos of a WWI era bottle, shipwrecked, then salvaged; De Haartman & Co Cognac. This cargo met a similar fate. The freighter SS *Kyros* was overtaken by a U-boat. In this case, the Germans pulled alongside the ship and commandeered the vessel. The submarine was short on supplies, so they raided the galley for food and fresh water before setting the crew and captain adrift in lifeboats, then used the empty ship as target practice. Other than what the Germans took for themselves, the manifest, including the cognac, went down with the ship.

The wreck was salvaged, bottles analyzed, but the cognac was undrinkable. Wine can age in glass bottles for over a hundred years, but due to the high level of alcohol in a distilled spirit, the beverage eventually turns. Although the cognac bottles themselves were collectable, they weren't necessarily highly coveted at auction compared to our 1907 Heidsieck & Co. Monopole Diamant Bleu Cuvée champagne.

From the photographs of the cognac bottles, I could see the glass was pitted in what appeared to be a fine haze. It reminded me of the windshield of my first car—a rusty 1967 Chevy Nova. I guess I've always been a Chevy guy. Years of sand kicked up from Florida roadways pitted the windshield. When I'd turn into the late afternoon sun, there would be so much glare on my windshield I could hardly see.

First, I found a sandblaster on Amazon, a tool primarily used to remove graffiti from stucco, brick, and concrete surfaces. I figured by using sea salt mixed with fine sand, I could pit the glass bottles, much like the windshield of my first car.

When the sandblaster gizmo arrived, I practiced on a few dummies. There was some trial and error, but once I was confident I "salt-blasted" our pair of Heidsieck champagne bottles.

To mimic the blackish residue, I mixed tubes of oil-based paint to get the color right, and lightly dabbed a few splotches with a brush here and there. The next challenge was getting the cork in the bottle.

I had practiced both extracting and replacing corks on dummy bottles with the PVC pipe suppression rig I'd made. Finally, when I thought I was ready for our vintage bottles, Mona and I filled them with common Heidsieck we'd purchased at Vons. She watched me, amused, as I went about the work. It took time, but the corks behaved. The transfer worked, and we had our counterfeit bottles.

Later that evening, Mona hacked into emails from Kenneth's

executive secretary. The intercepted airline itinerary confirmed Kenneth was coming to the Bay Area. He had bought tickets to attend the Monterey Jazz Festival.

Mona said, "It's time to let him know we have what he wants."

She micro-managed as I photographed the champagne bottles—using different lighting and backgrounds. We settled on one of the first images I'd taken—the bottles side-by-side against a white seamless backdrop.

She crafted a text message reminding him we'd met in Lexington and added we had obtained an unexpected gem from the Kentucky cellar. *"This champagne appears to have been ship-wrecked."*

He texted back, *"Tell me more."*

We sent the photo.

Kenneth called immediately, and Mona improvised. She said the bottles were buried in a crate along with a receipt from an auction house.

"Heidsieck?" Kenneth asked.

"There's no label, but that's what the paperwork says." Mona apologized she didn't have it in front of her and would have to go to the warehouse to confirm. It was clear he knew the wine's storied history. Mona feigned ignorance. Kenneth said he wanted to see the bottles. He'd be in California and wanted to meet us. They ended the call with pleasantries, and the price for the bottles was never discussed.

"Looks like we need to come up with an auction receipt," I said.

She bit her lip. "Let me work on that."

First, Mona researched the Swedish auction house that, many years ago, had offered the first cases of the shipwrecked Heidsieck. Twenty minutes later, she mocked up a convincing bill of sale with the authentication paperwork. Her talent as a graphic artist astounded me.

Another hurdle. We didn't have a warehouse full of wine, our supposed place of business. Mona suggested, "Suppose we're keeping the brick-and-mortar location a secret."

"What do you mean?"

"What if a year ago, our warehouse was burglarized. We've since found a new location, but the whereabouts of our temperature-controlled vault are kept under wraps."

I'd read about heists at fine wine stores and finished her thought, "And only our most trusted clients have ever been there."

"Creates an air of exclusivity."

We were two peas in a pod.

Mona had a friend who worked at a winery in Napa Valley's town of Rutherford, renowned for their Special Collection Cabernet Sauvignon. A backdoor deal was made for a meeting location in the private tasting-room of a family-owned vineyard. That afternoon we sent her friend a thousand dollars cash, plus a handful of select "edibles" purchased at a marijuana dispensary on L.A.'s trendy Abbot Kinney Boulevard. We'd have the entire tasting room at our disposal for the entire day.

The Chevy Super Sport was not a fit for our wine broker personas, so I searched for a luxury rental. Tourists who fly into Los Angeles fulfill fantasies by renting exotic cars to drive through Hollywood, Malibu, and Beverly Hills; sort of like *The Beverly Hillbillies* theme song; "*...swimming pools, movie stars.*"

I found a Bentley Continental GT at a rental agency near LAX. The convertible was the most expensive vehicle in the pool at one thousand dollars per day. We decided we'd check it out first.

The car was huge—a beast. It had fine leather upholstery and a crafted wood dashboard. In the back of my mind, I worried if Kenneth got cold feet and decided not to purchase the bottles, the expense of everything would be for nothing. I had to remind myself this was Mona's deal. If the scam fell apart, it wouldn't have been the first time a mark backed out. So far, Mona had done everything right. Who was I to doubt? But still, I had a premonition there was a loose end.

Kenneth phoned to inform us he'd be in California in a few

days. Mona got him to agree to meet at the Rutherford winery location without having to explain our lack of warehouse. "Wait until you see these," she said. "They're like something from the Titanic." After she finished the call, Mona turned to me, her eyes sparkling, so beautiful. "The stage is set." She was in the zone.

Two days later, we rented the luxury Bentley convertible. We packed the counterfeit champagne in a plain cardboard wine box—but a specific brand Mona had hunted down—and placed it in the trunk before we set out for Napa Valley.

CHAPTER 38

Because it was a convertible, Mona brought a wide brim hat. She claimed it as "sun protection," even though the top was up for the entire drive north.

Wine tourism is a big deal in Napa Valley, and hotel rooms do not come cheap. Even mid-level, corporate chains are shakedowns for a standard room night. Because of the Bentley convertible, I'd booked the Marriott since it offered underground parking. As we checked in, they gave me a parking pass for the dashboard. I made sure to bring the champagne bottles, our precious cargo, inside.

Mona hung the clothes she had picked out for us—khakis and a sports jacket for me and a pencil-skirt suit for herself. It felt like we were waiting out the calm before a storm. We grabbed an early dinner at a French restaurant within walking distance from the hotel, so she put on an evening dress and looked great. Behind her at the mirror, I helped Mona clasp her silver butterfly necklace and couldn't help but kiss the nape of her neck. I felt like the luckiest guy in the world.

Restaurants in Napa celebrate how dishes are paired with wine, so I let Mona order. The waiter brought a foie gras and cheese appetizer, then opened a bottle of local Syrah.

I followed Mona's gaze outside the window to a young family with a toddler. The boy was playfully running around while the mother was trying to catch him. He hid behind his father's legs as the mother tickled his belly—a moment of family bliss.

Mona asked, "What do you think of kids?"

"What do you mean?"

"Do you see yourself being a father?"

"Have I thought about raising a kid? Not lately."

"Ever?" she asked.

I had considered it, but said to her, "The responsibility. I'm not sure I want to take that on." I was thinking about my incarcerated father, not a stellar role model. "I wouldn't want to make my dad's mistakes."

"Which were?"

"Turning me out." I told her more of how I'd assisted my father with several scams, often serving as a lookout and escape hatch.

"Escape hatch?"

"If dad got the feeling the deal was going sour, and the mark suspected he was being scammed, he'd cue me to intervene with an emergency. I'd stand outside, watching hotel windows. If he adjusted the drapes, that was my cue. I'd run up, pound on the door, and say mom had an accident. He'd apologize to the mark before scrambling out of there. On more than one occasion, as we were making our escape, cops would pass us going the other way. Nobody looks twice at a parent with a child."

"And you never knew your mother?"

"She went back to her old boyfriend, a guy who would never consider having a kid in his home."

"So sad."

"My gut tells me there's more to the story."

"Like what?"

"I don't know," I said, honestly, because I didn't.

"You don't think your father is entirely honest with you?"

"Hard to say. Telling lies is what he did for a living. Girlfriends lived with us over the years. To my friends, I'd say they were my mom, even though my dad never was married to any of them."

Mona asked, "Say you'd grown up in a stable household. A middle-class cliché. What do you think you'd be doing now?"

"Hard to say."

After she watched the family for a moment, Mona said, "Have you ever considered going legit? I mean, could you be happy with a corporate job, standing on the sidelines of your kid's soccer game?"

I said, "If it means sharing a life with you? Absolutely."

She reached across the table and took my hand. I'll never forget the hopeful look in her eyes. The moment was interrupted when the young boy came up and peered through the window. The boy waved at us before his parents retrieved him.

That evening, after making love, Mona dozed off, and I tried to envision how being a father would change my life. Would my past catch up to me? In the middle of the night, I awoke in a sweat. At first, I assumed it was the tannins from the red wine. But my joints ached. I felt flu symptoms coming on and sat on the toilet for most of the night. Could it have been the foie gras appetizer? Mona seemed fine. She slept peacefully.

At dawn, she ordered room service. When it came, I couldn't watch as she ate the fruit covered yogurt. My only salvation was the lukewarm tea made from the hotel coffee machine.

We had time to spare, so spent the morning in bed watching television as I tried to sleep it off. No luck.

As we checked out of the hotel, she was on the phone, arranging the delivery of a lunch spread from a local restaurant. Just the mention of smoked salmon made me quiver.

We arrived at the winery before noon—a picturesque hillside property surrounded by rows of vineyards. Mona's friend Beatrice met us with open arms. She was a jovial, curly-haired woman. Mona referred to her as "B" and explained she had known her since junior high. "Thank you for the special delivery," Beatrice said. "Da Kine," referring to the marijuana we'd shipped.

Our plan was Beatrice would be behind the counter, offering glasses of the winery's famed Sauvignon Cabernet. Mona explained Kenneth was a big client of ours and asked Beatrice to have a bottle of the signature Special Reserve on hand. They agreed on which vintage to uncork.

I moved our Bentley right outside the tasting room. I put the top down. All was on display.

The venue had an impressive view of the valley below. Coffee had been made. I sipped some of it, but it made my stomach feel worse. When the catered lunch arrived, I had to avoid it and stepped out to the deck. In the distance, workers tended to the vines. Mona joined me. "You alright?"

"I'll manage."

"Do you think you're coming down with something?"

I hadn't told her yet, but I'd booked a pair of open-ended plane tickets to Maui. My plan was to surprise her with the spontaneous exotic getaway, but my symptoms worried me, among other things. "You trust Beatrice?" I asked.

"What do you mean?"

"When Kenneth discovers the bottles are fakes, he may send some people back here to snoop around. Could Beatrice lead him to you?"

"I hadn't thought of that," she said.

"We may have to cut her in."

"B and I go way back. She wouldn't give me up."

"Does she know your family?"

Mona nodded. "But I'm not in touch with my folks. They don't care about me." She gazed over the vineyards with a look of sadness. "After my parents divorced, they went their separate ways. I think each of them thinks the other stays in touch with me. Unless I contact them, they don't know where I am."

I thought about the phone calls with my dad from prison, my one and only family connection, and said, "I bet they'd be thrilled to hear from you."

Mona said, "I don't want to talk about my parents right now."

Back to the business at hand, I said, "We'll engage the good cop, bad cop routine. You'll play the positive one. I'll play the curmudgeon."

"Shouldn't be a stretch," she teased.

"When it comes to negotiating a price, let me handle that. If he balks and doesn't agree, we'll part ways. And we'll wait for him to come back to us."

"I get it," she said. "Desperation is the worst cologne."

"We need to have the confidence we hold the cards."

Mona twirled the butterfly pendant on her necklace. I noted that by saying, "Your butterfly is our good luck charm."

She smiled. "Butterflies are free."

The agreed upon meeting time of 1:00 p.m. came and went. Mona considered texting Kenneth, but thought better of it, repeated the phrase, "desperation is the worst cologne."

Forty-five minutes later, a white Lincoln Navigator slowed on the highway and pulled into the vineyard. We stepped out to the driveway as it eased to a halt next to the Bentley. Kenneth emerged, followed by his fiancée, Rebecca. I hadn't expected her to come. She wore tight-fitting leather pants and a stylish western top, country attire, and appeared different than when we'd seen her last. To Rebecca, Kenneth said, "You remember Richard and Leslie from Lexington."

Saccharine as a pack of Sweet'N Low, Rebecca said, "Nice to see you again."

As we made small talk, a portly, middle-aged man carrying an aluminum sample case emerged from the front passenger seat. Kenneth introduced him as "Our friend Eugene."

The driver stepped out, too. He was a muscular guy in a dark suit, hair cut short. My instincts told me he wore two hats, both as a driver and personal bodyguard. I wondered who of them needed the bodyguard, Kenneth or Rebecca.

We invited all into the tasting room. Kenneth eyed the Bentley. That's when I realized I'd mistakenly left the hotel parking pass and car rental packet on the dash. I wasn't sure if he saw it, or if it registered.

Beatrice greeted everyone and offered samples of wine. All

three declined, however, Eugene helped himself to sparkling water. He chugged the entire Perrier while the driver/bodyguard found a seat in the corner—a strategic position to study the proceedings.

After Kenneth and Rebecca took in the view from the outdoor deck, I invited them inside. Kenneth, Rebecca, and Eugene assembled at a round table set in the center of the room. The bodyguard remained in his corner.

I retrieved the cardboard wine box, and Eugene's eyes lit up. This seemed to have something to do with the brand of wine printed on the cardboard box. I had no idea what the significance could have been but smiled inwardly; that was Mona's handiwork. I said, "It was quite a surprise discovering shipwrecked Heidsieck in a Kentucky cellar." With that, I pulled the two bottles out and carefully set them on the table.

Eugene dried his hands on his pants and reached for one of them. He turned it upside down and studied the base of the bottle. He opened his sample case and pulled out a magnifying glass.

It was obvious Kenneth had brought along a professional.

I had a sudden, uncontrollable urge to find the men's room. I thought I had purged everything that morning. Apparently not. Out of necessity, I excused myself. My biggest worry was Mona would be alone with them when they discovered the bottles were fakes.

CHAPTER 39

As I shat my brains out, I was one hundred percent certain the professional appraiser would determine the bottles were counterfeit. As soon as I could, I emerged from the men's room to face the aftermath.

Eugene had set the champagne bottles out on a white linen cloth while he illuminated the glass with a flashlight. He pulled some sort of scientific device out of his sample case. A bored Rebecca asked, "What's that thing?"

Matter of fact, he stated, "a mass spectrometer." He went about preparing the instrument. They'd brought a Crime Scene Investigator. Was a lie detector next?

Meanwhile, our host Beatrice had opened a bottle of the signature cabernet, and said, "It would be a crime for everyone not to sample." All agreed, and she poured for Kenneth, then Rebecca, and finally Mona.

I politely refused.

Beatrice offered the bodyguard a pour, but he too turned it down.

Meanwhile, Eugene worked the device and made notes on a legal pad. To pass the time, Mona and Kenneth swapped opinions about varietals—all Greek to me. Rebecca spent the time with her nose in her phone. Eugene examined the fake auction house receipt Mona had created.

I never expected Kenneth would bring a pro and wondered why he hadn't spotted the counterfeit bottles immediately. It didn't matter. I'd already come up with a plan. Upon learning the champagne was fake, I'd surmise someone must have duped the deceased matriarch when she bought them. I'd say that would explain why the bottles were found in a common cardboard box. Kenneth and I hadn't talked money up to that point, so I'd simply apologize for wasting his time.

Meanwhile Mona had Kenneth engaged in colorful descriptions of the cabernet they were sipping. I overheard words like, "chocolate," "oak", "flinty," and something about "struggling vines."

Eugene had not revealed the verdict.

It was their bodyguard who concerned me most. There was something about the guy's energy—or edge. He studied us like a cat on a windowsill watching birds on a wire.

A bored Rebecca asked Eugene, "So what's the deal?"

There was an awkward moment of silence before Eugene set his magnifying glass down. "Short of opening a bottle to test the PH level," he said, "these appear to be authentic." With that, he nodded to Kenneth.

The endorsement came as a surprise.

"A cause for celebration," Mona said.

Another bottle of cabernet was opened. Kenneth said to me, "Let's discuss logistics."

To negotiate in privacy, we moved out onto the redwood deck. Over my shoulder, I could hear Mona engage Rebecca in small talk. Somehow she got the ice princess to laugh. A miracle.

Leaning on the rail on the deck, Kenneth looked out over the valley as he took a sip of the cabernet before saying, "What price did you have in mind?"

"Market," I said bluntly.

"Which means?"

"Two hundred fifty thousand."

He shook his head. "I can offer fifty thousand for the pair."

I knew who I was dealing with. Kenneth had made a career as a master negotiator. "Two hundred fifty thousand *each*," I countered.

He studied me. "That's a lot of money. Maybe at one time someone paid that but…"

Laughing, Mona and Rebecca emerged from inside, each carrying their refilled glasses. Kenneth appeared to brighten at the sound of Rebecca's laugh. It must be rare. He acknowledged them before turning back to me, saying, "Had I known that was the amount you had in mind, I would have never come. Sixty thousand."

"I'm sure you're aware of the collectible value."

"One hundred thousand dollars is as far as I'll go for the pair. The family you bought these from had no idea what they had in their cellar."

"No different than an antique furniture dealer finding gold coins tucked under a dresser," I said, "or a bookseller discovering bank notes stowed in pages. I'm sorry we didn't talk numbers before."

"I am too."

At that moment, Mona came to my side. "Excuse me. Sorry to interrupt," she said, handing me her cell phone. "It's Lester," she said. "He said it's urgent."

I didn't know anyone named Lester but read into her angle. Mona's interruption could not have been better timed. I pretended to take the call and stepped away, saying, "Lester, how are you?" I acted as if I was listening. "Give me a second."

I turned to Kenneth. "Excuse me for a moment," and stepped inside the tasting room.

At the bar, Eugene sat across from Beatrice in conversation while the bodyguard had not moved from his perch in the corner.

I feigned conversation into the phone, said aloud, "Another customer has made an offer and I'm in discussion with them at this very moment." I could see Kenneth craning his neck from outside. I said, "Is that the best you can do?" After a moment, feigning pleasantries, I told the fictional Lester I'd get right back to him and finished the call.

Returning to Kenneth, I said, "I've got interest from another party, a longtime customer. I'm sorry, but five hundred thousand for the pair, or I'll have to take his offer." The perception of urgency was what Mona's fictional phone call had created.

Kenneth shot a glance at Rebecca. He smiled to himself, and said hushed, "Having two bottles is a plus." Then, even more under his breath, "I'm going to open one of them on our wedding night and save the other. She doesn't know that yet, so for me, this is an emotional purchase." He struggled. "I try to keep emotion out of business, but…I'm familiar with the market value, but I honestly can't pay that price. I can offer two-hundred thousand each."

I stood firm. "I can't. Five hundred K for the pair."

I could tell not getting his way was killing him. But I also knew he could afford it. A good day on the stock market would cover the entire expense. With the assumption he'd take the bait, I added, "I work with a team who transports fine art. It's a Sunday, so the banks are closed, but once payment is confirmed, shipping will take less than forty-eight hours." It was more fiction and hoped he didn't ask for any details because I'd made it up on the spot.

Kenneth bit his lip, closed his eyes for a moment, as if in meditation. It was an uncomfortable silence. Finally relented, "Okay. You drive a hard bargain, but we have a deal."

We shook on it.

I forwarded him my account and routing number. Thankfully, he didn't ask why my bank was offshore. He sent me the address to ship the bottles. I assumed it would be his home in Connecticut where he'd store them in his prized cellar, but instead, it was his office in New York City.

We joined the ladies. By then, they appeared to have become fast friends. The last of the wine had been consumed, and as Kenneth and his entourage prepared to depart, Eugene approached me. He handed me a business card, the edges frayed, and said, "If you are ever in need of my services," revealing red wine stained teeth I hadn't noticed before, "I'm available to assist." From the bump of his elbow against mine, I got the feeling he may have suspected the bottles were not authentic, even though he claimed they were. I thought of age-old gambling wisdom, some say attributed to the actor Paul Newman, "*if you're playing a poker game and you look around the table and can't tell who the sucker is, it's you.*"

Minutes later, as they set out in the Lincoln Navigator and drove down the hill, Mona turned to me with her mischievous smile. "Well," she said, facetiously, "*they* were nice." There was that look of mischief in her eyes.

I kissed her. "You are brilliant. That phone call...perfect."

She said, "One hell of a team, you and I."

"I've got a surprise," and pulled out my phone to show the open-ended boarding passes. "Assuming the payment lands, and we ship the bottles tomorrow, how about we skip off to Maui to celebrate?"

She was ecstatic. I'd never felt so good. Mona thanked Beatrice and bid her goodbye.

We tucked the two bottles of counterfeit 1907 Heidsieck & Co. Monopole Diamant Bleu Cuvée on the back seat floorboard of the Bentley convertible and set out for Los Angeles.

CHAPTER 40

Present Day

After my sitdown with Trevor, driving northbound in Nevada, Madeline called. From the sound of her voice, I got the impression she had been drinking. "I got the stuff from Mike's phone. A number looked familiar. That bitch Christine texted Mike that night. I know because it's the same number she's texting from, pressuring me to take the money."

"What did she text?"

"*Meet me in the theater.* Why would they go to a place full of asbestos?" Madeline became emotional. "Mike stopped telling me things. He was afraid the stress would trigger another miscarriage."

"Another?"

"I've had three," she confessed. "God hates me."

In the back of my mind, I wondered if the exposure to chemicals could have contributed to her bad luck.

Madeline turned to anger. "Those motherfuckers killed Mike to shut him up."

I suggested she get some sleep, and we'd look into it in the morning. She bid me a tearful goodbye.

Driving through the night, I made good time through Nevada, reached Reno, and climbed up over Donner Pass. Dawn was breaking by the time I pulled into Amarillo Slims. As I fed Suzie, my phone rang. It was not a number I recognized. Alexandro had been arrested.

"Fireworks *and* nunchucks," he said. "They searched my van."

"Who?"

"Cops. Who else?"

I knew those fireworks were a bad idea. "What's the bail?"

"They said I'm not eligible because I'm a minor."

"Who said that?"

"Some fat-assed lady. Said I need to go to some detention hearing, which won't happen till Wednesday. So what? I'm supposed to just sit here and rot?"

"Where are you?"

"Juvenile Detention in Auburn. You've got to get me out of here."

I told him I'd do everything I could and suggested he call his mother.

"Mom can't afford no plane ticket. Dude, get me out of here."

My next call was to Oscar. I explained the situation. He confirmed, "That's right, there's no bail release when it comes to minors. How old is this kid?"

"Not sure. Fifteen or so."

"Priors?

"Not sure."

"Gang affiliation?"

"I really don't know that much about him."

"And you say he was in possession of an illegal weapon?"

"Nunchucks and fireworks."

"At the hearing, a judge will determine if the boy will be held or released to his parents or legal guardian."

"And what if there's nobody?"

"Then he'll probably be in juvie until the issue is resolved. How do you know this boy?"

I explained how he had been tailing me for the last couple of weeks.

"Tailing you?"

"It involves Mona's ex-boyfriend trying to settle a score."

Oscar was well-aware of my accident, and Mona's death. He didn't press further. Instead, he referred me to Claudia Myers, a defense attorney in Marin County. "Juvenile defense is her racket."

I thanked him and suggested he put somebody else on that retail theft case.

"I don't have anybody else, Jack. Don't dilly-dally over there," he said, sounding like my dad. "Finish what you've got to do, and get back home, pronto."

"There'll be no dilly-dallying," I assured.

My next call was to Claudia Myers and Associates. Claudia was familiar with Placer County Juvenile Detention Center. She explained she'd handled tons of juveniles arrested in the Lake Tahoe ski resorts on drug-related offenses. I explained the situation and that I worked with Oscar.

"Some of these places," she said, "you've got to keep them honest. Small town cops can get away with murder." She mentioned her retainer. I said, "This has to be a friends-and-family rate," echoing what Hector had said when he hired me.

"No worries. Oscar was a mentor when I was just starting my career, fresh out of law school. Let me look into it and get back to you."

Since I'd been up all night, I laid my head down to catch a brief nap before Hector called. "Dude, what's up with my sister? She's all freaked out."

I told him I'd spoken with her last night, and brought him up to speed, saying, "Madeline has a right to be upset. There are unanswered questions surrounding Mike's death."

"Tell her she needs to chill out. She should come home."

I told him that was the plan. Next, I called her, but Madeline didn't pick up. I wondered if she was sleeping it off, having drowned her sorrows.

Finally, I tried to grab a couple of hours' sleep. I was exhausted. But my mind was racing a mile a minute. I couldn't sleep a wink. So, I got up, and got busy.

Any rest would have to wait.

CHAPTER 41

As I set out for campus, Slim was outside tinkering with his motorcycle, the bike with the longhorns on the handlebars. Assorted tools and replacement parts were set out on a hotel towel. He greeted me, saying, "Mornin' chief."

"Got yours out today, huh?"

"Considering selling her," he said, waving his silver ring-fingered hand over the bike. "Runs okay, but got to fix her up some." He pointed to the bike rack I'd placed on the back of my Chevy, what I'd used to disguise the license plate. "Got yourself a peddle bike, do ya?"

I felt obligated to explain. "The rack avoids getting tagged by digital license plate readers."

"Ah…the government."

"And others."

He motioned to the motorcycle he'd lent me previously, and said, "That one still at your disposal." Considering the close-calls I've had, borrowing that motorcycle again made sense. I took him up on the offer.

Slim teased, "I'll make an outlaw biker out of ya yet."

As I suppressed a yawn, he retrieved the leather jacket and helmet. "Heard you pull in early this morning."

"Had some business in Nevada. Was up all night."

"Casino business?"

I laughed. "No. I've left the grind of craps and blackjack tables behind me."

"Private eye stuff, then. A stakeout?"

"You could call it that," I said, avoiding details.

"Where you headed?"

"Taking a look inside the theater on campus," I said as I straddled the bike. "I suspect the college is hiding toxic chemicals down in the mine."

"Sounds like a toxic work environment to me," Slim said.

"Something like that."

"Why not call OSHA?"

I kick-started the motorcycle and revved the throttle. "Got to see for myself."

"My advice, if you care to hear, is to not press your luck up in Argonaut. People tend to disappear around there."

"What kind of people?"

"Outsiders like you. You look a little tired. Sure you don't want to rest a bit?"

He was right, but I said, "No, I'm fine."

"I'll fire up a pot of strong-ass coffee. How's that?"

"I'm good. Thanks for lending me the bike." I pulled on the helmet and gave Slim the thumbs up. "Thanks for taking care of my dog." Then, I set the bike down the hill. My departure was far from graceful. Maybe I was extra clumsy from lack of sleep, or having very little experience on a motorcycle, but I slid sideways and almost went down. Reaching the pavement, I maneuvered, but over-corrected and almost went down again. Thankfully, I steadied the bike and set out for Bret Harte College.

Slim was right. I was tired. I could have used the jolt of caffeine he offered.

In Argonaut I parked the motorcycle in the parking lot of the general store, secured the helmet to the handlebars, and tucked the leather jacket inside the bike's saddle bag. My plan was to find Two-Dollar Bill. I didn't know if I'd already asked too much from him, but my hope was he would let me into the theater.

First, I tried the Eureka Tavern. The bar hadn't opened yet, but Laura saw me through the window. She unlocked the door and asked, "Have you seen Madeline?"

"Isn't she at your place?"

"No. We'd been drinking, and she got all weepy. She said she needed to get some of Mike's things. She was in no condition to drive, so I took her keys. But she tricked me because she had another set in the visor."

It was around midnight when Madeline and I had last spoke on my drive back from Vegas. It hadn't occurred to me she was not staying with her friend at the time. If she was home, then she would be under surveillance.

Laura said, "Madeline says her house is bugged, and that creepy folks are watching her. She took my sledgehammer. Said she was going to smash the hidden cameras." I wondered why Madeline hadn't told me when we spoke, and asked Laura if she knew where Bill was.

"Haven't seen him in a couple days," she said. "Not like him."

I said, "He told me he was in the doghouse with his wife and planned to go home to patch things up. Do you know where he lives?"

"He said that?" Laura said with concern. "Bill lost his wife to lung cancer years ago. That's when he started spending all his time here. He said his wife was still alive?"

"Yes."

Deeply saddened, Laura said, "He can be a delusional."

I asked, "Do you know where he lives?"

"A place on campus, I think. That's what he told me, anyway."

I thought of the squalid army cot in the basement of the maintenance shed, and how I'd assumed that was his temporary residence. "What do you know about the asbestos abatement in the theater?"

"Only that nobody can go in there."

"Have any workers or asbestos removal teams come in here?"

"None. I figured they haven't gotten around that yet."

I didn't tell her my plan was to look inside the theater. For that, I needed Bill. I thanked Laura and set out for the maintenance shed.

"Have Madeline call me," she said as I crossed the street.

On campus, I made my way past lawn mowing equipment to the cinderblock building. Lawrence, the buck-toothed guy I'd first seen in Madeline's office, emerged from the garage wearing his campus security uniform. He sized me up, asking, "Can I help you?"

"I'm looking for Bill."

"He doesn't work here anymore."

"Since when?"

"Since we caught him drinking on the job," he said with a gesture to indicate sipping a flask.

"I'm sorry to hear that."

He shrugged. "What can I do for you, stranger?" His forced smile revealed the severity of his buck teeth.

"I don't intend to be any trouble."

"No trouble at all."

The guy got on my nerves, mostly because of his arrogance. I sensed he wasn't the sharpest crayon in the box. Nor the brightest color. I thanked him, and as I walked away, I could feel his eyes on my back. Once I was clear of Lawrence and the maintenance shack, I looped back around to the theater building.

The doors were secured by heavy padlocks. The windows were boarded. There was, however, one small window over a door that wasn't covered in plywood—a horizontal transom above the entrance. There appeared to be a latch at the base. I'd need a ladder and some tools.

Giving Lawrence and the maintenance yard a wide berth, I went back down the hill to the town's hardware store. Thankfully, Sheriff Marsh wasn't parked there. I bought a six-foot aluminum ladder, a flashlight, a rubber mallet, some bailing wire, and a flathead screwdriver. Keeping a watchful eye for Lawrence, I carried the goods back onto campus. The students strolling to and from class seemed to pay me no mind.

Around the back of the theater, I went to work.

Leaning the ladder against the door, I climbed up to the transom. Using the screwdriver and rubber mallet, I was able to chip away at the molding. From there, I fashioned the wire into a loop and was able to spring the latch. Success. The window opened and there was just enough room for me to slip inside.

Standing in a narrow hallway, I recognized the familiar chemical odor from when I was in the mineshaft. There was no evidence of any kind of asbestos removal. I made my way into the auditorium.

The strongest odor came from the front of the stage. I could see the trapdoor beyond the stage footlights wasn't entirely closed, and there were remnants of muddy footprints surrounding. When I lifted the door, the chemical scent hit me like a ton of bricks.

With caution, I descended the stairs.

I turned on the flashlight to get my bearings. Down a concrete-walled hallway there was a metal door slightly ajar, and more muddy footprints. A padlock dangled free. I pulled open the heavy door. It creaked on the hinges.

Beyond, there were layers of hanging black plastic. Mountain Rescue guy Ty had mentioned tarps in the tunnels. Maybe the plastic was a temporary solution to keep the chemical smell contained.

Easing my way through the drapes, I came across a hallway with linoleum flooring and tiled walls. The space felt institutional, like a hospital, or old folks' home. There were security cameras perched above. I wondered if someone was watching.

I'd seen theaters with underground dressing rooms, but this was entirely different—a tech workspace. There was a half dozen portable tables in what appeared to be computer stations. The monitors displayed an assortment of surveillance. Some of it was on campus, but more than half appeared to be spying on living spaces. I assumed Madeline and Mike were observed from here.

First, I heard shuffling. One of the doors behind me sprung open. Marsh surprised me. He had his Glock in hand. Lawrence was behind him, a smirk on his face.

Marsh said, "Now you're really starting to piss me off."

Before I could reply, he ran up and smashed the pistol across my jaw. The next sensation was hitting the concrete floor. They dragged me to a storage room and locked me inside.

CHAPTER 42

Pressing my fingers against the painful gash on my skull, oozing, blood trickled into my eyes. I wiped it away and looked for something to put pressure on the wound, but there was nothing. I pulled off one of my shoes and peeled off a sock. Applying pressure, I hoped that might slow the pulsing hemorrhage. It would have to do. I pulled out my phone, but there was no reception.

I heard voices outside the door, so I slid my phone into my shoe, and slipped it on my foot without the sock. Marsh slid open the heavy door. Behind him, I could make out Chancellor Foster and Christine. Lawrence peeked out behind them.

"That's the guy," Christine said.

Marsh grabbed me by the collar, flipped me face down on the concrete, and frisked me. He took my wallet and tossed it to them. Had he taken off my shoes, he would have certainly found my phone.

Christine thumbed through my wallet and said, "I've looked into who you are, Jack O'Shea. A former swindler who wrote a best-selling book. Now a licensed private investigator? Absurd."

I said nothing.

She asked, "How did you get mixed up with Madeline?"

After dabbing at the bloody wound on my head, I said, "The night of the..." I was about to say *accident* but instead chose, "murder...you texted Mike. What was that about?"

She and the Chancellor shared a look.

I continued, "I've got to hand it to ya. I've been in the company of hustlers all my life. Ponzi-schemers. Card hustlers. You name it. Never have I seen a pair like you, cloaked in a virtue signaling world of higher education. Globalization for those that can afford it."

The husband and wife shared a look.

Pointing to Marsh, I said. "How much do you pay this assclown to do your dirty work?" From the look on Marsh's face, it was clear he didn't like being referred to as an ass, nor a circus performer.

I went on, "You've got a big problem with that toxic waste you've been stockpiling. And Mike was about to blow the whistle, wasn't he? That's why you killed him."

Chancellor Foster asked, "Who was he in contact with?"

I ignored that, and asked, "How does one jump from the recycling business to running a liberal arts college? How'd you make that jump? I suppose academia is good business, and far more prestigious than getting rid of people's trash." I nodded to his trophy wife, "And far better in certain social circles. It's all about how you're perceived, isn't it? But I suppose both rackets are riding the coattails of government spending. Especially if you know how to play the system."

A clearly angered Christine said, "Bill told us you took photos."

Lawrence nodded behind her.

"Where are those?" Chancellor Foster asked.

In retrospect, I probably shouldn't have admitted I'd sent them to the Environmental Protection Agency, but I did. And that was not good.

Christine said, "That's unfortunate for you." She nodded to Marsh and ordered, "Flush this interloper. Flush twice."

The clearly henpecked husband tried to reason with her, "No. We can't keep doing this."

"Have a better solution?" she snapped back. It was clear who wore the pants in this family.

Relenting to her demand, he nodded to Marsh.

Lawrence yanked me to my feet. They pulled my arms behind my back and pushed me towards a black plastic tarp. The drape parted to the edge of the mineshaft.

"Sayonara," said Christine, the last thing I heard.

CHAPTER 43

In complete darkness, I bounced off the sides of the mineshaft before hitting water. Torpedoing underneath, my feet did not hit bottom. I flailed my arms and feet to come up to the surface. In pitch black, I could feel the liquid surge from side to side, the energy swirling around me. As the water settled, I treaded to keep my head above water.

Above, I could see the faint silhouette of someone looking down—presumably Marsh. He ducked out of sight, followed by the sound of a metal door slamming. I was left floating in complete darkness.

I reached around for the walls, trying to find something to hang onto. The stone was slippery, like they doused it in grease.

My phone.

I reached for my shoe and held it above water. I dug out my phone from the toe. Miraculously, it lit up. I thumbed 911, but there was no cell phone reception. I turned on the flashlight. With legs kicking, one arm wading, and the other holding the phone above water, I was able to keep afloat.

With the light on, I could see the shaft was about fifteen feet in diameter. I searched for something to hold onto. There was nothing. I felt something bump against me. Shining the light, a body was floating face down. I frantically pushed it away. The corpse bounced off the wall and returned. I flipped it over to discover Bill. His face bloated, eyes bugged, and skin ghostly white.

I pushed him away, but there was only so much room. The sway of the water brought him back again. I wondered who else could be floating in this foul-smelling swill.

Keeping the phone above water while still staying afloat was a challenge. I screamed for help. If Bill hadn't heard Mike that night, nobody would have known. I realized exhaustion would eventually get the best of me. And like Mike, I'd drown.

Putting my phone in my teeth, I felt around the walls of the shaft with my feet underwater for a foothold, around the perimeter. There was nothing. I was like a rat stuck in a greased sewer pipe, clawing at the sides.

From the light on my phone, I could see there was a stone icicle on the wall about six feet above my head—a stalagmite stone mineral deposit. It was one of the geological anomalies Bill had pointed out when we toured the tunnels. If I could latch onto that, it might give me leverage to keep my head above water. But it was too high and there was no way I could reach it.

Then it occurred to me—my belt.

Maybe I could take off my belt to hook the buckle between the stalagmite and the cavern wall.

Struggling to keep my phone above water, I returned it to my teeth and reached with both hands to remove my belt. Then, kicking to stay afloat, I made a loop with the belt buckle.

I tried to lasso the stone formation. I cast the belt loop above again and again, but the mini stone protrusion on the shaft above me was out of reach. I needed another two feet of length.

Then it occurred to me. Bill might have been wearing a belt. Maybe I could buckle the two together.

At the edge of exhaustion, kicking my burning legs to stay afloat, with my phone in my teeth, I felt around Bill's waist with both hands. Thank God he had one. I maneuvered his belt off, but in the struggle, I'd swallowed water. It made me gag. I coughed my guts out.

Entirely winded, I had to float on my back for a while to recover, the phone still clinched in my teeth. Meanwhile, Bill's body bumped against me. I nudged him away, but he drifted back like a dog playing fetch. There was only so much room.

When I felt I had regained enough strength, I connected his belt to the end of my own and resumed my attempt to hook the stalagmite. The belt buckle clanged against the wall, but I couldn't get it to catch—an impossible game of carnival ring-toss.

I took more of the nasty water in my mouth.

Finally, it caught.

I held onto the belt with one hand and shined the light with the other. The loop had caught around the indentation, but barely.

Returning the phone to my mouth, I knotted the belt around my armpit and, with my other hand, held on for dear life.

It worked, but I'd only bought myself time.

I resumed calling for help.

The light from my phone began to dim. I turned off the flashlight to save what little battery was left and called out, into darkness.

The pain in my shoulder from holding up my weight was overwhelming, and I was convinced I was going to die. Maybe I'd join Mona in the afterlife. Maybe she was waiting for me, assuming there was an afterlife.

Admittedly, I prayed for God's forgiveness. My life had been one of sin and selfishness. Why would a Higher Power spare me? I didn't deserve redemption. I accepted my fate.

I thought of my father.

And I prayed for him.

You can always tell the sound of a Harley.

I heard something rumbling above. Could that be Slim? He and Madeline were the only ones who knew I'd gone to campus.

I yelled at the top of my lungs. The sound of the engine stopped. I screamed again. I heard the plastic tarp above rustle and saw the distant beam of a flashlight. "That you, Jack?"

It *was* Slim. Emotion overcame me. "Down here!"

"Hold on, brother."

I was expecting he'd call the fire department. Instead, I heard something scraping against the stone above. Turning on the light of my iPhone, I could see he was sending Madeline's garden-hose down, the one she'd laid out to water the flower box memorial.

I was certain there wouldn't be enough length as the hose swung from side to side, the metallic fixture clanging against the wall.

As luck would have it, the hose reached me. There was enough length, but barely.

"Got it!"

Slim disappeared from the rim above. A moment later, I heard the motorcycle fire to life. That's when I realized he'd secured the other end of the hose to his bike. The engine running, he returned to the rim and said, "Tie on!"

I pulled what little slack I had.

While floating on my back, phone in my teeth, I weaved the end of the plastic hose through my belt loop. I tied a crude knot—and held on for dear life. "Got it," I said.

A moment later, the slack tightened. He was pulling me out of the watery muck.

I slid up the walls of the shaft. If any part of the hose gave way, I'd tumble back. Miraculously my phone's light hadn't given out, clinched in my teeth, illuminating my ascent.

Hoisted past the interconnecting tunnels, there were more of them than I'd imagined. I remembered what Bill had told me, that this was the mine's elevator shaft.

Finally, near the top, I dangled near the tunnel that I'd been thrown down. There was a metal door, like a bulkhead on a ship. That's what connected to the theater. Another fifteen feet, and I'd be at the edge of the shaft.

Twisting and wriggling, like a fish out of water, I was able to maneuver myself over the lip. Slim grabbed my collar and dragged me across the dirt, presumably for good measure. He shut off the rumbling bike. I gasped for air, grateful to be alive, and coughed my guts out.

Slim said, "Had a bad feeling when you set out."

I tried to speak but couldn't. My throat was on fire yelling and all the caustic liquid I'd swallowed.

Students had gathered and were looking on, mouths agape. Some of them were capturing video of my agony with their phones.

Slim wiped his hand across my shirt and smelled it. Winced. With a grimace, he said, "Gonna need a sheep-dip, my friend."

CHAPTER 44

In the veterinarian's office, Doc Reibach held a bottle of hydrogen peroxide. "We're going to need to induce vomiting and pump your stomach."

"Is that necessary?" I muttered, bent over, bleary-eyed.

Slim stood at the doorway and said, "And a pressure-wash."

She said, "That too. You need to purge," and directed me to the stainless-steel washtub on the floor-level, the same one Suzie had been cleansed in only days before. In a coffee cup, she mixed a cocktail of hydrogen peroxide and warm water into a foamy broth and handed me the cup.

Slim, clearly uncomfortable, said, "What do you say I run back and fetch some dry clothes?"

"Thanks," I said, and searched my pockets.

"I've got a key," Slim said, which made sense since he owned the place. Besides, Marsh had taken my room key, wallet, and everything else in my pockets when he frisked me. Slim wished me luck.

I trusted Dr. Reibach's expertise, so swallowed the nasty brew in three gulps. I started coughing, and then up came the contents. I hadn't vomited that hard since drinking binges in my college days. Next came a series of dry heaves. But I was in store for more torture. She had a suction tube ready, the sound of an electric motor humming, and said, "Lay on your side."

In the fetal position prone on the stainless-steel tub, I braced myself as she lubricated the plastic tube and worked it down my throat. The gag reflex was painful, and through coughs and more dry heaves, she worked the tube down. I thought there was nothing left in my stomach, but the suction proved otherwise. As the machine gurgled, I suffered through the uncomfortable humiliation. None of it was pretty.

When the procedure was finally over, Doc had me remove my clothes, which were still damp and smelled like rot and solvent. Doing so revealed the scars across my torso from the car accident. "Bear attack," I said with false bravado.

Doc Reibach said, "Think of this as a Silkwood shower. Ever see that movie?"

I nodded with, "Meryl Streep."

"Just try to relax." She adjusted the water and then started in. The spray was scalding hot. But I suffered through it. She used a brush on me clearly intended for animals and not human skin.

Finally, when the torture was over, she brought a stack of pet towels. I had to use three of them to dry myself off.

Slim returned with a long-sleeve polo and pair of jeans, plopped them down on the table, then went out for a smoke. Thoughtfully, he'd brought my toothbrush, toothpaste, a comb, and flip-flops.

In the restroom, I gingerly dressed. Only then, looking in the mirror, did I realize how close I'd come to death. It was a miracle Slim followed me and devised a way to pull me out of that hellhole.

The clock read 11:37AM. My father would call in less than a half an hour, so I asked Doc Reibach for my phone. She dug into my pants and dug it out. Unfortunately, by that time my phone was dead. I couldn't tell if the battery had expired or if the device was ruined forever. She directed me to her charging cord. It did nothing. When my father called from prison, it would likely go into voicemail. I wouldn't have a chance to explain anything about the short story he'd receive, and what to do with it.

What was left in my pants pocket was the index card Trevor had given me with the phone number to call once I'd spoken with my father. But the ink on the soggy card had smeared beyond recognition—the handwritten number a blur. If I were to contact Trevor, it would have to come from the phone number Alexandro had given me. That would compromise my source and certainly put the kid in harm's way.

Doc Reibach consoled me with a cup of chamomile tea. The warmth of the liquid soothed my jagged throat. She asked, "How'd you end up in there?"

"Sheriff Marsh. Chancellor Foster. His charming wife. And there's a body down there."

"Who?"

"Everyone knows him up there as Two-Dollar Bill."

Her eyes glassed over.

As if on cue, emergency lights appeared out the window. I recognized Sheriff Marsh's car as it pulled up. He stepped out, hand on his holster, and addressed Slim, who was smoking on the porch. I overheard him say, "Where is he, Tex?"

Slim extinguished his cigarette and said, "Who are you talking about?"

"Don't bullshit me. You gave him a ride. Where is he?"

Doc Reibach pulled me away from the window, and said, "I'll deal with this. Stay inside." She left me in the examination room and closed the door. I heard a cabinet open, followed by a heavy metallic click that sounded like a gun.

I peeked out the window to see her step out to greet Marsh, saying, "Aren't you out of your jurisdiction?" The veterinarian had an over-and-under double-barrel shotgun in her hands, and I had no doubt the champion skeet shooter knew how to use it.

I could see Marsh was taken aback. "Set that down," he ordered and pulled the Glock from his holster.

There was a moment of hesitation before she laid the shotgun at her feet. Doc Reibach said, "What do you want from us?"

"Where is he?"

"Where's Two-Dollar Bill?"

"You need to mind your business." He turned to Slim. "I know he's staying at that cripple camp of yours. I was just there."

"What'd you call it?" Slim said.

"You heard me."

Doc Reibach interjected, "That student who killed Eddie...the hit and run...why'd you let him go?"

"Special Ed the retard?" he said. "There was no proof."

"Blood all over the grill of that car wasn't enough?"

"You don't know the details."

"I know the killer's daddy was rich."

"Look...I don't tell you how to spay and neuter cats," Marsh said, "so you don't get to tell me how to do my job." He stepped towards the door.

"You got a warrant?" Doc Reibach said.

That stopped him in his tracks.

Slim said, "Whoever you're looking for is not here. You want to arrest us? Then go ahead."

Sheriff Marsh studied both Slim and Doc Reibach for a moment. He holstered his gun and checked his watch. Without saying a word, he returned to his car and backed out of the parking lot.

When he was gone, Doc Reibach and Slim came back inside.

She put her shotgun away, and I said, "These are my problems, not yours."

"Marsh has been our problem long before you arrived."

CHAPTER 45

Keeping an eye out for Sheriff Marsh, Slim and I walked back to Amarillo Slims. When we got there, Sandy was in distress. Marsh had barged in and threatened her. She said, "I didn't tell him shit."

Slim said, "He saw my bike at the vet office. That's how he knew I was there."

To me, Sandy said, "He asked for you."

I told them my plans were to head to Los Angeles. On the way, I'd contact authorities to report Two-Dollar Bill's body, dumped in the mineshaft. But first, I had to get my phone working again. As luck would have it, there was an AT&T store not far, and Doc Reibach drove me in her pickup.

After transferring my SIM card from my water-logged phone to a new device, and setting it up, I checked for missed calls. There was my father's call from prison. There was another voicemail from Agent Williams at the Environmental Protection Agency. She said, "Our team has been reviewing the photos you sent. It appears most of the containers are rusted and crystallization has begun. There is a barrel marked sodium cyanide stored next to a container of acid, and that presents a potential for deadly cyanide gas. Another concern are the barrels of Trichloroethylene. Please give me a call immediately once you get this message."

Next, I called Oscar and his receptionist put me through. As I began to tell him all that had happened, Oscar interrupted. "Wait. Back up, Jack. Who threw you down a mineshaft?"

"It's a long story. It's a miracle I got out of there."

"Christ almighty. Get your ass back home. Nothing needs to be solved now. Live to fight another day."

He made a good point.

The movie—I remembered Madeline was shooting her scene and texted her, *Call me.*

My phone rang a minute later. She said, "We're almost done here. I'm all packed so we can head out right after they wrap me, and...Wait a second..." and in a lowered voice, "*They* just pulled up."

"Who?"

"Macbeth. Lady Macbeth." I assumed she was talking about the actors until she said, "Chancellor and Christine."

"Stay on the phone," I said. "I'm on my way."

Risking Sheriff Marsh again, I jumped into the Chevy and sped to the film location while keeping Madeline on the phone. Chancellor Foster and Christine had joined the onlookers and were eyeing her. "How am I supposed to perform with them glaring at me?"

In the background, I heard Louis's voice giving direction, and she said, "I've got to go. We're about to shoot."

"Don't hang up," I said. "Keep the line active."

I figured as long as they were shooting Madeline in the scene, she was safe. I heard rustling as the phone was set aside, and the echo distant voices. Then the phone suddenly cut off. I didn't know if it was a break in reception, or if she had ended the call. I called back. Madeline's phone went to voicemail.

CHAPTER 46

Google Maps estimated twenty minutes. The Chevy got me there in ten.

I pulled up among the cluster of RVs and camper vans. At first, I didn't recognize Madeline in costume, but then was able to single her out.

As I made my way inward, a scruffy production assistant stopped me. He motioned silence with a finger to his lips, and said, "Hold up, pal. We're rolling."

Seemingly annoyed by a nearby distraction, Chancellor Foster turned back and saw me. His mouth dropped. He tugged at Christine. She turned. Her face registered shock, then fear, as if she'd seen a ghost. Metaphorically, they both had since I'd beaten death. The irony is Macbeth is haunted by ghosts of those he killed.

Sheriff Marsh's car pulled in. He got out. I didn't have much time, so rushed to the set and ruined the shot.

"Cut! Cut! What the hell!?" director Louis shouted.

I ignored him and went straight to Madeline's side. "We have to go."

She stammered—didn't know what to do.

Louis came up, "What the fuck? You just ruined that take?"

I took Madeline by her arm. "Grab your phone and let's go." I pointed to Marsh, who was in conference with Chancellor Foster.

Madeline darted for her bag, retrieved it, and we ran for my car.

Marsh drew his gun and shouted, "Hold it!"

I gambled he wouldn't shoot, not in front of everybody. Madeline climbed in the passenger seat, and I jumped behind the wheel.

As I sped away, I could see Marsh running back to his car. The flashing lights of the squad car lit up.

"Hold on," I raced the Chevy down the curvy mountain road. We were able to keep a blistering pace.

The area was not familiar to me, but Madeline knew the fire roads. I could hear the distant echo of Marsh's siren and kept an eye out for helicopters above.

At a fire road, I was able to elude him.

Back on pavement, I told Madeline how I'd come close to meeting Mike's same fate at the bottom the mineshaft. I told her Two-Dollar Bill hadn't been so lucky.

She said, "The mine is how they make problems go away."

"Just one stop," I said, "for my dog."

CHAPTER 47

At Amarillo Slims, Doc Reibach was there. I thanked them all. To Slim I said, "You saved my life."

As I gathered my things, Madeline was on her phone. I settled the bill for the room nights, and she waved me over. Madeline had Clara Frey on the line, the investigative reporter Mike had been in contact with. Clara had just learned of Mike's death. She'd called to offer condolences.

Madeline switched her phone to speaker-mode and introduced me. Clara enlightened us Silicon Valley has more toxic Superfund sites than anywhere else in the country.

I asked, "How can that be?"

"Before most computer chip manufacturing moved offshore, chemicals used to make semiconductors weren't regulated, or disposed of properly. That manufacturing legacy left acres of contaminated soil. In Santa Clara County alone, the heart of Silicon Valley, twenty-three sites are tagged as extremely toxic. The Google Campus in Mountain View sits on one of them. Sunnyvale is another hot spot. You won't find those in-the-know drinking the tap water there. The most dangerous compound is Trichloroethylene, a chemical known as TCE, which was used in the cleansing process of chips. The tiniest bit has been proven to significantly increase the risk of miscarriages, birth defects, and developmental issues in children."

Madeline gasped. That point hit her hard.

Clara went on, "Mike informed me there are discarded barrels of TCE in the mines. He was working to confirm that."

A devastated Madeline, tears in her eyes, looked to me and said, "Why didn't he tell me?"

I explained to Clara I had seen drums of various chemicals, and that I would share photos of them, but stressed Madeline and I had to get on the road. We scheduled a time to resume our conversation when she and I were back in Los Angeles.

Doc Reibach had jotted down instructions for Suzie's care. She warned, "Marsh will come after you."

"What makes you think so?"

"That's what he does, Cleans up the mess."

Slim added, "And you two are the latest."

Madeline said, "Is something burning?"

I smelled it too.

Slim went behind the counter to investigate. He shouted, "Damn! The back porch is on fire." White smoke wafted outside.

Suddenly, there was a gunshot.

The wall behind me exploded. White plaster rained down. The glass pane of the restaurant's front window crackled and blossomed like a spider web before the safety glass fell away.

More gunshots.

I yelled, "Get down!"

Doc Reibach and Madeline dropped to the floor. It was far more difficult for Sandy. She struggled to wriggle out of the wheelchair.

Slim pulled her down just before a round ripped through the backrest.

Up on my knees, I could see Sheriff Marsh across the road, crouched military style, aiming a short-barreled rifle. He took a moment to adjust something on the side of the weapon before taking aim. Next came a barrage of semi-automatic gunfire. Glass shattered. Bottles of barbeque sauce pulverized.

A yelp—Sandy's service dog had been hit.

CHAPTER 48

The gunfire ceased for a moment. I assumed Marsh was loading a new clip.

Sandy, lying beside her riddled wheelchair, army-crawled over to her suffering dog. It pained me to see the poor animal writhing on blood-smeared tile.

I inched up to see Marsh marching toward us, rifle slung over his shoulder, adjusting body armor at his collar. He wasn't wearing his uniform but rather hunting camo, dressed to kill.

Smoke started to fill the restaurant. Slim got up. At the broken front window, Slim met Marsh with fists. The Texan was able to land a punch before Marsh pistol-whipped him back.

"No!" screamed Madeline.

Marsh turned to her. He aimed his Glock. That's when my dog Suzie attacked. A distraction. Her jaws clinched his leg before he kicked her away.

I rose to my feet.

Marsh stepped up to me, raised his pistol, and—

The shot was deafening.

Marsh jolted sideways, a look of surprise on his face.

Prone Sandy had a pistol in her hand. It was the gun I'd seen earlier, what she kept concealed in her wheelchair—a short-barreled, stainless steel .357 Colt Python.

The gunshot put Marsh back on his heels. The protective vest had shielded his vitals. Sandy's next shot struck him in the neck, above the torso, and above the body armor. The wall behind him splattered in blood. He dropped the pistol to put his hand on his neck. With one hand attempting to suppress the bleeding, the other hand reached around for the assault rifle strapped over his shoulder.

Sandy's next shot was even louder.

Headshot.

Marsh spun to reveal a chunk of his skull missing, the crevice exposing chunks of brain matter.

He dropped in a heap.

Sandy fired the remains of the revolver. The cylinders of the revolver spent, she kept pulling the trigger over and over, the sound of the hammer clicking upon empty casings. The mild-mannered paraplegic had saved our lives.

Slim gently took the gun from her hand. The restaurant filled with more and more smoke. He picked his wife up in a fireman's carry.

Doc Reibach cradled dog Harley.

And I helped Madeline to her feet, Suzie at my heels.

Clear of the burning restaurant, with Harley in her arms, Doc Reibach shouted, "I've got her," and ran off with the wounded animal.

Slim held a weeping Sandy as they both watched flames engulf Amarillo Slims.

By the time the firetrucks arrived, the restaurant was burning like a tiki torch. Thankfully, the building was far enough from the trees not to spread, although burning-embers threatened above. I informed a fireman Sheriff Marsh was inside, and the team expedited their efforts to put out the flames, not that it would have made a difference.

CHAPTER 49

Three Years Ago

Post-traumatic amnesia. That's what they called it. This is what I remember from after the car accident.

Through one eye, I saw the fluorescent lights inside the ambulance, and then different lights on the ceiling of the hospital as they wheeled me through corridors. Apparently, my other eye had swollen shut. They said it was a miracle I didn't lose it.

I have a vague recollection of being in surgery as cloaked figures and strange voices hovered above me.

I woke covered in bandages, alone in the middle of the night. When I tried to get up, the nurses stopped me. They said I was in Providence Queen of Valley Medical Center in Napa, and that I'd been in an accident. I asked where Mona was. One of them said something about how I was the only one admitted. In my haze of confusion, I thought that was good. It meant Mona *wasn't* in the hospital. And she was not hurt.

The cocktail of drugs knocked me out, and when I awoke, there was soft daylight coming through the window. I asked for Mona. There was no response from the staff. Only then was I able to piece it together. Mona didn't survive. I'd soon learn they pronounced her dead at the scene.

It is called heartbreak because that's exactly what it feels like.

I wanted to die. For a while—I don't know how long—I was in and out of consciousness. When I was lucid, the staff asked for family members. My father wouldn't be released from prison to sit at my side, so I told them there was nobody.

The guilt, and remorse, crushed me.

Things went from bad to worse when I was informed the police had requested permission to interview me, and the doctor had granted it. I figured they had finally caught me. I'd eluded the law all these years. Now it was time to pay for my sins.

One of the nurses propped up the hospital bed, and I found myself in front of a squat woman who introduced herself as Forensic Detective Josephina DePaul of the Napa Valley Police Investigations Bureau. I noticed there was a uniformed officer standing at the door, and I was convinced they knew every-thing—my history of deceit, aliases, and life of crime. Fate had finally come to collect.

She began by offering her condolences for my loss, and then asked me to recall the details leading to the crash. I said Mona and I had been at the vineyard selling wine to a collector. From the look on her face, it was clear she already knew that. She asked, "So you'd been drinking."

"No." I sensed where this was leading. There was a death involved. Had my blood alcohol been over the legal limit, they would charge me with vehicular manslaughter. I told the truth, "Nothing."

"Not a glass or two with lunch?"

With images of that pink salmon spread I couldn't stomach, I told her, "I didn't have lunch."

"But that fruit-forward cabernet," she said. "Not even a glass?"

I shook my head no.

"When was the last time you had a drink?"

"The night before, with dinner." I sensed she didn't believe me.

The detective said, "I'll be frank with you, Mister O'Shea. With all of the wineries in this area, DUIs are common. And when there's an unfortunate fatality…as protocol, my department has the medical staff draw blood. We'll get your results back in a few weeks, so—"

"—You're asking me to incriminate myself?"

There was an awkward moment of silence before she said, "I'm trying to piece this together." Detective DePaul pulled out notes. "From the officer's report, it claims you were soaked in champagne. That would suggest an open container."

I said, "There was nothing open."

"It's not like you'd just won the World Series, so…why were you so doused in champagne?"

"There was champagne," I said, realizing what had happened. "In the back seat of the car."

"An open bottle?"

"No. The impact of the crash did that to them."

"Them?"

"There were two."

The detective made note of that. "We'll see what the toxicology report says."

"I'm telling the truth."

I could tell she didn't believe me. "Is there anything else you'd like to add?"

I shook my head no.

"Thank you for your time."

After they left, I stared out the window and thought about it all. As sick as that foie gras had made me, the curse was a blessing. The toxicology report would come back negative. Call it luck of the Irish. God had dealt me the saving "amazing grace" as the gospel hymn goes, and "saved a wretch like me."

I did not learn of any funeral or memorial service for Mona. In my condition, I probably could not have attended, anyway. I did learn her family arranged cremation. In a private ceremony, Mona's ashes were dumped into the San Francisco Bay.

I'd lost both my love, Mona, and a half million dollars. What I'll never lose is the image burnt into my mind forever—the way

Mona looked at me in the seconds before the crash, mischief in her eyes.

CHAPTER 50

Present Day

Eldorado County Deputies drove Madeline, Slim, Sandy, and me to the county seat of Placerville. I called Oscar and brought him up to speed. He arranged to have Claudia Myers, the lawyer he'd recommended to assist Alexandro, meet us there.

When I'd previously spoken to Claudia, my mind's eye envisioned a smartly dressed professional in a dark suit and heels, like a character from a television legal drama. To my surprise, Claudia was a robust, Birkenstock-wearing, boisterous motherly force of nature. She seemed to know everyone at the Sheriff's station by name.

They separated us, and investigators from Operations Division of the El Dorado Sheriff's Office began interviews. I didn't know where to start. Over the last thirty-two hours I hadn't slept a wink, almost drowned in a toxic bath, had my stomach pumped, was scrubbed like a potato, and been shot at. So I began at the beginning, the day my friend Hector asked me to look into his brother-in-law's death, which led me to Argonaut and the darkness of a long-abandoned gold mine. It was after midnight by the time we finished.

Agent Williams from the Environmental Protection Agency insisted we meet at the mineshaft first thing in the morning, so

Slim and Sandy arranged a room for Madeline at the inn for the night, and I returned to mine.

When we returned, Doc Reibach greeted us with good news. Luckily, Harley had only been grazed. She had the dog in a two-wheel contraption to support hind legs. "It's only temporary," she said. "Taking weight off the leg to speed recovery."

"Both of us on wheels," Sandy said in grateful tears.

Slim grew emotional too, although he tried his best to hide it.

Finally, I was able to lie down to sleep, but couldn't. Something told me Chancellor Foster and Christine would shield themselves with defense lawyers before agreeing to any kind of questioning. My word against theirs.

When I finally dozed off, whatever hours I got were blissful. Suzie licking my face awoke me the next morning at dawn. Like with Mona, a little affection goes a long way.

By the time Madeline and I arrived at the mineshaft, it was already surrounded by authorities, including a team from the Environmental Protection Agency's Criminal Investigations Unit. I was greeted by no-nonsense Agent Williams and directed them to the entrances in both the bowls of the theater and maintenance shed.

Men and women in layers of protective gear began an inventory of the toxic waste below.

I learned Chancellor Foster and Christine had remained elusive. Their luxury mountain home had been searched, but it appeared the couple had grabbed essentials and skipped out.

Buck-toothed Lawrence was brought to me in order to make an identification. Agent Williams asked, "Is this the man who pushed you into the mine?"

"One of them. Yes."

"That's bullshit," he protested.

Madeline asked Lawrence point blank, "Where's Foster and Christine?"

"Hell if I know," he said.

"You pushed Mike down there too, didn't you?"

"No."

I asked, "What about Bill?"

He dropped his head without a reply. To me, it was clear he had. Marsh's trusty sidekick was taken into custody. When they emptied Lawrence's pockets, they found two-dollar bills.

With the assistance from the fire department, they pulled Bill's body from the bottom of the mineshaft, stiff from rigor mortis, skin discolored gray. As they searched for identification, by no surprise, there was a two-dollar bill in his breast pocket. Lawrence must have missed that one.

It became painfully clear the investigation would take time, more than a few days—weeks, even months. My plan was to retrieve Suzie, thank Slim, Sandy, and Doc Reibach for their care and generosity, and head back home.

The authorities told us there would be additional interviews and requests for formal statements. By eavesdropping, I over-heard the San Francisco police had gone to Chancellor Foster's townhome in San Francisco's Castro District. Neither he nor his wife were there, by no surprise.

It was midafternoon by the time Madeline and I were allowed to go about our business. Our plan was to make the drive south in tandem, one car following the other.

Madeline's Honda was packed, but she'd forgotten some of the jewelry Mike had given her, plus keepsakes and photos. She asked me to accompany her to her home to get them. From there, we'd swing by Amarillo Slims, collect my dog, and finally head home.

On the way to her house, Madeline said, "I couldn't sleep last night, so read your book on my Kindle, or...most of it. You were a thief?"

"Not proud of it."

"Then you understand Foster and Christine, to some degree."

I said, "I've lied. Cheated. Stole. But money can be replaced. I'll never understand how anyone can take a life."

"What do you think will happen?"

"I don't know. Sometimes rules are different for people with a lot of money."

We drove in silence for a moment before Madeline asked, "What was it like down there? I've been wondering what Mike was thinking before he…"

"You called down to him, right?"

She affirmed with a nod.

"And he responded?"

"I told him I loved him."

"Then he was thinking of you." As I said that, I thought of Mona in the fleeting moment before our accident. Other than the split second when the tractor trailer was suddenly in front of us, her thoughts were of me.

I said, "I admire your courage. You could have taken their money, but you didn't."

Madeline's eyes glassed over. "Mike was way more courageous than me."

"You've honored him with yours."

She wiped her eyes as we pulled up the driveway. "I'll just be a minute," she said, and got out.

I was turning the car around on the gravel when I heard Madeline's scream.

CHAPTER 51

I ran to the house. Christine met me at the door, a small silver pistol in her hand. I recognized the weapon. It was the Jimenez JA-22 Saturday night special Sheriff Marsh had planted in my car.

Behind Christine, Chancellor Foster had Madeline in a choke-hold.

"Let her go."

Foster looked to Christine. She shook her head no, clearly the one in charge here, and said to me, "You've made one hell of a mess."

I noticed a stepladder in the corner. The surveillance cameras disguised as smoke detectors had been taken down. I motioned to that and said, "You've been spying."

To Madeline, Christine said, "Our right. It saddened me to see hear ungrateful you and Mike had become, everything you said...and how you betrayed us. Whistleblowers are never heroes. They're disgruntled employees, like you and Mike. Sour grapes. Whining about this or that, "Give me more money. Give me more money" she said in a high-pitched, taunting voice. "And I've got news for you. Mike was no saint. He tried to blackmail us, threatened to go to the press."

Madeline said, "I don't believe you."

She raised the pistol. "Doesn't matter what you believe."

I said, "With that pea shooter in your hand?" I pointed to the samurai sword hanging over the mantel. "Maybe you'd get off a shot before I pull that Ginsu knife down."

Christine considered the weapon on the wall, then challenged me with, "Go for it, tough guy. Let's see what happens."

I told them, "Sheriff Marsh is dead. They found Two-Dollar Bill's body in the mineshaft. And Lawrence is squealing like a pig. It's over."

The muscles of her jaw clinched. She aimed the gun at me. I lunged. Christine fired. There was a sharp sting on my shoulder—a sudden jolt of pain.

Her next shot was aimed at my face. Luckily, the pistol jammed. I could see the tiny .22 shell protruding sideways in the semi-auto ejector.

Madeline spun and kneed Chancellor Foster, separating herself from his grasp.

I grabbed the samurai sword. Unfortunately, there was no blade in the sheath—the thing an ornamental prop.

As Christine attempted to unjam the gun, Chancellor Foster came at me swinging. He was clearly an amateur. Pathetic. I landed an uppercut. He yelped, flailed backwards, and fell.

Madeline grabbed a piece of framed art off the wall and smashed it into Christine's head. Glass shattered, and the pistol flew across the room. Christine staggered before Madeline kicked her and she went down.

Call it bottled-up rage—that's when Madeline went "postal."

Madeline's steel-toed boot was the weapon. She kicked Christine into the corner. The woman's head jolted with each violent kick.

Foster tried to protect his wife.

Madeline went back and forth between them, both wedged against the wall, and let them have it with all her might. All her might.

I picked up the pistol and unjammed it.

In pure rage, she unleashed.

They became submissive, and I could have held Madeline

back, but chose not to. She needed this. Call it boot therapy.

When it was clear Christine was unconscious, bleeding from the mouth, and Chancellor Foster was whimpering with each blow. and obviously going nowhere, I finally pulled Madeline away.

I'll never forget the look in her eye—pure satisfaction—revenge as a dish served cold. As Madeline caught her breath, I held the unjammed gun on them, and called 911.

CHAPTER 52

They shuttled me to the hospital in Auburn. Thankfully, the .22 bullet had missed my collar bone. Madeline sat in the waiting room as the doctor juiced me with painkillers and stitched me up. They bandaged me in gauze, gave me antibiotics, and ordered I stay overnight for observation. All the while I wondered how Doc Reibach had treated dog Harley's gunshot wound.

There was no reason for her to wait for me, so I convinced Madeline to head back to Los Angeles on her own.

"My brother was right about you," she said. "You're a good man. Thank you for everything."

"Simply returning a favor."

I asked her for a favor. "Would you take Suzie back to L.A. and look after her for a few days?"

"Of course."

I'd weighed my options. Should I call Trevor to say I'd missed my father's call from prison? Or do nothing? It would be another day before my dad would have the opportunity to phone again.

I'd already planned my next move—return to Las Vegas.

After Madeline set out for Suzie, I phoned Oscar and asked him to do me a favor.

"Anything to get you to come back to L.A.," he said. "You need to get your priorities straight."

I said I had one last thing to do. "Thumb through that Rolodex of yours. I need you to make a few calls."

241

CHAPTER 53

Ye Olde King's Throne Tattoo Shop was only two or three blocks from where Mona had attempted to pick my pocket the day I met her. Ironically, it was just a stone's throw from the Las Vegas Federal Bureau of Investigation field office.

Accompanied by agents from the Crimes Against Children Task Force, we interviewed the tattoo parlor's proprietor. Sammy was all the cliché; a wiry, beady-eyed, and straggly haired character one might expect to run such an establishment.

Tough-as-nails FBI Agent Anne Simms led the team, and Sammy the tattoo guy was surprisingly cooperative. With a pencil, I sketched the double-crown tattoo I'd seen on Daniela, the young brunette with Trevor.

"That means she's Rex King's lady," Sammy said. "All his girlfriends had to get one."

"Girlfriends?" Agent Simms questioned.

"Dude's a player," he said.

I said, "We're looking for a brunette who goes by Daniela. She has an Eastern European accent."

"Yeah, I worked on her. She shares an apartment with a bunch of other girls in Henderson." The tattoo artist explained his wife Lola was a nail service and hair extension technician who offered in-home, 24-hour service. "Lola's been out to their place."

After Lola was contacted to provide the address, I accompanied the team to the apartment building in the suburb of Henderson. They left me waiting in the car. When Daniela was escorted out, I got out.

She had a black eye. That didn't surprise me. Daniela said, "You're the guy who came in the kayak."

"Trevor hit you?" I asked.

"I uh…fell down the stairs."

"You don't have to lie."

Her eyes welled up in tears.

Next was the ride out to Lake Las Vegas, to Trevor's luxury home. The caravan of agents had grown by then. I suggested they intercept the armed security guards outside Trevor's gated community so he was not tipped off. Agent Simms radioed ahead.

Outside the mansion, they brought Trevor out and paraded him past the darkened vehicle with Daniela inside—tinted windows cloaking her identity. Apparently, she made a positive identification, and he was arrested.

In the back of my mind, I wondered if Trevor had kept Mona's cell phone after all these years, so informed Agent Simms about it. It was added to the search warrant, and once granted, I accompanied them inside.

In Trevor's office, sure enough, Mona's cell phone was in his drawer, the same device I'd handed over while Mona hid inside my Santa Monica condo. From that, the Feds were able to access the victims Trevor had blackmailed, but the coup de grace was his laptop. The computer was full of child pornography, including the "Trojan Horse" email attachment he'd implanted on those who wouldn't pay the blackmail.

Trevor's possession of that material, combined with underage Daniela, proof of human trafficking, and the fact he was a potential flight-risk being Australian meant the judge refused bail.

Mona said Trevor's biggest fear was to be incarcerated. Now it looked like his worst nightmare had come true.

But before I returned home, I had one last thing to do.

I'd bought Alexandro's mother a plane ticket from Kona, Hawaii, and met her at Sacramento International Airport. She was a small-framed Filipino woman who apologized for her boy, blaming her deceased husband for her son's reckless behavior. "His father was a crook," she told me.

I didn't tell her I too was the descendant of a crook, and had been one myself, but assured her Alexandro had a good head on his shoulders.

She said, "He needs to go back to school."

Claudia Myers met us at Juvenile Detention in Auburn, presented his mother as the legal guardian to the court, and Alexandro was released. The mother wept when she saw him. Apparently, it had been years since they'd seen each other.

After paying the storage fee for his impounded van, I gave Alexandro the balance of what I owed him for his services. He claimed it was "tyranny" they confiscated his fireworks and nunchucks.

I said there'd be, "No more double-agent billing," and filled him in on how Trevor was arrested.

"Brah, doesn't surprise me," Alexandro said. "Live by freaky, die by freaky. All that nasty shit came back to bite him."

I said, "You need to go back to school."

"That's what my mom says. Not for me."

"Consider it."

He shrugged in reply. I had to admit I saw a little bit of myself in that kid—his lust for freedom and penchant for scheming. "Then at least pursue your creativity as a photographer," I encouraged. "That can lead to something."

"That would be cool," he said.

Oscar called it "a government shitstorm." I thought of it more as *the chickens had come home to roost.*

In addition to murder, Chancellor Foster and Christine were slapped with racketeering, conspiracy, money laundering, tax evasion, and the transportation and illegal storage of hazardous waste. They would be investigated by the Environmental Protection Agency, Immigrations and Customs Enforcement, Department of Homeland Security, Internal Revenue Service, and the California Department of Education.

As the Department of State investigated student visa fraud, all classes were suspended. The production of *Macbeth* was put on hold. Dozens of Renaissance Faire, Medieval Times performers, and hangers-on drifted off to new horizons.

When Two-Dollar Bill's wallet was found in Lawrence's car the buck-toothed part time security guard admitted everything. Apparently, Bill knew too much. Chancellor Foster ordered Sheriff Marsh to take him out.

I was surprised when my dad phoned outside our regular day and time. "Jack," he said, "what's with this story you sent me about rats?"

I explained the circumstances.

"All because of Garret Luth?"

"No need to pass it on."

My dad understood Garret was trying to make a deal for an early release. "It's not gonna happen. Those of us on the inside see how it goes down," he said. "Pedophiles are the bottom of the barrel in here. It's rare for a chicken licker not to serve their full stint." I was glad to hear that. It meant Trevor's troubles were just beginning. I asked my dad, "Any luck for some leniency for *your* good behavior?"

"Who told you I behave?"

As usual, he wrapped up the call with the fatherly advice, "Don't take any wooden nickels."

Rex's double crown tattoo connected him to several underage sex workers. He was investigated in a human trafficking ring, and the pimp is facing twenty years.

***

Insurance covered the loss of Amarillo Slims BBQ. Slim and Sandy planned to rebuild the restaurant. Sandy said they'd add vegetarian and vegan choices. I was pleased to learn dog Harley was out of the hind-leg contraption and walking on her own.

Back in L.A., my dog was glad to be home. I got into Oscar's retail theft case. The job meant impersonating an employee as a shipping and receiving clerk. The undercover job wasn't much of a challenge, but corporate reconnaissance paid the bills. At least until the next case came along.

I was back a few days when Hector texted me, *"Let's grab a beer. Meet me at Backstage."* So we were back where we started, beers at the bargain happy hour.

"Thank you," he said. "Here," and slid me an envelope.

"I can't take your money."

"It's not mine, it's Madeline's. She wants pay your book rate and compensate for the pain and suffering."

I scratched the itch under the bandage on my shoulder and inched the envelope back to him with, "Nah."

He pushed it back to me. "You almost got yourself killed, so you're going to take this or I'll donate it in your name to some bullshit charity."

"What's that mean?"

"Like…Children's Last Wish For Better Smiles International, or one of those, maybe five cents of every dollar goes to the kids, and the rest pocketed by bullshit administration fees."

"You wouldn't."

"You'll get on a mailing list of gullible suckers and then junk mail for life. Don't test me. I'll do it."

There was no arguing with him. We sat in silence for a moment before I said, "Your sister was right about a lot of things."

"I'm man enough to admit when I'm wrong. Happens on rare occasion, but…"

"You're lucky to have a sister."

"That's right…you don't have a sibling."

"Just my old man."

"Tell ya what…I'll be your brother by proxy. How's that?"

We toasted, and Hector asked, "Does that mean I can ask my best bro for a temporary loan?"

I waited for him to elaborate.

"The deal is…I'm owed on a script rewrite by these bottom feeding producers, and they're dragging their feet, claiming financing difficulties. My rent is coming due, so…"

I picked up the envelope. "How much ya need?"

The late afternoon sun through the window in my second-floor office meant I could see my reflection in the glass, angled off the window. There it was—my scar. No hiding from it. I didn't have what it would cost for the next phase of plastic surgery, to make me "whole again," but that had become less of a priority.

I thought about Mona. I thought about my dad.

There was no going back. I'd come to accept my flaws and imperfections, physical and otherwise.

It's who I am.

Flawed, but still standing.

Jack O'Shea. Deception Specialist.

ACKNOWLEDGMENTS

I am first and foremost thankful to Linda Landrigan (editor of *Alfred Hitchcock's Mystery Magazine*) for pulling my short story *Ghost Negligence* from the slush pile and introducing the world to detective Jack O'Shea. I read the magazine as a teenager. To be printed in it (then honored with the Shamus Award presented by the Private Eye Writers of America) was a dream come true.

I'm incredibly grateful to editor Laura Apgar for her keen insight and guidance on this journey. And thanks to editor Tom Hottle for assisting this admittedly "grammatically challenged" storyteller.

I must thank Steve Jankowski, Lawrence Maddox, and my wife Jennifer for suffering through my tirades, reading chapters, and providing thoughtful feedback.

I'm incredibly grateful to Lance Wright of Crimson Gate Books for all his tireless effort, dedicated professionalism, and inspired posts of truly stunning ocean sunsets. I'm proud to be part of the team.

High-five to my East Coast crime writer colleagues Scott Adlerberg, Jason Starr, Wallace Stroby, Dennis Tafoya, Steve Hamilton, Linda Sands, and filmmaker Doug Katz for the their belief and inspiration.

Grateful to all.

Onward.

JOHN SHEPPHIRD is a Shamus Award-winning author, two-time Anthony Award-finalist, and writer/director of television films.

Mystery Scene Magazine calls his novel *Bottom Feeders* "A fast-paced, fun read that explores a part of the movie business that often gets overlooked... from 'Action!' to 'Cut' it's a pleasure to read."

His award-winning short fiction has appeared in *Alfred Hitchcock Mystery Magazine, Coast to Coast Noir: From Sea to Shining Sea, Down & Out: The Magazine*, and numerous anthologies.

As director film titles include *Jersey Shore Shark Attack, Chupacabra Terror, I Saw Mommy Kissing Santa Claus* and *Teenage Bonnie and Klepto Clyde*.